S0-BYE-951

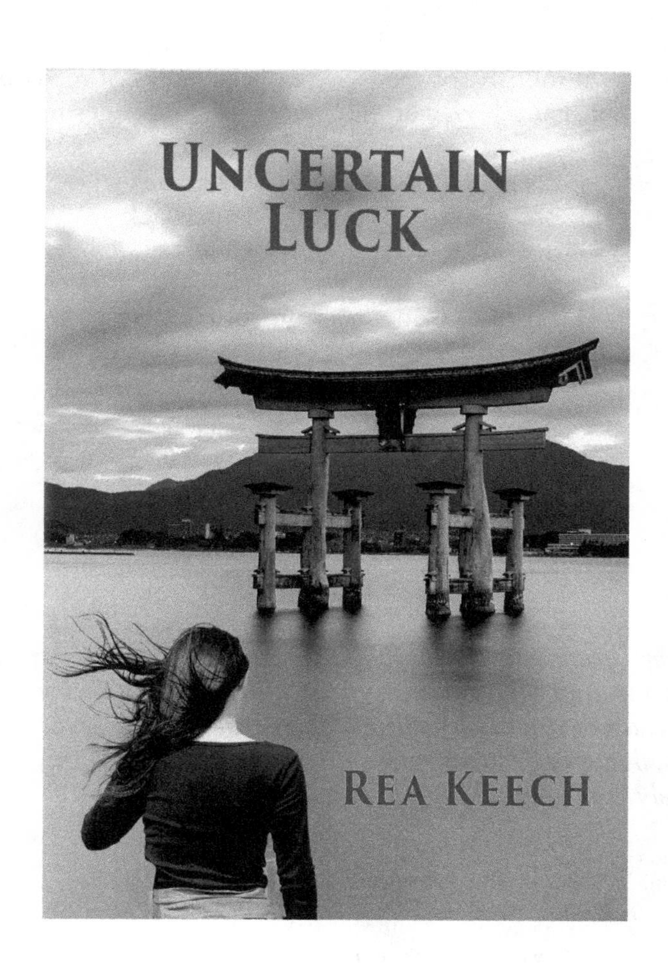
UNCERTAIN
LUCK
REA KEECH

ISBN 978-1-7330524-9-8 Hardback
ISBN 978-1-7355938-0-7 Paperback
ISBN 978-1-7355938-1-4 Ebook

Library of Congress Control Number
2020944542

Published by
Real
Nice Books
11 Dutton Court, Suite 606
Baltimore, Maryland 21228
www.realnicebooks.com

Publisher's note: This is a work of fiction. Names, characters, places, institutions, and incidents are entirely the product of the author's imagination or are used fictitiously, and any resemblance to actual persons, living or dead, or to events, incidents, institutions, or places is entirely coincidental.

Cover pictures:
"Japan Torii Arch"/Jonesy.dave/Shutterstock.com
"Back View of Young Asian Woman"/akiyoko/Shutterstock.com
Map:
"Vector Map of the City of Tokyo"/Nyker/Depositphotos.com
Sketches:
"Hands Holding Japanese Fortune"/Gustav O. Mittlemann/Depositphotos.com
"Crowded Metro Subway in Rush Hour"/robzs/Depositphotos.com
"Fushimi Inari Shrine, Kyoto, Japan"/Nyker/Depositphotos.com

Set in Sabon.

Uncertain Luck

—another novel of foreign love and intrigue
by the prize-winning author of *A Hundred Veils*.

ALSO BY REA KEECH:

The Shady Park Chronicles:

- *First World Problems* (Book 1)
- *Shady Park Panic* (Book 2)
- *Shady Park Secrets* (Book 3)

Sapporo
"Kitayama"
"Nakakuni"
Tokyo
Yokohama
Kyoto
Osaka
Kagoshima
Amami-Oshima
Yoron
Okinawa

Japan

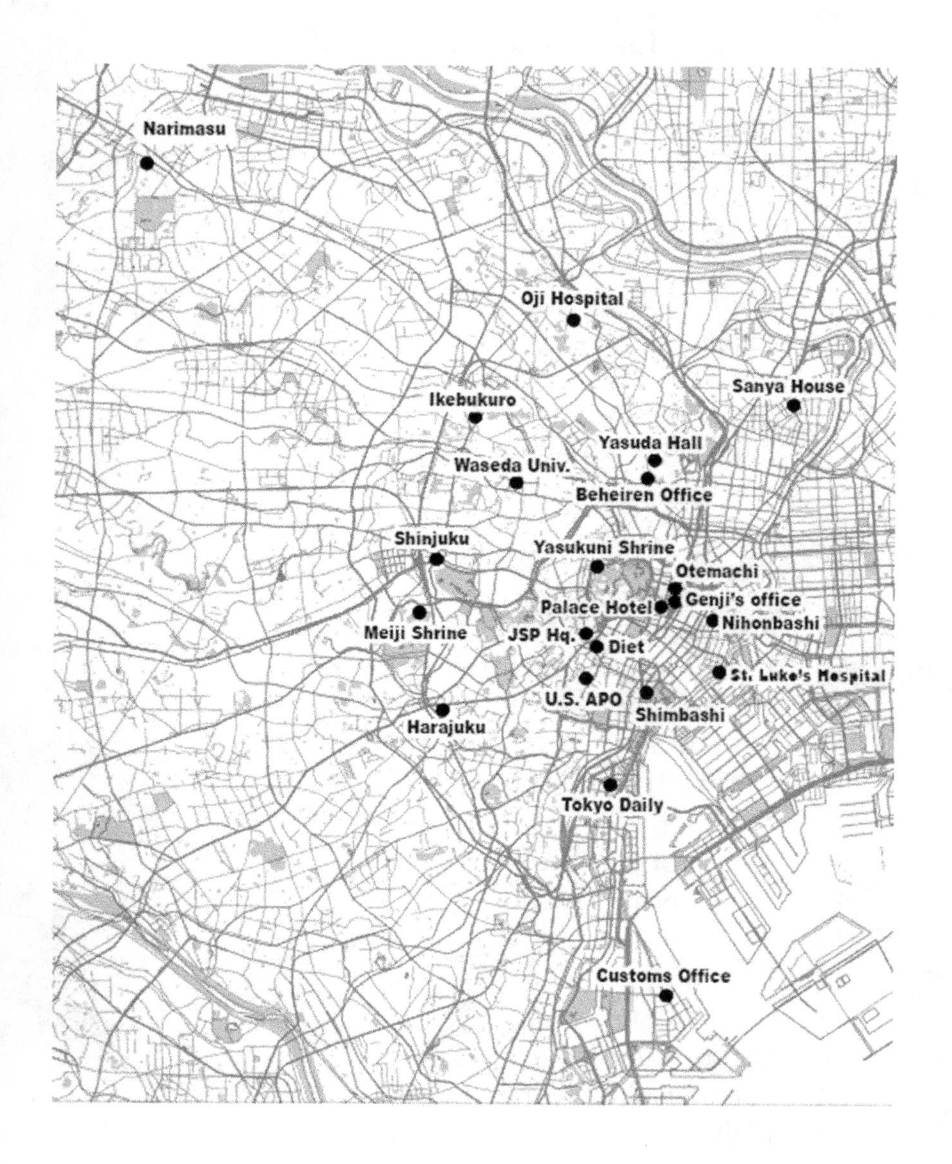
Narimasu
Oji Hospital
Sanya House
Ikebukuro
Yasuda Hall
Waseda Univ.
Beheiren Office
Shinjuku
Yasukuni Shrine
Otemachi
Genji's office
Palace Hotel
Nihonbashi
Meiji Shrine
JSP Hq.
Diet
St. Luke's Hospital
U.S. APO
Shimbashi
Harajuku
Tokyo Daily
Customs Office

Tokyo

List of Chapters

Map of Japan 4
Map of Tokyo 5

I 9

1 Lavender 11
2 Uncertain luck 20
3 Welcome to Tokyo 28
4 Potential witness 33
5 Evaporated people 38
6 Unfinished business 49
7 Tokyo runaways 55
8 The little-girl voice 63

II 73

9 Just like home 75
10 The face in the mirror 81
11 Gainful employment 89
12 Little America 99
13 Codfish fritters 104
14 *Tadaima* 110
15 Along for the ride 119
16 Giving peas a chance 125
17 *Mono no awaré* 135
18 The dark pond 139
19 *Korareta* 145
20 Tea for three 153
21 The unspoken word 159
22 *Wabi-sabi* 169
23 Dead souls 177
24 A fanatical cause 183
25 Time to go 189
26 An unwelcome passenger 198

27	Another good-bye	201
28	Destroying evidence	206
29	Killed in action	212
30	Confronting the enemy	219
31	Traveling alone	226
III		239
32	Taking a prisoner	241
33	Interrupted melody	248
34	Settling in	257
35	Flying pillows and boots	267
36	House scrubbing and money laundering	274
37	Merry Christmas	279
38	Car chase	289
39	Old friends and relations	297
40	The bell and the ring	306
	Epilogue	314
	List of epigraph translators	316
	Japanese words used in the novel	319

I

1

Lavender

The child must stand in the place of the one whom she so resembled.

—Murasaki Shikibu, *The Tale of Genji*

The caustic smell of electricity crept through her white surgical mask. The other women all said they didn't smell it any more. Emiko did, even though she'd been working in the factory almost two years, ever since she graduated from Kitayama High School. Her mother, in the back winding wires into coils, said she'd never smelled it.

Emiko picked up *Item A* with gloved fingers and placed it between *Tabs 1, 2, 3, and 4* on the circuit board. She eyed the higher pile of completed boards in front of the gray-haired woman next to her. "Did you ever wonder what these things are for?"

Jun-oba gave her a sideways glance. "No." She touched Emiko's hand. "By the way, a woman in the back said your mom went home early. Wasn't feeling well."

"Something serious?"

Jun-oba scoffed. "Come on. You know it's the only way we can get time off now and then."

The buzzer signaled the end of the shift. Emiko tossed her white kerchief, gown, and shoe covers into the bin, let down her long hair, and walked out into a town walled in by mountains on all sides. Snow Country. The mountain peaks glowed pink in the late summer sun. Tourists were awed by the scene. Soon the town itself would be wrapped in snow, and Emiko knew the low cover of clouds blocking the sky would give her the feeling of being trapped in a white cocoon.

Up ahead, standing under the red and white banner of the newly-renamed "Moon Landing" ramen shop, was a familiar scraggly-haired man in tattered clothes. She watched a by-passer stop, face him, and yell, "Attention!" The mind-shattered old war veteran snapped to attention as his tormentor grinned and walked on. The shopkeeper came out to shoo him away, but Emiko paused. She slipped a thin brown pay envelope from her jeans and gave the vagrant enough for a bowl of ramen. "Let him eat," she told the shopkeeper. "He can pay."

For all Emiko knew, her father could be standing hungry in the streets of some other city. The war had shattered his leg but not his mind. For over twenty years he'd supported their family as a watchman at the factory. But now and then he took brief trips to cities where protests for peace were being held. He'd never returned from his last trip even though he said he'd be back in a couple of days. Emiko's mother had a letter from him dated January 1969, when he arrived in Tokyo. And now it was the end of August. The police said men went missing all the time in Japan. *Jōhatsu*, they called them. Evaporated people.

As soon as she slid open her house door and stepped into the little *genkan* entryway, she knew something was wrong. Her mother's pink flowered handbag had been dropped on the edge of the step-up to the *tatami* mat area. "Mom!" she called. No answer. Emiko rushed into the bedroom and found her mother curled on the floor, sweat covering her forehead.

"Mom, is it your heart again? The doctor said you should cut back to part-time."

Her mother was gasping. "I will when your dad returns. Something must have happened to him. He's never been gone more than a few days."

Emiko wiped her mother's face with the sleeve of her purple blouse.

"He raised you to be strong, Emiko. If I die—"

"Mom. You're not going to die. I'm going out right now to call an ambulance." Emiko put a cushion under her mother's head and slid a coin for the phone from the dresser. But it was too late. When she looked again, her mother had stopped breathing.

Emiko threw herself on the tatami, sobbing. She pulled her mother's hand to her lips. It was gripping her father's guard whistle.

Fingers trembling, using long metal sticks Emiko lifted a thin, chalky bone from the tray of her mother's cremated remains and dropped it into the urn. She glanced at the funeral director through tears, and he stepped forward. "No need to go on, Miss. We'll finish the ritual. We're so sorry for your loss." After nearly two years of suffering with a weak heart, her mother was gone. She was only forty-three years old.

There were just a few mourners, friends from the factory and a few former high school classmates of Emiko who hadn't gone away to college or moved away to work in another town. They'd come to her house offering comfort, and they stood by her at the funeral. But now they had to go back to their own lives. Jun-oba stayed to walk home with her.

Emiko felt a strong hand grip her shoulder. The man wore an elegant black suit and tie, his hair graying slightly at the temples. "Emiko? I'm Genji Sato. A friend of your mother's." He slipped the funeral director a thick envelope.

Jun-oba's face paled. She turned and hurried away.

Emiko had heard Genji's name before. Her mother had told her all the men in Kitayama had returned from the war or been reported dead except her husband. Twenty-two years old and childless, she had met a handsome younger man, the son of the factory owner, who had come back to Kitayama after graduating from high school in Germany, where he'd avoided the draft. "Jun-oba and others disapproved," her mother had told her. "But my life felt so hopeless."

A few months after her mother began seeing Genji, her husband suddenly returned, finally released from a Russian prison camp in Manchuria. She immediately broke off with Genji, and Genji's father hushed the scandal by sending his son off to the university in Tokyo. The older brother took over management of the factory, and Genji stayed in Tokyo. That was twenty years ago. They said he'd started an import-export business of his own. Some said his father had disowned him. In any case, as far as Emiko knew, he'd never come back to Kitayama until now.

"Let me drive you home," Genji said.

Emiko waved her hand *no*, but her knees felt weak from the stress of the funeral. She wavered, and Genji took her arm. He gave a signal, and a black Mercedes pulled up. The driver held open the door with a white-gloved hand, and when Emiko refused to get in, Genji lifted her onto the seat.

"Stop. What are you doing? Let me out."

"Still living in Shiroyuki-cho?"

"Let me out. I want to walk."

The large sedan barely squeezed between the houses crowding the narrow lane. As they got out, Genji said something to his driver, who backed the car out to the main road. He took Emiko's arm again. "I'll help you inside."

"No." But her knees were still wobbly. She closed her eyes and took a deep breath, ashamed of her weakness.

He sat cross-legged across from her at the low table. "Is there tea in the carafe, Emiko-chan? Let me pour you some."

She drank some and, in fact, felt her strength starting to return. Looking at the photo of her parents on the dresser encouraged her. She'd moved it to a place of reverence on the tiny *kamidana* altar her father had built to honor their ancestors.

"Your mother was beautiful," Genji sighed. "I feel like I'm looking at her now."

Emiko tried to hide her embarrassment "It seems you paid for the funeral. I'd understood Kitayama Industries was going to pay."

He ignored that. "Your eyes," he said. "They're your mother's eyes."

Emiko had heard this often from her classmates and more recently her colleagues at the factory—from girls and women, mainly. But it disturbed her to be hearing it from a man who must be forty years old. Not to mention a man who'd had some previous relationship with her mother.

Genji looked around the room. Piles of clothes covered the floor in one corner. An ironing board was folded against the wall. Stacks of newspapers and books leaned unsteadily beside the sliding *shoji* door. He sucked in air through his teeth. "You deserve better than this."

"I'm all right."

"I wonder. You're alone now. Are you going to get by? The rent for these Shiroyuki houses can't be much, but with only you working now—"

"I'll work overtime."

"Still, I'd like to help you." He reached across the table and put his hand on hers. "So soft. So beautiful. Come sit next to me."

Emiko jerked her hand away. But she didn't get up. She'd been flattered, jokingly cajoled by boys before, but this was somehow more … real. Her heart was pounding.

"Your mother was twenty-two when I came back from high school in Germany. About your age, I guess."

"I'm twenty. I don't understand what you—"

"Let me be plain, Emiko. I have a wife in Tokyo whom I

respect. And a good business. But as soon as I saw you, I also wanted to take care of you. I want to buy you a nice place here in the new Mountain Luxe Apartments. You won't have to work. You can read your books, draw, paint, ski. I'll visit you as often as I can. Believe me, I'll be in agony when I'm away."

Now Emiko stood up. "You want to make me your second wife?"

Genji rose, brought her hand to his lips. "If you refuse me, I …."

Emiko had never been touched by a man as handsome as this. She was insulted but at the same time there was an undeniable thrill. She stood silent, staring at her feet.

"I know I'm older than you. But I'm still—"

"That's enough, Mr. Sato. I think you should leave."

His eyes looked genuinely sad. "I know this was sudden. It took me by surprise, too." He slipped a business card from his breast pocket and when she didn't reach to take it, dropped it on the table. Would you promise me to think it over? Just that?"

Emiko said nothing.

When he was gone, she collapsed on the cool tatami floor. It felt like all the energy had been drained from her, and she fell into a deep sleep until the next morning.

"*Gomen kudasai*!" It was Jun-oba announcing herself and sliding open the front door. With bowed head she handed Emiko a white envelope tied with black ribbon. "From the ladies at the factory. Our *okoden* funeral offering." She looked up, obviously waiting to be invited in.

Emiko knew she was expected to hold the envelope to her forehead and say something like "This is too much" or "I don't deserve your kindness," but she couldn't make herself do it. Empty courtesies, meaningless traditions left her cold. Her mother always said, "You're just like your father." Emiko took it as a compliment.

"Jun-oba, would you like to—"

"I'll just stay a minute." The old woman knelt at the table. "Emiko-chan, I hope you won't mind a bit of advice. Purple shoes at the funeral yesterday? I know I'm not the only one who noticed."

It was starting again. And her father wasn't here to say, "I guess she can wear any color she wants," and her mother wasn't here to change the subject and offer the old woman tea.

"I expect you'll be more careful now to obey the factory rules. You couldn't afford to lose your job." Jun-oba pointed to a glass bead necklace hanging on a knob of the tiny dresser in the corner of the room. "For example, as you know, jewelry isn't allowed in the sanitary room where we work."

Emiko poured her a cup of tea.

"You have to make more of an effort to fit in, Emiko. I loved your mother, but I wish she'd made sure you knew the way things are done."

"Yes, Jun-oba." Emiko wondered if the woman would object to her becoming Mr. Sato's mistress as much as she did to her sneaking books into the factory to read at lunchtime. Probably not. Becoming a rich man's mistress was rare, but it wasn't one of those things that "aren't done."

Jun-oba swallowed a bite of rice cracker and narrowed her eyes. "I came to bring the funeral offering, Emiko. But there's something else. The ladies and some of the men were talking. You probably don't know who that well-dressed stranger was, but some of us recognized him. He's the younger son of the factory owner, and he left this town in disgrace when he was eighteen. He's not somebody you should be talking to."

"He paid for Mom's funeral."

"I suppose you did have to thank him for that." Jun-oba said this with puckered lips as if she'd bitten into a crabapple.

"He seems nice."

"That's enough. We won't talk about him any more. My friend at the hotel says he's returned to Tokyo, where he belongs."

Emiko was feeling mischievous. "He wants me to become his second wife, and I—"

Jun-oba choked on her tea. "No! That can't be. You absolutely can't do that."

"Anyway, I'm definitely not going back to the factory."

"Oh? Well, not right away, of course. You'll want to take some time to mourn before going back to work. We'd all understand, Emiko-chan." The woman rolled her eyes around the room. "You probably can't afford to stay here. You can stay with me. In my sewing room."

The thought of doing that made Emiko cringe. "I don't deserve this kindness," she intoned. "I couldn't possibly put you to so much trouble."

Clearly taking this as polite acceptance of her offer, Jun-oba left with a satisfied smile.

Emiko sat cross-legged on the floor. Jun-oba was right. She likely couldn't earn enough even with overtime to stay in this house. And even if she could, being here would remind her constantly of her mother and father.

Her mother had died with her father's whistle clutched in her hand. Every day, he hung it around his neck as he limped off to the factory stockyard. One day he came home smiling. "There's been an incident," he announced. "Day after day nothing. But today something happened. A thief dug under the fence and I saw him filling up a bag from the charcoal pile."

"Did you blow your whistle, Dad? Get him arrested?" Emiko was excited. "Nah," he'd told her. "The guy was poor. I just let him take it. The whistle's still standing by for action."

Emiko and her mother knew the watchman job was boring. They didn't blame her father for occupying his mind with other things, which meant mostly politics. The war and his imprisonment afterwards had turned him into a fervid opponent of what he called imperialism. Japanese imperialism was basically defunct except for what he said was the economic variety. But he also opposed American imperialism, which he said had been played out in the Korean war and was ongoing in Vietnam.

Emiko read all the newspaper articles he showed her and all the books. In high school, she had learned that nothing but poor grades and scorn resulted from questioning the Education Ministry's version of history. It seemed that the only person she could speak her mind to was her father. Where was he?

She picked up the letter he'd sent from Tokyo. The police in that postal district told her mother they had no information on Hiroji Ozeki. It wasn't surprising since her father seldom used his real name on his visits with protest organizations.

Emiko took a deep breath. She had to find him. She put the letter into her backpack, added a couple bundles of clean clothes, and counted the funeral offering money—plenty for a trip to Tokyo and at least a short stay there. For insurance, she slipped in Genji's business card.

2

Uncertain luck

"... the Abbot has ordered that women are not to be allowed inside the temple courtyard .... Take care you obey his orders."

—Kanze Kojiro Nobumitsu, *Dōjōji*

Light snow was already dusting the town when Emiko bicycled to the station. The direct train to Tokyo wasn't until the following morning, but she wanted to leave now. She'd take the local to Nakakuni, and catch the Tokyo train there the next day.

She set the kickstand and stood her bike unlocked in the mass of others left there every day. She didn't know when or if she'd be back, but she was sure her lavender bike would still be there if she returned.

She'd only been out of Kitayama a few times. Once on a school trip to Kyoto, another time to Nikko with her parents, and once to Tokyo with her father. The swarms of vacationing high school students in jeans jackets and cowboy hats had already gone back to school, so the station was practically empty. She easily found a seat by the window.

The train rattled through the valley, snaking left and right as if probing for some unseen gap between the mountains. At the edge of town it made a curve so sharp Emiko could see the end of the train she was on. It seemed almost to be coming towards her. And then the train bored through a dripping tunnel. The only way out, Emiko thought.

The train emerged into a different world—bright sun,

clear skies, and warmer, humid air condensing on her still-cold window. She saw women in baggy *mompei* pants and wide straw hats harvesting rice in yellowed fields marked off by glimmering irrigation channels. In other fields men were digging up long *daikon* radishes, piling them onto a hand-drawn cart. These were the hard-working people Emiko's father had taught her to admire.

At Nakakuni station she got off and noticed a gaudy poster stapled to the wall advertising a guest house within walking distance. It wasn't expensive, but Emiko didn't want to spend that much. She walked along the gravel road through the town and looked around. Across a little river, up on a green hill, a huge red sun was setting behind the roofed *rōmon* gateway of a temple.

She crossed the river on a log bridge and followed a packed dirt path up the hill. Heavy stones were placed in the steeper parts as steps. By the time she reached the level ground at the top, the sun had set. She looked through the entryway at the temple. Its dark, aged wood and single curving roof unadorned with paint or gilding suggested indifference to attracting visitors. In fact, none of the posters in the station had even mentioned the temple.

She walked through the open door, slipped off her shoes, and padded warily up to the altar. Here there was some glitter. Gilded candlesticks with electric bulbs for flames, gold-trimmed hanging lanterns, and a painted statue of Buddha. She didn't know whether to bow to the statue, clap her hands, or what. To tell the truth, she thought anything like that was silly and was glad nobody was there.

On a gate in front of the altar was a wooden coin box with a tray of *omikuji* fortune papers beside it. Emiko dropped a coin into the box and took one. In the dark of the temple, she had to hold it close to read. *General prediction: uncertain luck. For starting a trip: uncertain luck*. Emiko shoved the paper into her backpack. "Thanks for nothing."

A shuffling sound behind her made her jump. She turned around to see a lanky teenage boy in an open brown robe over black pants, who also stiffened, obviously not expecting to find anyone in the temple. He had a rag in one hand and what smelled like wax in the other. Since he seemed to be frozen in the doorway, Emiko approached him. "Are you—"

"Hello," he said. It was more like a squeak. He bowed, presenting her with a view of his glossy shaved head. He was tall, with dark eyebrows and a pale, just-hatched look. Emiko finished, "—in charge here?"

"The abbot is away now, so ...."

"I see. I'm traveling and I wonder if I could stay here for the night."

The acolyte or whatever blinked and said nothing.

"I don't need anything. Just a place to lie down until morning."

He began mumbling what Emiko assumed was some kind of Sanskrit prayer. She waited. He cleared his throat and said, "We do have a tradition of accommodating travelers. I wish the abbot was here. I mean, it's usually men."

"I could just sleep right here. I guess that front door closes?"

"I'll be saying vespers."

"It won't bother me."

He was loosening up just a bit. "I can bring a futon, I guess."

The vespers seemed to be forgotten. Tōshin—his dharma name, he told her—not only brought a futon but offered her a bowl of rice and *miso* soup. She told him to call her Sachiko. "It's my traveling name."

They sat on the futon, Tōshin uttered some kind of prayer, and they ate side by side. "Where do you sleep?" she asked. "Just curious."

"There's another room through that door. That's where travelers can sleep, too, but ...."

"I understand. Here is fine."

When they finished eating, Tōshin took the dishes away, came back, and sat cross-legged at the altar to say some prayers. Emiko took a walk outside while he did. The stars flashed brilliantly in the moonless sky. Below, she could see a few lights of the town but there was no sound. The only thing she heard was the droning of prayers inside the temple. When she noticed that had stopped, she went back in. Tōshin was turning out the lights.

"Can you leave a couple on? It's pretty dark in here."

He nodded. "Not supposed to, but I guess it's all right. Well, I usually go to bed early." He bowed and went into his own room.

He'd laid out a blanket and a stiff buckwheat hull pillow on the futon for her. Emiko crawled under the blanket and fell asleep almost immediately. But it must not have been long before she woke up with no idea where she was. The wind had picked up, and swaying lanterns were casting flickering patterns on the high ceiling. Behind the dimly lit altar, the whites of the Buddha's eyes flashed out. The sliding doors rattled in their tracks.

When it came back to her where she was, she had to admit sleeping here was unexpectedly scary. As the rays from the lanterns flashed on the far wall, she saw the door to Tōshin's room. Trembling, she dragged everything towards it, then quietly slid open the shoji. Tōshin was asleep on his own futon. When she plopped her futon down next to his, he opened his eyes and gasped as if seeing a ghost. He sat up and started intoning what Emiko supposed from her reading of Noh plays was an incantation against demons.

"It's all right, Tōshin. It's just me, Emi- uh Sachiko."

Eyes closed, he intensified the chant. She rested her hand

on his shoulder to assure him, and he sucked in a lungful of air as if it would be his last. When he opened his eyes, he didn't seem to trust what he saw.

"I was scared, Tōshin. That's why I came in. I can't sleep alone out there."

He rubbed his hairless head, beginning to comprehend.

"So, I mean, can I just sleep in here?"

"You're not—"

"I'm not a demon. No. I'm just a girl trying to find her father."

He reached out with a shaky finger to touch her arm. "I'm not usually frightened like that."

"Let's just lie here and talk a bit." When she stretched out next to him, he cautiously leaned down on an elbow, then gradually put his head on his pillow. "You say you're trying to find your father?"

They talked until they fell asleep. When she told him her mother had recently died, he recited a Buddhist mantra and warned her to use only her mother's spirit name until her spirit had time to completely detach itself from the world. Using her real name would call her back to earth. Emiko's eyes always glazed over when she heard this kind of talk about the ghosts of dead people returning, unable to let go of something in their life.

The next morning Tōshin fixed breakfast for her—the same rice and soup, but with a raw egg added, and tea. When she left, he said, "I'll pray you find your father."

Passengers lined up on the platform long before the train for Tokyo was due to arrive—women with babies on their backs in *ombuhimo* carriers or toting bulky *furoshiki* wrapping-cloths filled with clothes or *omiyage* gifts for family or friends, a few children running and shouting but never straying far from their parents, men smoking cigarettes and reading newspapers, some giving Emiko covert glances. She saw no one her age. They were probably away at college or working.

Hating to stand in line, she went to a snack shop by the station and bought a *bento* boxed lunch to take on the train. She pulled a copy of the *Asahi Shimbun* newspaper from the trash can and sat on a bench. September 2, 1969—yesterday's paper. *Ho Chi Minh Dies of Heart Failure at 79*. She tried to read the article, but her eyes were clouding over. Her mother had been only forty-three.

As soon as the train door opened, the orderly lines of passengers on each side of the door broke into a single-minded shoving match to get a seat. Emiko was the last one to get on the train. She'd resigned herself to standing for the whole two-hour trip to Tokyo but saw an empty seat bypassed by everyone. Nobody seemed to want to sit beside a googly-eyed youth with a tangled crop of bleached orange hair sprouting atop his head and sparse black hairs springing from his chin. Two women who preferred to stand gave Emiko a disgusted glance as she nodded to the young man and sat down.

"Interesting shirt," Emiko said. It was a white T-shirt featuring a crude drawing of a girl putting a flower into a rifle. Below it was written *Give Peas a Chance*. "Are you a vegetarian?" she asked.

His onyx eyes registered surprise that she was talking to him. He probably hadn't heard correctly. "Satoru," he introduced himself.

The train lurched forward, slipping the newspaper from Emiko's lap. Satoru picked it up. He blinked on seeing the headline, stroking the hairs on his chin.

"Keep it," Emiko said.

"Pardon?" He was scanning the Ho Chi Minh article with glazed eyes. When he finished reading, she said, "I take it from your shirt you're opposed to the war in Vietnam?"

He nodded, handed the paper back to her.

"So. You going to Tokyo to find a job? To join some protest movement? Just to have a look around?"

"Mm." He seemed to mean all of that. "I'm going to enroll in a computer training school." His pursed lips might indicate he meant this as a joke. Emiko couldn't tell. She asked which school.

"Haven't found one yet."

"Here." She opened the back section of the paper. "Some ads for training programs. I think I saw one for computers. Right. Here."

Satoru tilted his head back and forth doubtfully as he glanced at the ad.

"You don't seem very interested."

He shrugged. "I'll see when I get there."

"You just graduated from high school this spring?"

"Mm."

He didn't seem to want to talk, so Emiko turned through every page of the paper hoping to find some description of a Peace-in-Vietnam activity her father might be involved in—anything that might be a clue how to find him. Of course, she'd been doing that every day with her mom for almost eight months. Never anything. The biggest protests had been back in mid January, the time her father had sent his last letter. He'd probably taken part in them. But why didn't he come back?

"Can I see the Help Wanted ads again?" Satoru finally spoke. He ran his finger down the *Part-time Male Help Wanted* column. "I couldn't get any of these."

"No?"

"No driver's license. No trade license. I didn't do well in school. I guess you did?"

"Me? Not bad. English was my favorite subject. I'm not planning to stay long enough to get a job."

"I have a place to stay. The Sanya House. Not luxurious but it's cheap." He looked at her.

"I'm staying with my father."

The train stopped at another local station, and Emiko noticed Satoru look away as several passengers passed money through the train windows to buy snacks from vendors. She wasn't hungry yet, but when the train started off again, she took out her bento and shared it with him.

Satoru shook himself awake. "Ah. The transfer announcement. I get off here and take the train to Minami-senju." He pulled a small green furoshiki bundle from under the seat. Emiko expected him to take a backpack or something else from the rack above, but the little bundle—that was it.

She followed him onto the platform.

"What? Your father lives here?"

Emiko walked alongside of him, realizing she'd have to admit something. "Truthfully, my father's missing. I have no idea where I'm staying. You said the Sanya House is cheap, so ...."

Satoru looked doubtful. "They do have a women's wing, my friend told me. I don't know if you'd like it there, though."

"We'll see."

3

Welcome to Tokyo

After all, Tokyo was a vast boarding house for all sorts of people from all parts of the country. Hardly anyone thought of it as home ....

—Osaragi Jirō, *Homecoming*

Satoru's friend had said the Sanya House was off the main street. They had to ask a few people for directions, and every time they got strange looks. They found it on a narrow street covered by a maze of electric wires and lined with bicycles in front of two- and three-story stucco buildings crammed against one another, all with slightly different designs and colors, grays and creams predominating. The buildings were so narrow and close they advertised with vertical signs jutting over the sidewalk. Emiko wasn't feeling the broadening of her possibilities she'd hoped for when she left Kitayama.

They stepped over a bearded man sleeping on the sidewalk. If Satoru's outfit clashed with what was expected on the train, Emiko stood out here in her hip-hugger jeans. "People are staring at me," she said.

"Of course. Because you're so pretty."

The sign was in Roman letters, which looked painted on by hand. The door was open, and a pale-faced, gray-haired man sat on a wooden chair bent over a tiny table in the narrow hallway. "Three hundred fifty yen per night, payable in advance." It was about the cost of a large bowl of ramen. "Guests must leave by 8 a.m. each day and cannot return until 8 p.m. No exceptions. *Sabisu* tea in the morning."

"Free tea," Emiko smiled. "How wonderful."

The hotel man narrowed his eyes to slits at her sarcasm. The clock on the table said 10 a.m. "Pay now. Find your room, then come back after 8 p.m. Women that way, men that way." He tilted his head left, then right.

Emiko walked through an open door into a narrow room—lobby?—with a black and white tile floor and another little table set with two chairs and a teapot. A woman in a long gray apron shuffled towards her with a tiny towel, looking her over carefully. She pointed to an open doorway. "Bed number nine."

On either side of a corridor only wide enough for a single person rose bare wooden structures with futons on platforms, three-high. Emiko calculated that eighteen women could sleep here, although only one could get into bed at a time. Bed number nine was on the top. She climbed a ladder and crawled in, bumping her head on the ceiling when she tried to sit up. There was only enough room to lie down.

When she'd come to Tokyo with her father, they'd both slept the night on vinyl couches in the makeshift office of Beheiren, the Citizen's League for Peace in Vietnam in the Hongō district, not far from Tokyo University, where she'd watched her father urging on a crowd of anti-Vietnam war students. She was in high school then, and watching him stand on those stairs and shout through a bullhorn to a roaring crowd gave her a feeling of pride. She'd helped make some of the placards and handed them out to masked protestors, who carried them into the street, forming a single-file line and weaving snake-like back and forth to take up the whole street. On the train ride back, her father explained terms like *complicity*, *escalation*, and *agent orange*. After that, she read the newspaper constantly and talked with him during dinner about things like the Japan-U.S. Status of Forces agreement, the security treaty, and the continued occupation of Okinawa until her mother clapped down her chopsticks and moaned.

Unable to sit up in the bed, Emiko turned on her side and took out her father's last letter and a subway map. The letter had been sent from the Hongō Post Office. She saw it was near the little Beheiren office where he'd taken her five years ago. She'd go there first. The police had already told her mother it was almost impossible to find somebody in Tokyo. But it was like when somebody tells you they've already looked everywhere in the room for your lost pen or something, yet you're not satisfied until you go look for yourself.

She counted her funeral offering money. At three hundred fifty yen per night, and if she ate mostly ramen, which she loved, she'd be able to stay in Tokyo a week or so. It would have been nice to lie in the bunk a little longer, thinking, but she heard the apron woman shuffling towards the room. "All right in there? Guests can't stay here during the day."

She crammed her backpack into a wooden box at the foot of the bed, turned its tiny key, and climbed down the ladder.

"Is there a phone?" she asked the man out in the hallway. She wanted to call Jun-oba, tell her she'd come to Tokyo so she wouldn't wonder what happened.

He looked annoyed, as if tired of being asked this question. "Not in here. There's one down at the corner in front of the bar."

Emiko stood on the sidewalk looking at her subway and train map. She felt someone bump her, then tap her behind. A greasy-haired man with a gold tooth and snake tattoos on both arms stopped and looked her over. "Pardon me, Sister. This sidewalk's narrow, isn't it?" He grinned, and she saw a second gold tooth. Emiko backed up to the Sanya House wall and kept studying the map, ignoring him.

"Here, here, that's not polite, Miss. I was talking to you." He rolled his Rs *yakuza* gangster style.

Emiko in high school had amused her friends talking like

a yakuza. "*Damarrre bakarrro*," she shot back at the man. Shut up, fool. Although she said it with a smile just to be safe.

The man stood gaping at her, his grin gradually widening. "Just the type," he said. "You'll be perfect. Those long legs. That butt. And that sassy mouth. Throw that map away, Sister. I've got a job for you that'll change your life." He handed her a business card. *Hi Crass Bar.*

"Sorry," Emiko said. "I don't do *crass*." She rolled the R on the English word, too.

The tattoo man laughed and flicked the card she still held. "*Kashikoi*. Smarty. Call me when you're hungry." He set off down the street with an exaggerated swagger.

Satoru came out of the hotel still holding his green bundle and stopped beside her as if he'd expected her to be waiting for him. He ran his fingers through his bleached hair. "What's so funny?"

"Nothing." —Except was she ever going to come across a normal guy on this trip? But maybe that wasn't fair. None of the "normal" guys she knew from high school interested her, to tell the truth.

Satoru looked down at the sidewalk. "My friend says there's a place in Shinjuku where I ought to hang out." He shifted on his feet, seemed a little scared. "You could come, too."

"Thanks. But I need to make a phone call and take care of a few things. We'll probably meet up again here tonight—at Sanya House bedtime."

Satoru stood looking up and down the packed street, then shrugged. "Sure. Eight o'clock, right?"

"Maybe you should call your parents, tell them you got here all right."

"Can't. I need to get the name of some computer school first. I had to promise I'd enroll. Did you throw that newspaper away?"

"Yeah, but you can find them in the trash cans everywhere." This is what it must be like to have a younger brother, Emiko thought. She kind of liked it, but at the same time it was annoying. Finally, Satoru said "Bye" and walked towards the station.

She found the red pay phone on the corner. Not knowing how much it would cost to call, she put in all her change, a whole handful, and called the Kitayama factory.

"*Moshi moshi*. Hello. Emiko Ozeki here. I need to speak to—"

"Emiko! Just a minute. I'll get Jun-oba right away. She's so worried."

It turned out *angry* might have been a better word. "Emiko, what do you mean going missing like this? Where are you? They saw your bicycle at the station. You can't just—"

"I'm fine, Jun-oba. Just listen. I came to Tokyo to find my father. With Mom gone, Dad's all I have left. You have to understand. He's here somewhere. I have to find him."

Jun-oba sniffed. She might have been crying. "Emiko-chan," she said. "I hope you find him. I really do. But, Emiko, he's not your father."

"What? Jun-oba, what do you mean?" Was she saying a man who suddenly disappears like that is no father to you?

The phone clicked off. The time had run out. Emiko had no more change. Oh, forget it. One advantage of coming to Tokyo was that she didn't have to deal with Jun-oba any more.

4

Potential witness

The others go home.
With the fireworks over,
how dark it's become.

—Masaoka Shiki, *haiku*

The red flash burst up behind the ridge before they heard the explosion. Juan dropped flat onto the prickly grass, the ground vibrating beneath him. His ears were ringing. He lifted his head to look through the cloud of dust and smoke. All the men were lying flat, face down, gripping their rifles. He saw a few heads pop up like his, but not all of them. The ridge was supposed to have been abandoned. Somebody had made a mistake.

Another flash, then the boom, and dirt shot up behind him. Some of the men were slithering back down towards the trees at the base of the hill. Juan fired some shots at the top of the ridge and started backing down, too.

"Take out that mortar." It was Lieutenant Joss. "Spread out. Up the hill, ladies. Up to grenade range." Hunched over, Joss started zig-zagging towards the ridge of the hill, grenade in one hand and waving his men on with the other.

In Puerto Rico, Juan was a high school center fielder. Now in his early twenties, he could still throw farther, more accurately than anyone in the platoon. He stood up, ran, cocked, and threw. A blaze of white blinded him. It was the last thing he remembered.

He awoke strapped into a sitting position in a hospital

bed. His chest throbbed with pain. He noticed a wide bandage there and broke into a cold sweat wondering what it was covering.

"You're going to be all right, soldier." A young medic with a clipboard peered at him through thick glasses. "Three broken ribs. Some lacerations. Give a shout if you need any pain medication."

"Lacerations?"

"No big deal."

"I want to see."

The medic looked at his clipboard. "Almost time to change the bandage anyway." He peeled it off. "You'll have a few scars when it heals. That's all."

"Where am I?"

"U.S. Army Field Hospital, Camp Oji, Tokyo. You've been here two days. Little break from Vietnam."

Juan remembered trying to take the ridge, knock out the mortar. Nothing after that. "The rest of the platoon?" he asked.

"Don't know. CID guys were here to question you. You've been unconscious till just now."

"Criminal Investigation Division?" Juan couldn't imagine what he'd done.

"They'll be back."

As the pain killers kicked in, Juan felt better. He realized the pain in his chest was the broken ribs, not the lacerations. They told him there was nothing to do for the ribs except wait it out. He started to eat the mushy food they gave him. A nurse came to give him a bedpan to pee in. She was heavyset and kind of butch. But she was a woman, and he was aroused at her touch—until she gave him a quick smack. Anyway, that was good. He was still functioning down there.

Later, the nurse brought a walker. This was humiliating.

He eased out of bed, keeping his upper body straight, and held onto the handles, light-headed, making his first sortie to the toilet. He felt stronger the next day and was soon walking step by step on his own.

"Feel up to going downstairs?" the nurse asked. "There are some people who want to talk to you."

She led him into a bare office that smelled like Clorox. Two men in army haircuts and tan suits showed him their CID badges. The first stage of their interview seemed to be glaring at him as he maneuvered himself, flinching, onto a metal chair. Were they waiting for him to fall on his knees and confess to something? Juan raked through whatever memory he had left of the battle. Still nothing after the flash. He hadn't even been able to find out if the ridge had been taken or not.

The two tan-suits sat close in front of him flipping notes. "Tell us about the Bighorn Ridge battle," the one with a unibrow said.

"You mean ...."

"You don't know what we're talking about?" the one with a twisted ear said.

"We were taking a ridge. Mortar on top. I guess I got hit. I remember that much."

"A ridge your lieutenant told you was held by a single enemy soldier. Is that correct?"

Juan nodded.

"Would you say *yes* for the record. This is being recorded."

"Yes. That's what our lieutenant thought."

The one with the ear said, "To be clear, that's what he told you?"

Juan nodded, then said, "Yes." He couldn't imagine where this was going. Had he done something wrong he didn't remember?

"And did Lieutenant Joss brief the platoon on how he knew there was only one man on the ridge—and that the ridge needed to be taken? Neither of which was correct."

"No, Sir." Juan recalled that Joss had gotten key details wrong previous to this. He didn't say anything about that but asked, "Was anybody else hurt?"

The unibrow guy chipped in, "Two men killed. You really don't know that?"

"I remember a white flash. Then I woke up here in the hospital."

The investigators eyed each other, flipped through pages in their notebooks. One read out, "traumatic amnesia."

"OK," the other said. "Let's turn to the months before the battle. Have you ever witnessed behavior by Lieutenant Joss that unnecessarily put his men's lives in danger?"

The answer Juan hesitated to give was yes. Joss often ignored parts of his orders simply because he loved a fight. And of course there was the Vietnamese farmer Joss shot in the face. He'd said he thought the guy was armed. "Um, I couldn't say" was what Juan came up with.

Both investigators started to speak at once. They told him others in the platoon had accused Joss of being criminally reckless but were starting to walk back their testimony. "They're still under his command," one said. "We have to assume they're afraid of repercussions."

"But you're safely out of his hands here," the other explained. "So you'll need to tell us everything you know about this man."

Juan shifted in the chair, which sent a sharp pain through his rib cage. He flinched, emitting a little cry.

The unibrow frowned. "You're hurt. There's time. We don't need to do it today." He flipped back a page in his notes. "Broken ribs. You could be sent home for six to eight weeks, but we need you to recuperate here in Tokyo so we can talk to you again. We'll extend your time here as a potential witness as long as necessary."

That was OK with Juan. He didn't have much reason to go back to Puerto Rico. His mother and father were divorced and remarried to people he hardly knew. Both parents had turned a cold shoulder to him when he insisted on enlisting. He had no brothers or sisters.

"Get some rest for now," the unibrow said. He clicked off the tape recorder, and Juan was dismissed.

Two MPs were escorting a soldier down the corridor. Juan turned to look. It was Lieutenant Joss. Joss stopped, the aggressive red flush that Juan knew quite well coloring his face. "Gomez. You. I should have known why they brought me in."

"Come along, Sir," ordered an MP big enough to be a bouncer. He took Joss's arm. "You're not to talk to any witnesses."

Through his teeth Joss grunted, "Witness all you want, Gomez. Just remember. I'll see you back in Nam."

5

Evaporated people

Of course, missing persons are not really uncommon. According to the statistics, several hundred disappearances are reported every year. Moreover, the proportion of those found again is unexpectedly small.

—Kōbō Abe, *The Woman in the Dunes*

Emiko took the subway to the Hongō district. The lunchtime sidewalks were full of men in gray or dark blue suits hurrying in all directions, none making eye contact with each other. In jeans and her lavender V-neck sweater, Emiko walked at the slower Kitayama pace while the "salarymen" surged by on either side as if she were a rock in the stream. In the rush of humanity there was no chance of asking for directions—or even of stopping.

It had been only a few years since she'd been here with her father, but the buildings were higher and the streets were jammed with cars and taxis that seemed to sound their horns constantly for no apparent reason. The air smelled of liquid petroleum gas exhaust. Finally, the throng of pedestrians stopped and bunched up at a traffic light. Emiko turned to the man next to her and asked where the Hongō Post Office was. His fixed, blank stare seemed to indicate he hadn't heard, or couldn't imagine he was being spoken to. She repeated the question, and he turned his head, waving his hand in front of his face as if her Kitayama accent was a foreign language.

The Walk signal lit, and the throng surged on, pulling

Emiko with it. She kept walking until, luckily, she saw the post office, the one her father had sent his last letter from. The Beheiren office she'd been to with her father should be nearby, if it was still there. She wondered if she'd recognize it.

The horde of suits gradually thinned out, replaced by young men and women in jeans, probably Tokyo University students. The pace was somewhat slower, some of the young men ostentatiously clumping along in tall wooden *geta* clogs as if to flaunt their difference from the salarymen. Emiko noticed some going into or coming out of *soba* noodle shops or coffee houses. In the distance, she saw the tall clock tower of Tokyo University's Yasuda Auditorium, which had been occupied by protesting students when her father sent his letter. She and her mother had clung to each other, crying, when they saw the televised news coverage of police firing water canons into the building and student protestors throwing concrete slabs and Molotov cocktails from their barricade high in the building. The battle had lasted two full days before the protesters were cleared out. Hundreds were arrested.

Emiko leaned back against the wall of a soba shop and bent over, her head in her hands. Finding her father seemed hopeless. She couldn't even find the Beheiren office he'd worked out of. She might as well go back to Kitayama and keep working in the factory.

"Are you hurt, Miss?" A tall young woman in a jeans jacket stopped before going into the shop.

Emiko straightened up. "No. I'm fine. Just a little hungry, I guess."

"The soba in this shop is the best. Coming in?" The young woman spoke in a raspy voice.

They sat together at a counter. The young woman placed a novel she'd been carrying beside her bowl. She'd written her name "Kasumi" on the cover. It was about a man who'd fallen into a hole in the sand, where he came under the control of a woman who lived there. Emiko had read it. She asked if Kasumi was a student.

"Yes. You?"

A lump rose in Emiko's throat. She had passed the Waseda University entrance exam, but her family couldn't afford the tuition. Without answering, she looked down.

"Anyway, the soba's good here. You said you were hungry." Kasumi gave her noodles a loud slurp by way of encouragement.

Emiko noticed a flyer protesting Japanese involvement in the Vietnam war folded into her book. "Are you in Beheiren or …?" There were lots of leftist organizations, but her father had been most closely associated with Beheiren.

Kasumi gave a single nod *yes*, studying Emiko for a reaction.

"I'm looking for their Hongō office. I wonder if you could—"

"What for?" Kasumi cleared her throat.

"I'm trying to find my father."

"I see." Again Kasumi cleared her throat and looked down, silently stirring her noodles.

Emiko persisted. She opened her map on the counter. "Could you show me where the office—"

"It's locked up now. We don't use it much."

"I'd really like to find it anyway."

Kasumi gave her a stare. "You're from the police, aren't you?"

Too shocked to reply, Emiko felt her face flush. "No, no," she finally managed. But Kasumi hurried out of the shop.

Emiko ran after her. "Wait, wait. I can prove it." She handed her the letter from her father.

As Kasumi read a bit, the frown faded from her face. "Sorry," she apologized. "I didn't know your father, but there were some older men helping us during the Tokyo University demonstrations. Come on. I'll show you."

The Beheiren office was on a street off Hongō-dōri Avenue crammed with used book shops. Emiko remembered the area but not the unmarked wooden door that opened to a hallway and a windowless room in the back. The fluorescent lights hummed when Kasumi flipped them on. A neat line of white helmets stood against the wall, megaphones hanging on hooks above them. Stacks of books, magazines, and newspapers covered the tables, chairs, and half of the floor. Emiko recognized the couch she had slept on when her father brought her here, now littered with piles of protest placards.

"Since the police crackdown last January, we mostly use this place for storage," Kasumi explained. She coughed, cleared her throat, and Emiko wondered if she might be suffering from a long-term respiratory effect from breathing tear gas that her father had told her about.

On a table was a batch of flyers reading *U.S. Must Get Out of Vietnam*. This was her father's main cause. On another table was an open box of gas masks.

"Those are new," Kasumi coughed. "We didn't have them during the Yasuda Auditorium protests."

Emiko tried to describe her father to Kasumi but realized his features didn't really distinguish him from any other middle-aged man.

Kasumi twisted her jaw, shook her head. "Sorry. There were so many demonstrators. We didn't always know each other's names."

"He walks with a limp, if that helps."

"Eh? A limp?" Kasumi put a hand to her cheek. "There was a man. Yes. I remember. He was very nice."

"Do you know ...?" Emiko didn't have the heart to finish.

Kasumi lowered her head. "I'm sorry. Everybody scattered after the arrests. I never saw him again."

It was exactly what Emiko feared. He was probably somewhere in jail. With a lump in her throat, she caught Kasumi's eyes. "Could you ask other Beheiren members the next time you meet?"

"The thing is we don't run protests from here any more. We're just storing those supplies for now. I've been using the place to oversee a special group your father wouldn't have been involved in. I can't—"

Steps sounded in the hallway and a squinting, square-chinned man clumped into the room. He stood studying the two women. "You left the door unlocked."

Kasumi said they were just leaving. She didn't introduce Emiko. He didn't seem interested.

"Where are the foreign newspapers and the Beheiren reports? I'm setting up new quarters near Grant Heights."

Kasumi slid a box of papers across the desk towards him.

"That all?" He scratched an address on the back of an envelope. "If you find any more, send them to me at this address." He turned to leave. "And secure all the weaponry." He left without another word.

Kasumi gave Emiko an embarrassed glance.

"I guess he's the boss?" Emiko asked.

"He thinks he is. We don't have any bosses. We work together."

"Weaponry?"

"Typical Takashi. He uses words like *ambuscade*, *counter offensive*, *campaign*." Kasumi pursed her lips. "I'm glad he's moving to new 'quarters.'"

"So he's in Beheiren?"

"Not really. He seems to be out there on his own. He acts like Beheiren is some kind of army and he's in charge of it."

"What are those reports he took with him?" Emiko remembered her father mentioning reports he'd helped Beheiren members write.

"I don't know. After the arrests, somehow they got dumped

here. Takashi thinks he can make use of them, it seems."

As Emiko was leaving, she noticed a shelf filled with face covers of various types. She picked up a scarf that looked familiar. It was a deep blue striped one her mother had sewn for her father.

Kasumi had said the nearest police office was close to where Emiko was staying, and although Emiko was tired, she decided to walk all the way back. She and her mother had called the Tokyo police several times to ask if there was any arrest record for her father, but this time she would give them a list of aliases he might have used.

The man at the information desk said Emiko would have to request that information at the central office. He sucked some air through his teeth. "But I'm sure you'll only be able to ask about your father's actual name because you'll need to provide evidence of family relationship. Privacy laws," he explained, tapping a pile of papers on his desk as if they contained the very laws he referred to.

"You can't be serious. I just want to know if my father's in jail." Emiko must have raised her voice because a woman at another desk looked up, startled. She came over to the information desk. "Have you filed a missing person report?" she asked. "That might be the first step."

When Emiko said they'd done that almost eight months ago, the woman breathed out a concerned "Heh ...." She said it was seldom possible to locate a person who'd been missing that long. "The problem is a lot of times people don't want to be found. Men in particular feel trapped by family obligations, social expectations. They reach a point when they feel their individuality has been crushed. They can't handle it any more. They disappear."

The man at the desk nodded agreement. He said there were private detectives specializing in locating missing persons. "You might be wasting your money, though. They're seldom successful."

"My father's not like that. He's not hiding out. Something happened to him."

Emiko walked slowly back towards the Sanya House, the thought of her missing father bringing tears to her eyes. As she stopped to take a tissue from her pocket, a man bumped into her from behind, exclaiming, "Hey! Watch out! People are trying to walk here."

"Sorry." When Emiko stepped aside, she jostled a woman carrying a net shopping bag trying to squeeze by. The woman dropped her bag, Emiko stooped to help her retrieve it, and the woman yelled, "Thief!"

A policeman in a blue patrol cap and uniform came out of his little *kōban* police booth.

"She tried to take my bag!"

"Now, now." The policeman lowered his hand in a calming gesture. "I saw the whole thing." He turned to the few people who had stopped to look. "It's just a mistake." Emiko held her face in her hands. The policeman spoke to her. "Miss, you seem upset. Would you like to come into the kōban for a minute and sit down?"

Emiko sat on the plastic chair wondering if she was being arrested. Obviously not, though, since he poured her a cup of tea. He had a gentle, round-cheeked face and silver-framed glasses. His nametag read Oizumi. "Just rest here a bit, if you want," he told her.

"I will if you don't mind. I never imagined a police box would be a place to calm down."

"Stay as long as you like. You can see I'm not too busy."

Emiko glanced around at the gray walls—bare except for a few maps—and at a gray counter holding a microwave, a rice cooker, and some kind of radio. The only other items in the booth were his gray metal desk and a few gray chairs.

"You seemed confused on the street. Are you lost?"

Emiko shook her head. "No."

"I see." The policeman pulled open his desk drawer and emptied a bag of seaweed-covered crackers into a dish as if to signal he wasn't meaning to interrogate her. "Please. If you like them. They're good with tea."

Emiko felt she needed to explain. "I was distracted," she told him. "I'm looking for my father."

Sergeant Oizumi's face seemed to radiate sympathy. She told him everything.

"I see. I see." He scratched his head. "You say you have a list of names he might have used?" He looked at it and said he might be able to help her. "A neighborhood officer doesn't need to go through the red tape you mention. It will take two or three days, but I think I can get an answer for you. You say you're staying … did I hear correctly? The Sanya House?"

"It's all I can afford."

"Well, good, in this case. It's only a two-minute walk from here. You could stop by in a few days. I'm here most afternoons and evenings until 10 p.m."

It was just six o'clock when she walked towards the Sanya House. Satoru was already standing in front of the door.

"Going to wait out here for two hours?" she teased.

He shrugged. "I guess. And you?"

"Me? Of course not." Although she hadn't really planned what to do until eight o'clock. She changed the subject. "Any luck finding a computer school?"

Satoru shrugged again. "I applied to one in Nihonbashi. Didn't get in."

Emiko wasn't surprised. How could he with that bleached hair and that shirt?

"They didn't even let me into the building."

She looked at his bundle. "I guess you didn't bring a suit. In Tokyo, you know—"

"I can't see myself wearing a suit."

Emiko couldn't picture that either. "Maybe you could look for some kind of job."

"Yeah. I'm out of money, just about. My parents won't send me any until I show I'm enrolled in a school."

"I see. Well, have you eaten dinner? We could go get some ramen."

They found a shop, and Satoru stared at the menu on the wall. "Hmm. It's more expensive than back in Nakakuni."

"I'll pay. Salt-based or soy?"

Satoru scratched his head, embarrassed. "Soy."

"So how did it go in Shinjuku? Did you find the place your friend told you about?"

"Mm."

Emiko tilted her head for more details.

"Some of the guys have places they can sleep for free. I might stay there instead."

"You mean on subway benches or whatever? Even the Sanya House is better than that."

Satoru greedily slurped up some noodles. She wondered if he'd eaten anything since he got to Tokyo. She said, "I could lend you a little money if you need it. Not much." He looked so grateful, she gave him more than she should have.

After eating, they walked along the streets of honking car horns and stopped at the thin bronze statue of Matsuo Bashō writing one of his haiku poems.

"I never read any of those in school," Satoru commented.

"I did." Emiko grinned, remembering one in particular that had struck her. It seemed appropriate to quote it:

Bitten by fleas and lice,
I slept in a bed,

A horse urinating all the time
Close to my pillow.

Satoru didn't laugh. Too close to home?

Emiko took her pajamas from her backpack and found the bath—no tub, just low plastic stools, faucets, and plastic pans along the walls. It was early, and she was glad to be the only woman in the room. Quickly she hung her clothes on a hook, held the little towel in front of her, and sat down to wash. Pouring warm water over her head from the pan brought a sudden memory of her mother washing her hair when she was a little girl. Her arms trembled as she rinsed the soap from her body.

Shivering, she lay in her bunk, tired but unable to fall asleep. No fleas, lice, or horse urine, but the woman in the bunk below was snoring so loud it echoed from the bare wood walls. She held her father's scarf to her cheek.

She must have finally fallen asleep because she was awakened by the noise of women struggling to get dressed in the narrow lane between the bunks and leave by the morning deadline. Nobody talked. They bumped against each other without apology—every woman for herself. Emiko looked down wide-eyed from her bunk as if she'd been transmitted into an alien world.

Most of the women were old and wore loose house dresses or plain kimonos tied with a simple *obi* sash. They rushed out carrying furoshiki bundles—to where, Emiko couldn't imagine. She struggled into her jeans lying on her back. When she climbed down, one last lodger who looked only a few years older than Emiko was just getting up. "Ugh," she croaked. "What time is it?"

"Time to leave, it seems."

The young woman buttoned up a shimmery white mandarin blouse that hung below the waist. "You're new here.

Wonderful place, isn't it?"

"Mm." Emiko said she wouldn't be staying long.

"Me either. I'm saving money for an apartment." She pointed towards her nose. "Mariko."

Emiko introduced herself, and Mariko suggested a cup of Sanya House green tea before they left. The clock in the women's "lobby" showed they had ten minutes. Mariko found chairs and poured for them. The day's *Asahi* newspaper lay folded on the table. Emiko picked it up, but Mariko wanted to talk. "Are you saving money for an apartment, too?"

Emiko told her she had no income.

"Hmm." She gave Emiko an embarrassingly close look. "You're pretty. You could get a job where I work."

"Where's that?"

"At the Hi Crass Bar."

"Oh, I don't know."

"It pays better than being a tea girl in some big company." Mariko checked the clock. "Anyway, I have to be going. See you tomorrow morning, maybe."

Emiko opened the newspaper and read the headline. "U.S. Army Brings Charges against Lieutenant Calley for the My Lai Massacre."

The stern lady in the gray apron approached. "Uh, Miss." Time was up. Emiko waited on the sidewalk until the last of the lodgers had come out. No Satoru. She waited a little longer. He didn't appear. She hoped this was a good sign, a sign he was managing without her help. She didn't need an aimless boy to worry about. If she was going to stay in Tokyo much longer, she *did* need him to pay back the money she'd lent him, though.

6

Unfinished business

They were the ghosts of men drafted from the valley who had been killed in battle. The number of them in uniform increased every year.

—Ōe Kenzaburo, *The Silent Cry*

Juan's nurse clicked her tongue. "All right. No more blood or urine tests. You're cleared."

"No infection?"

"Not what we've been testing for. We were testing for drugs."

Immediately, Juan thought of Lieutenant Joss. His lieutenant was definitely high on cocaine when he called for the attack on what was being called Bighorn Ridge. When they brought him here for questioning, did they give him a drug test?

"And we're going to move you to a bunk in the hospital staff quarters. We need your bed for another patient. No more breakfast in bed. You'll eat in the staff mess hall."

"So this is good-bye, Nurse?"

She smirked. "Report back here again at 0700 the next few days to get your bandage changed." She checked her clipboard. "You're to report downstairs to CID at 0800."

Juan's chest bandage had gotten smaller each time they changed it. He felt more itch than pain there now. The ribs still hurt when he moved, but the nurse told him he shouldn't just lie in bed. "Do some walking. You're young. You'll heal fast."

Juan walked—slowly—down to the hospital waiting room and picked up a copy of the military newspaper *Stars and Stripes*. The headline said the army was finally bringing charges against Lieutenant Calley for the My Lai massacre. For the first time, Juan read some of the details of what Calley was accused of. Compared to him, Joss was a small fish. Juan wondered if the army was ready for any additional public embarrassment after My Lai.

The CID guys looked chagrined when Juan came in. *Stars and Stripes* was open on the desk. The unibrow looked up. "Private Gomez, the Lieutenant Joss inquiry has been put on hold. Your orders now are to take medical leave in Tokyo until further notice." Juan could leave Camp Oji, but he needed to sign out every day, sign back in, and sleep in the male staff quarters every night. He could stop at the purser's office to pick up his back pay.

He went to check out the hospital staff sleeping quarters. Beyond the swinging doors, a massive blue laundry bin reeked of a now familiar smell—iodine, silver nitrate, and alcohol used to treat wounds and burns. He shuffled in his slippers cautiously across the waxed floor and found his bunk. It was on the top.

Somebody tapped him on the back. "I seen you walking pretty slow. Guess you're wondering how you're going to climb up there, am I right?" The Spec-4 hospital orderly held out his hand. "Walter Jones."

"Juan Gomez. Yeah, having a little problem with some fractured ribs right now."

"Tell you what. This here on the bottom is mine. I'll switch with you." Walter spoke with an accent Juan hadn't heard before. He told Juan he was from a little South Carolina island named Coosaw. "Gullah, they call us. The way we talk, that's Gullah, too."

Juan said he was from a bigger island, farther offshore.

Puerto Rico.

Walter heaved his own blankets up onto the top bunk. "There you go." He glanced at Juan standing in his light gray hospital pajamas and chuckled. "Medivac patients don't travel with much luggage, do they?"

"I guess my fatigues are somewhere."

Walter shook his head. "No. I cleaned up after they brought you in. What was left of your fatigues got dumped in the garbage. Boots, too. Everything."

Juan looked down at his slippers. "They said I could leave base. Walking would do me good."

"You wouldn't be wearing your boots anyway. We're required to wear civilian clothes off base."

"How come?"

"Don't want the locals to see us all over the place, I guess. We're supposed to blend in." Walter gave a high-pitched laugh. "You have dark hair. That's good, but you're a head taller than any of the locals. And, me, I'm black." He said Juan could buy some "blend-in civvies" in the post exchange downstairs when he cashed in his paycheck.

They sat on the bottom bunk. Walter had been in the country for over a year with plenty of time to look around. He took a map from his pocket. "Let's see. What's close by? Here you go. The Oji-jinja shrine. You got to see that. Everything around it was destroyed in the World War II fire bombings, but the main shrine was left standing." Walter pursed his lips. "Some things you can't kill, I guess. The locals say a spirit lives in it. And the big old ginkgo tree next to it survived. Supposed to be about six hundred years old."

Walter went back on duty, and Juan looked for some clothes in the PX. When the Japanese store clerk held up a shirt in front of him checking for size, she said, "Ooo, yes. Very nice."

He also picked out pants and shoes, a shaving kit, and a

duffle bag to put it all in. The clerk added a tie to his pile of purchases.

"No thanks. I don't want to look like a Mormon missionary."

He had Walter's map, but before long, he got lost and hailed a taxi. He had to say the name of the shrine twice before the driver understood. A towering Japanese-style gate marked the entrance. Juan followed some school girls in blue uniform skirts up to the ancient wooden shrine and paused, wondering if he could go inside. The school trip group stopped at a little structure to run water over their fingers, then went in. Juan did the same and followed. He stood aside while they took pictures of each other with two fingers held up in a V. Walter had told him the Japanese got this from seeing GIs take pictures of themselves after the war. V for victory. Little did these girls know what they were signaling in their photos. The victory, Juan thought, was now complete.

And yet when he examined the darkened old wood of the shrine that had survived the bombing, he wondered if that was true. Walter had said there was a spirit living in the shrine. Juan didn't have to believe in gods or spirits to imagine a spiritual strength that survived in a people who had experienced so much devastation.

This link to ancient values for Juan seemed to be symbolized in the ginkgo tree. He sat on a low stone wall wondering how deep the roots had to be of a tree that had stayed alive over six hundred years. The other trees had been destroyed and replaced, and shiny new shrines had replaced those that were burnt down. But in the midst of the new, the modern, and the changed, the old ginkgo and shrine survived. Who knew what old ideas managed to survive as well?

The excursion tired Juan more than he expected. His ribs were hurting. He ate an early dinner in the mess hall, changed back into his pajamas, and lay in his bunk studying Walter's map until he fell asleep.

He woke up when Walter came back for the night. The room was dark. He could only see the whites of Walter's eyes moving towards him. He felt Walter's fingers on the side of his neck.

"Sorry. Just wanted to check."

"That I'm alive?"

"It wouldn't be the first time .... Never mind. Hey, I want to show you something."

Juan sat up, no longer sleepy. Walter led him into a dark, cavernous storage room with a skylight. "Fall's the best season for looking at the night sky," Walter said. "Look at those stars."

They sat on boxes, gazing through the skylight. "Sometimes the sky's like that in Vietnam," Juan said. "I liked to lie on my back in the fields looking up."

"I been over to Nam," Walter told him. "You talk about fields. In the daytime, I guess you've seen that wavy air rising up over the hot grass?"

"Yeah."

"I'll tell you what that is. Haints."

"What?"

"It's what we call ghosts on Coosaw Island. Nam's a country crawling with ghosts these days."

If there was such a thing as ghosts, Walter was definitely right about Vietnam. So many dead. They never completely disappeared. They kept haunting the minds of the living.

"Here in Japan they call them *yūrei*. You know what the Japanese say it is that calls the ghosts back? Unfinished business. Something like that." Walter rocked back and forth on his box. "I guess there's a lot of haints in Nam that have unfinished business."

"That's for sure. Other places, too, I guess. How about

here in this hospital?"

"Oh, yeah. You know it. Plenty of them."

Juan felt a tingle in his chest. "I wonder, do you happen to know if anybody else from the Bighorn Ridge battle was evacuated to this hospital?"

Walter gave him a slow nod. "A Private Riggs. Same day you were brought in." Walter let out a deep breath. "Sorry to say he died."

"He was in my platoon," Juan murmured.

Walter put his hand on Juan's shoulder. They stopped talking and stared up at the stars until they were tired, then went to bed.

That night Juan had a dream about Alan Riggs. Alan was standing stiff and motionless in a rice field, not in fatigues but in gray pajamas, his eyes fixed on Juan in a fiery stare. Juan strained to hear what he was saying, but Alan's mouth never opened. The only communication was through his eyes.

7

Tokyo runaways

"I shall be nothing, the wind, the sky."
—Dazai Osamu, *No Longer Human*

Emiko was running out of ways to search for her father. Back home in Kitayama, when she needed some information, she'd always gone to the little library next to the post office. There were libraries of all types and sizes all over Tokyo. She decided simply to try the nearest, the Arakawa Ward library, only a short walk away.

The main room was filled with mothers and their children. A librarian with a string of pearls and a brown dress looked surprised when Emiko approached her desk and asked her a question—probably, Emiko assumed, because she hadn't given the traditional little bow before speaking, something she couldn't worry about right now. She was here to check death reports for her father.

"The newspapers are on microfilm," the librarian told her. "That's where you should search."

Emiko had checked the major newspapers in Kitayama regularly since her father was missing. She told her mother she was looking for possible "news" of him. No need to mention exactly in which section of the papers she dreaded finding that news. Now with microfilm, every newspaper in the country was available. She took a deep breath as the librarian showed her how to load the reels.

Emiko figured she had about eight months of reports to go through—the time her father had been missing. She sneezed as she scrolled through reel after dusty reel. After a few hours, she'd gone through reports covering just the first two months after her father was missing. No arrests, no death notices under his real name or any of the aliases she knew he used. It was mostly notorious criminals or famous people who were reported on. She rubbed her eyes and sighed.

The only articles with any relation to her father's disappearance described the increasing number of men going missing in Japan. She also found a series of articles about young Japanese, mainly males—possibly rejecting pressure to excel in school or start a prestigious career—who left home, went to Tokyo, and became addicted to sniffing glue. When she read that a favorite place for them to congregate was a decrepit neighborhood of Shinjuku, Satoru's face flashed before her mind.

Emiko winced at the tall stack of reels the librarian had brought. She'd never be able to go through all that. Her head hurt. Her eyes watered. She had to give up.

She was hungry and opened her purse to decide how much she could spend on lunch. Not much. Out on the street, she followed the smell of roasting *takoyaki* octopus fritters to a sidewalk stand on the corner. This was one of her favorites, and cheap. Three of the breaded balls filled her up. She hadn't eaten rice since she'd come to Tokyo. Her mother would tell her she was going to lose her strength.

Since Satoru seemed to have disappeared, Emiko decided to go to Shinjuku to look for him. The Yamate line was above ground, giving her a view of the city. As masses of unfamiliar buildings passed by, her hands became moist, and she wondered what she was getting into.

She had copied down the district and even the two block numbers identified in the newspaper article where "rebellious youth" tended to congregate. But when she left the station, she was overwhelmed. Shinjuku was teeming with people and so expansive she didn't know which way to turn. Her first instinct was to find a police box and ask directions there, but she quickly thought better of that.

The corner buildings had block numbers on them, but that wasn't going to be enough. She was looking for an open area, not a specific building. She started to wonder why she was even bothering to look for Satoru. It wasn't as if he was any relation. But somehow he had become attached to her in her mind.

About to give up, she walked in the direction of the Takashimaya department store. If she couldn't find Satoru, at least she could do some window shopping. Just then a tall, skinny teenager carrying a clear plastic bag crossed in front of her, wobbling unsteadily.

She followed him. At first she hung back considerably so he wouldn't notice. At each corner, he lifted the bag to his nose and took a breath. Soon Emiko realized there was no way he would be aware of anybody following him. Nor would he care. He was in his own world.

When the glue sniffer neared the edge of a small city park, he headed for a bench and sat down. His arm moved in slow motion, now and then lifting the bag to his face. Emiko stood at the edge of the park until he seemed to notice her. But she couldn't tell for sure. His face was blank. She moved up to the bench and stood in front of it. He showed no more concern than if a pigeon had landed there.

"I'm looking for somebody," she stated. "Orange hair. From Nakakuni. His name's Satoru. I wonder if you know him."

The teenager looked up to the clouds. "Satoru," he repeated. "Satoru. Satoru." It was as if he liked the sound of the word.

Assuming she'd get nothing from him, Emiko turned to

leave.

"I know him," the boy mumbled. He pointed towards the station. "Down by the tracks."

"Where?"

He stretched out his arm out, then jabbed down with a finger. Emiko saw there was a small incline where the trains entered the station. She didn't bother to ask any more questions.

Satoru was lying with some others on a slope of warm white rocks beneath the level where they could be seen from the street. He was asleep, a clear plastic bag still gripped in his hand. Emiko squatted, shook his shoulder until he blinked and gave her a languid smile.

"Get up." She punched his shoulder. "This is disgusting."

Satoru sat up, flicking the bag aside. He had the same emotionless look on his face as the teenager on the bench.

"Talk to me," Emiko insisted. "Why are you doing this?"

Her voice seemed to call him back partly from wherever his mind had flown. The other glue sniffers stirred and climbed up the slope towards the park. Emiko picked up Satoru's bag and tossed it away. A crow flew down and picked it up but dropped it immediately, letting out a blood-curdling squawk.

Satoru lifted his eyes towards the crow flying up into the sky. "I want to be free of the cares of world."

"Um-hum. Looks like you're on the right track."

"Don't laugh." His voice was tranquil. "I want to purify my life, like my friend. He's giving up everything and becoming a monk. I wish I could be like him. He's smart. He can memorize the prayers, learn all the ceremonies. I always knew I couldn't. But I don't want to wear a suit and write computer programs." He sighed. "I was going to give it a try anyway. But then I found this."

Tōshin, the novice monk in the Nakakuni temple—he must be the friend Satoru was talking about, Emiko thought.

A monk's life had always seemed rather absurd to her, to tell the truth. But she understood the concept of rejecting worldly ambitions. On the contrary, what Satoru was doing to himself was just wrong.

And yet, what was his other choice? Force himself to become a computer programmer or accountant or whatever, then find himself trapped in a job he hates in order to support a wife and children, feeling unable to be himself? This was exactly what the psychologists, the writers, the police had said created the phenomenon of runaways that was currently plaguing the country.

Is that what Emiko was doing, running away? After all, she'd run away from mind-numbing work in the factory. From the expectations of people like Jun-oba about how she must act, how she must order her life. And here she was sitting on a bank of stones beside a railroad track. She wasn't sniffing glue, but she was sitting beside someone who was.

"Can you lend me some more money?" Satoru's voice was squeaky.

"Sorry. I'm broke." Just admitting it made her stomach sink. "But unlike you I'm going to get a job. I don't know what. Maybe I'll go to work as a bar hostess. A girl at the Sanya House already suggested it to me."

Satoru seemed to be sobering up, or whatever you called it when the effect of glue fumes wore off. He breathed out a long, incredulous "Heh ...."

Emiko had to look away. "That is, just until ... I don't know. I'm hoping to get some information on my father."

"You mean the Hi Crass Bar near the Sanya House?"

She nodded. "But Satoru-san, the important thing is you have to stop sniffing glue and get some kind of job, too. Any job. You don't have to be a computer programmer."

He looked away. "I don't know."

A loud, wavering shriek rang out as a train approached

the station. "Let's get out of here," Emiko urged. "We're too near the tracks. Besides, we must be on Japanese National Railroad property."

"You go on," Satoru answered. "They know people hang out here. Nobody bothers us." He looked down the bank towards his plastic bag. Emiko left him there before she had to watch him go and retrieve it.

Exhausted, depressed, Emiko stood at the door of the Sanya House once again, waiting for it to open. Sergeant Oizumi had said it might take two or three days to get the police report. She'd been too generous with Satoru and now worried that her money might not last that long.

When the Sanya House opened, there was no sign of Satoru. She decided to skip dinner and shuffle in for the night with the cluster of women also waiting for the lodge to open. She washed, climbed up to her bunk, and fell asleep at once.

She was awakened by a sound of clumping and stumbling in the dark.

"*Itai. Kuso. Chikushō.*" Ouch, shit, damn.

"Hsss." The scratchy voice of an old woman called out for quiet.

"Emiko, are you awake." It was Mariko, the girl Emiko had met that morning. Talking too loud.

"Hsss. You girls go out to the lobby. It's the middle of the night. People are sleeping in here."

When Mariko tapped her on the arm, Emiko rubbed her eyes, got up, and followed her to the little table in the lobby. Mariko was wearing a tight powder-blue dress, her hair set upstyle with bangs. When she sat on the little chair, the short dress rode up to reveal most of her upper legs. She told Emiko, "After I was paid tonight, I have enough for the *reikin* key money and the deposit."

"For an apartment? That's great."

The yakuza manager flashed a vindictive grin over his gold teeth. "So. You're not too good to work here after all?"

Emiko's desperate wish to stay longer in Tokyo and the prospect of quick money had won. She'd allowed Mariko to bring her for an "interview."

"Yoshidama." The manager waited for Emiko's name, then tilted his head. "I hope you have decent clothes. You look like you're dressed to sweep up, not entertain guests."

Emiko turned to go. "I knew this was a bad idea."

"Wait a minute. Don't leave. If you need it, I can give you an advance to shop for something to wear. It'll come out of your pay."

And that was it. She was to start that night.

Mariko took her arm. "Let's go. I'll show you a fantastic place to get clothes in Harajuku."

Emiko was hesitant. She'd read about the gaudy shops in that section of town.

"Come on. One transfer and two stops and we're there. You'll love it."

Most of the things in the "Montmartre Boutique" Emiko couldn't even imagine herself wearing. Finally, not wanting to seem difficult, she picked out a lavender blouse. Mariko nodded and held up a white skirt. "This will go perfectly with it."

Emiko felt her cheeks burn. "You're kidding. Look how short it is."

"It's the style, Emiko-chan. Perfectly suited to your long legs. Hi Crass Bar customers aren't coming in to talk to a school teacher or housewife."

With new belt, shoes, and underwear, the bill came to more than the Hi Crass Bar manager had given her. Her palms were sweaty when she paid.

"Don't be so nervous," Mariko teased. "You'll have plenty

of money soon."

Mariko took Emiko with her to Shimbashi to pay the real estate agent, then to see her "apartment"—a single room, really, with a toilet in the hallway. It was on a second level overlooking the Yamate line train tracks. The room rumbled whenever a train went by and, with no curtain yet, was lit by a blinking blue neon sign advertising *Kirin Beer – Kirin Beer – Kirin Beer*.

"I'm going to move in tonight," Mariko said. "We could share the room, but …."

There was hardly space to spread out a single futon on the floor. "I'm fine at the Sanya House for now," Emiko assured her.

8

The little-girl voice

"Good evening, my sweet gentleman, so glad to see you."

—Sōseki Natsume, *Botchan*

Before the Hi Crass Bar opened for customers, Yoshidama needed to see Emiko's new outfit. She and Mariko changed in the little room behind the bar that served as an office. There was no mirror, but Mariko took a little one from her bag. Yoshidama knocked on the door and came in. "Ah! Yes. This will do."

Emiko's only knowledge of bars was from television shows. "What exactly should I—"

"Flatter the customers. Keep them ordering drinks and *otsumami* snacks," Yoshidama instructed. "And keep them buying drinks for you."

"But I don't think I can drink very much."

"Don't worry. There won't be any alcohol in yours."

Mariko put in, "And if they take out a cigarette, light it for them."

"Your pay depends on how much they spend," Yoshidama warned. "That's all you really need to know."

A bent old man came in to mop the floor. The girls, four of them altogether, spread tablecloths and put ashtrays and Hi Crass Bar matchbooks on the booth tables. The domesticity both calmed Emiko and at the same time annoyed her. It felt a little like they were setting traps.

"*Irasshayimase!*" The girls sang out in a high-pitched

chorus of welcome when the first two gray-suited salarymen came in. Emiko stared at the floor in silence. She found it demeaning to fake enthusiasm like this.

The salarymen looked to be in their forties. Yoshidama took their orders and brought them their drinks. They weren't regulars, so weren't looking for any particular hostess. Yoshidama tapped Emiko on the shoulder and pointed his chin towards their booth.

Emiko took a deep breath and approached. "Welcome, gentlemen. I wonder, may I sit with you?" It was what Mariko had told her to say. One of the men slid over, and she sat down, already feeling uneasy at asking to sit next to a stranger.

The man next to her had thick glasses that magnified his pupils. The one across from her had hair that stuck up in random places and large ears that bent forward. Emiko realized that in the real world not many twenty-year-old girls would be eager to talk to them. So maybe this was all right. She was getting paid to make them happy.

She studied their suits to see if she could discern any difference between them. Design? Material? Texture? Tone? No. They looked like mirror images. She studied their ties. Same material and texture, but here there was a difference: one was navy blue and the other was a lighter blue.

She told them her first name, as Mariko had instructed. They gave their last names, as expected. Mr. Oha next to her revealed two buck teeth when he spoke. Mariko hadn't told her what to talk about. "Where do you work, Mr. Oha?" she asked.

"A trading company," he answered, tapping a cigarette from a Seven Stars pack and dropping the pack on the table.

"I see," Emiko said. "What is it exactly that you do there?"

Mr. Oha looked at Mr. Kagyo as if for the answer but got no response. "Um," Oha told Emiko, "I work in the international exchange department."

"Oh, really?" Emiko tried to feign interest. "And what do you do there?"

Oha seemed surprised at the line of conversation and lit a cigarette. "I monitor the hourly exchange rates and change the figures on the board. Actually, I give the exchange rates to an office girl, and she goes to the contract room to post the figures." He took a long drag on his cigarette and let it out slowly.

"And how about you, Mr. Kagyo. What do you do?"

Kagyo took the unlit cigarette from his mouth and almost inaudibly mouthed, "Same thing."

"I don't understand."

"I do Western countries," Oha explained. "Mr. Kagyo does Eastern."

Somehow Emiko felt depressed by this answer. "I see. Do you ever feel that your job is monotonous?"

"Eh?" Oha responded. Kagyo put the unlit cigarette back in his mouth.

"I mean, you know that Greek myth of the guy constantly rolling a rock up to the top of the hill, only to have it roll back down again?"

"Eh?" said Mr. Oha.

"I just wonder," Emiko explained. "Do either of you ever wonder if you could do something more constructive or meaningful?"

"You sound like my son," Kagyo retorted. He held his unlit cigarette and gulped down his *mizuwari* whiskey and water. As if on cue, Oha finished his. Both men seemed to be getting more uneasy rather than relaxed. Emiko decided it was time to change the conversation topic.

Sensing his magnified eyes on her, she asked Mr. Oha, "What is your opinion of the Japan – U.S. Status of Forces Agreement?"

"Eh?"

Kagyo chimed in, "We didn't come here to talk about that."

"About what, gentlemen?" It was the manager, Yoshidama, now standing beside the booth. "Another drink, Sirs? The young lady is new and must have forgotten to ask. I'm very sorry. My apologies." He caught Emiko's eye and made a sign of striking a match.

"Hm?" Emiko frowned. "Ah, yes. She picked up a book of Hi Crass matches, but Kagyo waved his hand *no*. "I think we'll be going. Thanks. We've had enough for tonight."

The chorus of hostesses, sans Emiko, sang out *Arigato gozaimasu*, thank you so much, as the two men left the bar.

"Back room," Yoshidama commanded Emiko. He saw that Mariko wasn't with any customers at the time. "Mariko, you too."

The back room was stuffy, smelling even more like smoke and beer than the bar itself. A small rice cooker—Yoshidama's dinner?—steamed on a shelf that must have also served as a table. Mariko and Emiko were squeezed together against a wall facing the manager. "What the hell was that?" he bawled at Emiko.

"I did something wrong?"

"I heard the way you talked. You're supposed to talk *cute*."

"Seriously?" Emiko couldn't believe he wanted her to speak to customers in the high-pitched, fawning, little-girl register that women often used. It just wasn't her.

Mariko cut in. "And remember, Emiko. I told you to flatter them, light their cigarettes. The worst thing you can do is contradict or tease them."

"I understand," Emiko conceded. "I'll try to do better. Can you give me some ideas of what to talk about?"

"It's not what but how. Just act as if anything they say is brilliant."

Yoshidama barked, "So what *were* you talking about, Missy? I was watching. They seemed to be getting more and more uncomfortable."

"About their jobs," Emiko said. "And the Japan – U.S. Status of Forces Agreement."

"Whaat?" Yoshidama and Mariko yelled out together.

"What's that?" Mariko marveled.

"You idiot!" Yoshidama was furious. "That's it. You're fired. You earned nothing tonight. You still owe me for the clothes."

Mariko grasped Yoshidama's arm. "Please. She was doing her best. Give her another chance. She can learn. I'm begging you."

Yoshidama turned to Mariko. "Your friend's a pretty girl. Keep her with you tonight and teach her how to act, and I'll give her one more chance tomorrow night."

The next night was her second chance. Emiko had sat in with Mariko and some customers later the first night to see how it was done. She'd lit cigarettes and got Mariko's customers to buy her drinks, too, but Yoshidama paid her nothing for that night.

She'd rehearsed comments like "How fascinating!" and "I can't imagine; that must be difficult" when they mentioned their jobs. If they talked about their children, she would ask to see pictures and marvel at how pretty or cute or handsome they were. She practiced the obsequious intonation she would use. She even practiced using a Tokyo accent. It all made her feel a little sick to her stomach, but she was ready.

The first customers came in—three blue-suited men. Emiko managed to mumble *Irasshayimase* with the chorus, and Yoshidama sent her to their booth. In the high-pitched voice she'd practiced, she asked if she could sit with them. They smiled. Last night the men hadn't smiled when she said it. The little-girl voice was what they liked.

Her father hated it. He scoffed and grimaced when women on television simpered like that. Where was he? Not only had she failed to find him but she was on her way to becoming the kind of woman he laughed at.

The conversation moved past names to occupation titles. The men all seemed to have important-sounding titles. What could Emiko call herself, she wondered? Consumer Development Liaison Representative maybe?

"Something funny?" one of the men asked.

Time to think on her feet. "No. It's just that handsome men make me giggle, I guess." Was that going too far? Obviously not, the man's satisfied grin told her. "Buy me a drink?" she quickly added. Now, according to Mariko's instructions, she needed to flatter the other men so they wouldn't feel left out. She reached towards the man next to her, touched his tie. (This was permissible, Mariko had said. Even encouraged.) "Such a beautiful tie. It must be expensive." His embarrassed smile told her she was on the right track. When the third man tapped a cigarette from his pack, she lit it.

Her drink came—she'd asked for a White Russian, a drink whose name fascinated her. She held the glass up for a toast, then pointed out that one of the men had almost finished his drink. "Ah, before we toast, Mr. Nakaguri needs a refill." He nodded agreement, and she signaled Yoshidama to bring another.

Things were going along smoothly tonight. Emiko was on her third "White Russian," which tasted like watery cream, and the men's red faces attested to her efforts to keep them drinking. From the corner of her eye, she saw Yoshidama flash her a gold-toothed smile.

Then a noise at the door made everybody look up. The old man who mopped the floor and served as a doorman was scuffling with somebody, trying to keep him out. Emiko gasped as she recognized the bedraggled Satoru, bag of glue protruding from a pocket and a glazed look in his eyes, pushing past the old man. At the bleached hair, the filthy T-shirt, and the developing goatee, several hostesses screamed.

Satoru lurched into the bar, peering into each booth until he found Emiko. She stood and tried to lead him away.

"I need to borrow some money," he said loud enough for everybody to hear.

"Get him out," one of the hostesses shrieked.

Satoru said, "Emiko, Please."

Yoshidama had gone into the back room but came out when he heard the women yelling. He grabbed Satoru in a headlock. "You know this man?" Yoshidama growled at Emiko, his yakuza rolled Rs startling even the men in Emiko's booth, who scattered money on the table and slipped out of the bar.

"Let him go," Emiko said. "He won't cause any harm."

Yoshidama dragged Satoru towards the door, Emiko following. Out on the street, Yoshidama threw Satoru to the ground and kicked him.

"Stop it!" Emiko yelled.

Satoru struggled to his feet.

"Run, Satoru," Emiko shouted. "I can't give you any money."

Yoshidama turned to Emiko. "You! Don't think of ever coming into my bar again. I knew you were trouble from the start." He yanked open the bar door and slammed it shut behind him.

Mariko came out onto the street to hand Emiko her backpack. "I don't understand, Emiko. I didn't think you were friends with people like that. I'm sure you understand that kind of a scene can ruin a bar's reputation." When Emiko only hung her head, Mariko touched her arm. "Are you going to be all right?"

Emiko gave a single nod. "Yes. Thanks for your kindness and help, Mariko. I hope I didn't get you in too much trouble."

Emiko searched a few nearby streets of Sanya thinking she might find Satoru hiding somewhere, but he was gone. Now what? She'd already paid for the night at the Sanya House, so that was good. And she had her jeans and other things in her backpack. She remembered Sergeant Oizumi said he was on duty until 10 p.m. Yes, the light in his kōban was still on. When she walked in, the Sergeant did a double-take.

"Maybe you don't remember me?" she said.

"Emiko. Of course, I remember you. It's just ... you look different."

She realized she'd been walking around with a backpack in a very short silky skirt. Her blouse was partly pulled out, and her hair had probably been messed up in the scuffle in front of the bar. "I ..." she stuttered, pulling her hair from her eyes. "It's hard to explain."

"Are you all right? That's the important thing."

"I'm not hurt. Just ashamed to be standing here like this."

Sergeant Oizumi pulled out a chair. "Then sit, please. I can guess where you've been working. I know you need to support yourself somehow. Nothing to be ashamed of."

It was all she could do to keep from throwing her arms around this gentle man. She only said pointedly, "It's been three days."

He sucked in a concerned breath of air through his teeth, pulling out a folder from his desk. "Yes. I have a partial report. It's both good and bad, I'm afraid." He spread the paper on his desk. "This is a report for each prison, as well as the detention centers. The good news: he's not in jail." Sergeant Oizumi took off his glasses. "And in a way I suppose that's also the bad news since we still don't know where he is."

"You said partial report?"

"So far they've only checked under his real name. I was told it will take ten days or so to check under all the names on your list."

"Another ten days?"

"Yes, but they promised they could do it. If you can just wait a little longer."

She didn't see how she could stay in Tokyo that long, but she gave a stoic nod.

The policeman offered her tea, but she said she was tired and wanted to sleep. He walked with her to the door of the Sanya House.

It was late and once again the washroom was empty. She hung her new clothes on the wall and streamed pan after pan of hot water over her whole body. She wasn't sure what she was trying to wash away.

She'd lost her chance to finance her stay in Tokyo long enough to find her father. She probably could have stayed on at the bar if Satoru hadn't come in. She'd been getting good at pleasing the customers. But the job made her feel, well, somehow dirty. She scrubbed her whole body until her skin was red.

In the cramped bunk, she lay searching through her backpack. There was enough money for another night at the Sanya House, a couple bowls of ramen, and a ticket home to Kitayama. There would be no pay for her two nights working at the bar. In fact, Yoshidama might even find her and demand she pay him back for the clothes. She tucked her wallet into the backpack and stared at the wood ceiling above her head. It seemed to be pressing down towards her, trapping her in a tomb of hopelessness.

Wiping tears from her cheeks, she reached again into her backpack and took out Genji's business card.

II

9

Just like home

Every worm to his taste; some prefer to eat nettles.

—Tanizaki Junichiro, *Some Prefer Nettles*

Juan woke up to the shouts and clatter of the hospital staff getting up for work. In no time at all, he was sitting on his bunk in the big empty room—the only occupant who didn't have to report somewhere.

When the nurse changed his bandage at 0700, she said, "I think you can handle this by yourself from now on. I'll let the doctor know." She checked her clipboard. "CID needs to see you again."

The unibrow was alone this time. His face was flushed. "Take a seat, Private Gomez." He tapped a paper on his desk. "We won't be needing you as a witness any longer." He let out a long sigh. "The army has dropped all charges against Lieutenant Joss."

Juan, especially after reading about the My Lai incident, was disappointed to hear this—and it seemed the CID guy was, too. People like Calley and Joss should be exposed. And yet Juan couldn't help being relieved that he wouldn't have to describe things Joss had done.

"Lieutenant Joss is on R and R in-country for a month. Best to avoid him as long as you're here. He seems to think it's you that got him in trouble."

"But—"

"I know. We had multiple reports from other sources

and never finished interviewing you. He's got it in his head, though."

Juan met Walter in the mess hall for lunch. Walter was glowing. "Got my orders. End of active service. Two more days and I'm going home."

Juan congratulated him, swallowing his disappointment. "I'm going to miss you. It's lonely around here in the hospital. The war sucks, but I miss hanging around with the guys."

"Tell you what. I have the rest of the day off. Screw this chipped beef and toast. I know where you can get the best *yakitori* skewered chicken in Tokyo."

On the train Juan watched in amazement as the city flitted by his window. When they approached Shinjuku station, he caught sight of a young man and a pretty girl sitting on some rocks quite near the tracks.

"Glue-sniffers," Walter informed him. "Stay away from those types."

Juan found himself gawking at the neon lights, tall buildings, countless little shops, and sidewalks jammed with smartly-dressed people rushing in all directions. Some of the restaurants looked like gaudy fake palaces, but Walter took him down a side street and into a dark shop where the customers, mostly older men, sat at narrow tables along walls blackened by smoke. They found a table towards the back across from steaming skewers of chicken and chicken organs sizzling over a long brazier of flaming coals.

"Japanese soul food," Walter beamed. He ordered *shiro*, *reba*, *tebasaki*—two each—and saké. Juan, who'd eaten nothing but rations and mess hall food for years, was thrilled by the taste. It was only later that night that he found out he'd been eating small intestines, liver, and wing tips.

Walter had to work all the next day. The sleeping quarters were already empty. Juan walked through the swinging door and awkwardly up a flight of stairs to his nurse's station. She wasn't the friendliest person, but he felt like talking to somebody. When she saw him, she put down her clipboard. "Just the person I wanted to see. The doctor needs to talk to you. In here."

The doctor looked up from a pile of charts he'd been examining. "Private Gomez? How do you feel? I see you're chest lacerations have just about healed. In another day, you won't need a bandage. You're walking without assistance."

"I feel pretty good."

The doctor tapped his chart. "I'm estimating it will take at least another thirty or forty days for the ribs to heal. Ordinarily, we'd keep you here. Unfortunately, the hospital's preparing to move to a new location. So before that happens, we're discharging as many patients as we can. That would include you."

He wrote something on a form and handed it to Juan. "You're still on medical leave and will have to report back here for a checkup in thirty-five days. We'll be moving soon after that."

Juan asked where he would stay.

"You'll get your orders tomorrow morning. I got you special permission to billet at the Grant Heights military dependent housing area in Narimasu. You'll love it there. Just like being home."

Juan spent the rest of the day buying more civilian clothes at the PX. Also a map and a small black notebook he thought he was going to need. That night Walter couldn't stop talking about seeing his white-haired mother and father again, and his aunts and uncles and the nieces and nephews who still lived on the island.

When Juan woke up the next day, for the first time since he'd been in the country it was raining. He packed his things into his duffle bag and went down to the PX to buy an umbrella. Walter had already gone off to his job, and there was nobody to say good-bye to.

Using directions Walter had written in his notebook, Juan followed their previous route but got off at Ikebukuro. Walter had drawn his approximation of the *kanji* for the Tobu-Tojo line he needed to transfer to, but it still took half an hour for Juan to find the entrance in the massive, multi-leveled station.

So far, on every subway and train he took, Juan needed to stand. The jerking back and forth as he held onto the straps hurt his ribs. But as the Tobu-Tojo train droned on towards the northwestern reaches of the sprawling city, he was finally able to get a seat. The high concrete offices, department stores, and apartment buildings gradually gave way to low wooden shops and houses, still as crammed together as in the heart of Tokyo. Juan didn't see a square foot of land that was unused. Even tiny patches of dirt beside railroad tracks were planted with cabbages or daikon radishes.

The taxi from the station took him through narrow, winding streets barely wide enough for two cars to pass until it stopped at the guard post of Grant Heights. The guard waved them through, and they entered a different world. Acres and acres of green low-cut grass unfolded on all sides. In the distance, lines of identical duplex houses stretched out in the endless green lawn. Some larger buildings, the same putty color as the houses but higher than one or two stories, stood in what seemed random locations. This is not like *my* home, Juan thought.

The taxi driver knew where to take him. Juan showed his papers to the close-cropped "housing manager" in civilian clothes. "The post office is next door," the manager told him. "Your box will be 1264."

Juan chuckled to himself at the idea of getting mail.

"The PX and mess hall are just across the road," the manager said. "You might want to pick up some supplies. Then I'll take you to your billet."

Juan went into the PX and felt he'd entered the warehouse for all America. Shelves and shelves of Budweiser, Jack Daniels, televisions, LP records, comic books, electric razors, lipstick, Hershey bars, Corn Flakes, Cheerios, Rice Krispies, peanut butter. He bought a dozen eggs, some bacon, and a loaf of Wonder Bread. More than enough for a week's breakfast. He also bought a Japanese-English phrase book.

Since it was raining, the manager drove Juan in a huge left-hand drive American car for the short ride to a small one-story building behind the movie theater. "Temporary housing for enlisted men," he explained. "Have a good one."

Juan dropped his duffle bag on a plastic-covered couch. The little house was set up with late 1950s-style furniture like Juan had seen on re-runs of American television shows. He switched on the stale-smelling refrigerator and slid in the eggs and bacon. Now what? He gazed from his open door at the identical, colorless, sterile buildings dotting the fields of grass. It felt as if he'd been moved from one hospital to another much larger one. The isolation from the world of the Japanese was still in effect.

It had stopped raining, and the sun was breaking through the clouds. He decided to take a walk and check out the mess hall. When he was almost there, an army truck pulled up to the post office across the road, and the driver hauled a huge bag of mail inside. Immediately, American women in dresses and teenagers in skirts or khaki pants followed him in. Juan thought of his parents in Puerto Rico. They'd never sent him a letter in Vietnam. He wasn't sure they even knew he was in Tokyo.

He ducked into the post office anyway just to see if he could find box 1264. There seemed to be some mistake because there was a note inside it. He took it out: "Meet me in front of the Officers Club tonight at 1900." It was signed by Lieutenant Joss.

10

The face in the mirror

Truly the past returns to my mind
as though it were a thing of today.
—Zeami Motokiyo, *Atsumori*

Emiko awoke to the clatter of rain on the Sanya House roof. Swishing noises arose from the narrow aisle between bunks as women pressed against each other, covering themselves with transparent plastic raincoats. She heard a portable radio announcing that it was the first rain of the month.

She tied her father's scarf over her head and rushed ducking towards the station, where she found a telephone. Genji's card read *Gen-Sa Sōgō Shōsha*, the "Gen-Sa" presumably making it the Genji Sato Trading Company. It sounded impressive, and the address was in the prestigious Marunouchi business district, across from the Tokyo Imperial Palace.

With nervous fingers, she made the call. She had to give her name to two different people before she was connected to Genji's secretary. "I SEE," the woman intoned in her high-pitched little-girl voice when Emiko told her it wasn't a business call and she was just a friend.

"Emiko? It's really you? Where are you?"

She thought of hanging up but didn't. "I'm in Tokyo."

"Tokyo? Where in Tokyo? I want to see you."

"I'm in Sanya."

"Sanya! What are you doing there? That's no place for you. Listen, can you get to the Ōtemachi station?"

She took a breath. "Yes." This was really happening.

"All right. Call me again when you get there." He gave her a direct number.

When she got to Ōtemachi, the passengers crowding onto the subway were dripping wet. A hunched-up gray-haired woman was selling cheap umbrellas on the platform exit, but Emiko decided to hold on to what money she had. Genji's office was probably no more than a ten-minute walk from the station.

She dialed the direct number and asked for directions.

"It's raining," Genji scolded. "Stand inside the north exit. My driver will come by to pick you up."

Men with umbrellas and raincoats lined up to take taxis that pulled forward one by one along the stand in front of the station. Before long, a black limousine that Emiko remembered from Kitayama stopped, blocking traffic. A driver in a black uniform and cap got out holding an umbrella, ignoring the honking cars. "Miss Ozeki! Miss Ozeki!"

High school girls in blue uniforms stood in awe as the driver escorted Emiko past them towards the car. One of the girls snapped her picture—possibly assuming she was some movie star or celebrity. Genji's driver took her backpack and handed her a white towel to dry her face.

In front of the soaring modern building, a porter came with his umbrella to lead her through the sliding glass doors. Pots of white and yellow chrysanthemums lined the wide corridor. The elevator girl in a gray jacket and skirt sang out a welcome and asked which floor the honorable lady desired. Another girl in a similar outfit showed her into the Gen-Sa Trading Company waiting room and sat her beside an end table displaying a German newspaper. Immediately, yet another girl came to show Emiko into Genji's office.

She pulled off her dripping scarf and set her backpack on the carpet.

"Look at you. You're shivering. Who's taking care of you?

Nobody, it seems." Genji led her by the arm to a maroon upholstered couch embossed with his company's crest.

"The reason I came, Mr. Sato, is I'd like to borrow some money. I want to stay in Tokyo for a while before I go back to Kitayama."

"Emiko, you realize you disappeared before I had a chance to give you my okoden offering for your mother's death? I have it here." He opened a drawer in his desk and brought out a white envelope tied with black ribbon.

The envelope was heavy. She objected, "But you paid for the funeral arrangements. That's more than enough."

"That's different," he said. "This is my funeral offering for you."

"Truly? Thank you, then. I'm very grateful. And I'll pay you back."

"You can't pay back a funeral offering, Emiko. That would be an insult." He turned aside, his eyes glittering in the light from the immense window, and Emiko wondered if it was from tears. She recalled how impressed she'd been with his slightly graying hair and handsome face when she first saw him. He looked even more impressive now, standing before the tenth-floor window of his office overlooking the gardens of the Imperial Palace.

He turned back to her. "I don't suppose you have a change of clothes in your bag?"

"Pardon? No, I ... that is I—"

"No matter. Come as you are."

"I don't understand."

"It's almost lunch time. You must be hungry."

In fact, Emiko was starving. She hadn't eaten anything that day, and she hadn't eaten much at all since arriving in Tokyo. She let her silence stand for a yes.

He told her, "I usually eat at the Palace Hotel. A short walk from here."

Emiko put on her backpack.

"You're bringing that? Well, all right."

On the street, Emiko took Genji's arm and leaned close under his umbrella. The waitress at the Palace Hotel restaurant obviously knew him and led them to his "usual table." Floor to ceiling glass walls revealed the Imperial Palace moat, swans gliding across its indigo surface in the milky light.

"No Kitayama *donburi* rice bowls here," Genji joked, "but the *tempura*'s good."

Emiko nodded quickly. "And with some rice on the side?" She didn't feel up to conversation until she'd eaten more than half the tempura on their platter and two bowls of rice. Genji watched in what seemed frozen amazement, his chopsticks poised in the air.

"So," Emiko said, finishing her second cup of tea. "Tell me about your wife and children."

"No children, sadly."

"And your wife?"

"At the moment, she's not doing well."

"I'm sorry. She's sick?"

"Mm. Actually, she has a problem with alcohol. I want her to go to a rehabilitation facility in Germany." He looked silently out towards the swans. "So far, she refuses."

"Why Germany?"

"I still have connections there. A lot of trading business." The mention of business served to cheer him up. "That Mercedes Benz you were picked up in? The import tax on those is prohibitive unless you know how to get them into the country."

"You trade in cars?"

Genji beamed. "Cars, cameras, steel, wheat, medicine—anything at all. We're a trading company. We set up import-export deals all over the world."

This man was obviously a product of the economic boom

Emiko had been reading about in the newspapers. It was fascinating to sit face to face with someone who'd profited so quickly and unexpectedly. Genji seemed astonished at his own good fortune.

"My offer is still open," he said.

"What's that? You don't mean the second-wife thing? Absolutely not."

"I see." He took a sip of tea and slowly put the cup down. "How about I get you a job at Gen-Sa Trading?"

Emiko pictured the multitude of elevator girls, tea girls, door-opening girls, and other pretty girls that seemed to inhabit Japanese business offices. She didn't see any difference between them and the hostesses at the Hi Crass Bar. "No," she declined. "I can't picture myself in one of those tight skirts and jackets, simpering to men in a whiney voice."

Genji grinned. "I see what you mean." He picked up his cup, then put it back down. "In Kitayama they told me your English is good. We always need translators."

It wasn't something Emiko had ever though of. She needed a moment to let the idea sink in. Her first impulse was to jump at the chance. But the way Genji kept her in his gaze made her uneasy. Would he really give up the idea of making her his mistress so easily?

"Just an idea," he said.

Emiko wanted to keep the offer open but didn't want to commit until she felt more sure of Genji.

He took out a gold fountain pen and a black leather notebook. "You say you'll be in Tokyo for a while. Where are you staying? I'd like to have my assistant in the translation department give you a call tomorrow."

"Um. There's no telephone there."

"Heh .... You said the Sanya neighborhood. Where exactly?"

"It's sort of a dormitory."

Genji put the pen and notebook away. He got up. "Excuse me a minute."

Emiko finished the tempura left on the platter. Through the glass wall she saw the rain had stopped. Sunlight beamed through a break in the clouds, and a light wind rustled rows of red *higanbana* spider lilies along a winding stone path that disappeared from view. Back in Kitayama, at the Higan autumn equinox, Emiko's mother took spider lilies to her parents' graves to pay her respects to the souls that had passed over to the "other shore." Now it was her mother who had passed away.

"Daydreaming?" Genji slid a key across the table to Emiko.

"What's this?"

"I couldn't have you staying in that 'dormitory.' I got you a room here."

She objected, stood up, picked up her backpack. Genji took it from her. They were attracting attention, so Emiko reluctantly let him lead her to the lobby, then the elevator. "I'll go up with you," he said.

The elevator girl greeted them routinely, Emiko was relieved to see. She didn't know exactly what she was afraid of. But that wasn't true. It was the thought of going to a hotel room with a handsome man who'd professed his attraction to her.

Genji set her backpack on a stand and pulled open the curtain as Emiko stood beside him, spellbound at the sweeping view of the Imperial Palace and its gardens. He took her hand. "You're trembling."

"This doesn't seem right. I can't stay here. I appreciate it, but—"

He pulled her into his arms. She could feel his breath on her cheek. This was a moment when she was supposed to feel some kind of sexual thrill like she'd read about, like the women in the factory gossiped about. What she really felt, though, was apprehension. And, strangely enough, a certain sense of obligation. She took a breath and held it when he led her to the bed. "Please. I've never ... I told you I wouldn't—"

"I know. But you're so beautiful. Just this once. I promise." His hand was warm on her face.

A few of Emiko's friends in high school and afterwards had told her about their sexual experiences. In each case, it was something like this: The man wanted it. The girl was curious, at best. "It's over before you know it," they said. "And the guys are so grateful."

She felt his lips on her cheek, neck, lips. Was it really over before you knew it? Maybe she could let him have what he so badly wanted. But as he passionately unbuckled her belt, she resisted. "Wait," she begged. "I'm not ready to do this."

Breathing hard, Genji pressed her down. "Give up your futile hope, Nobuko."

The hair on Emiko's neck and arms tingled. She twisted from his grip and sat up, feeling an electrical charge as if an ethereal presence was in the room. It seemed that someone was behind her. She turned and saw in the mirror a face that looked as much like her mother's as her own.

"What is it?" Genji sat up beside her.

"I'm Emiko."

He seemed bewildered.

"You called me my mother's name."

Genji shuddered, entranced now by the mirror as if he saw an apparition. Emiko seemed to have vanished from his mind.

A thought made her heart race. "I know you and my mother were ... together. As I grew up, I couldn't help hearing some gossip. When I was old enough to understand, I asked her about it. My mother assured me, 'I was always loyal to Hiroji in my heart.'"

Turning again towards the mirror, Genji said, "It's true, I guess. That's what made it so sad."

"Made *what* so sad? I want the truth. Did you sleep with my mother?"

"So many were killed in the war. She finally gave in."

A chill made Emiko gasp. "Don't you realize—?"

"What?"

Goosebumps prickled her arms. Either he didn't know what the possibility was or, worse, he didn't care. She fought back the heaving of her stomach.

Genji's eyes were on her but didn't seem to focus. He seemed to be in another place, at another time. "Hiroji isn't in our way any more," he murmured. "Come here."

She struggled out of his grasp. "Have you lost your mind? Don't try to follow me." She picked up her backpack and ran out.

11

Gainful employment

"When you're held by the dead, you begin to feel that you aren't in this world yourself."
—Kawabata Yasunari, *Thousand Cranes*

Emiko ran without thinking until she was blocked by a crowd waiting for the light at Hibiya-dori Avenue.

Genji had to know he might be her father. Emiko shuddered to realize now that Jun-oba had always assumed he was. When Jun-oba heard Genji wanted to make her his second wife, she'd exclaimed, "You can't do that." When Emiko called her from Tokyo saying she was looking for her father, Jun-oba had said, "He's not your father." Emiko had assumed she only meant that a man who disappears like that doesn't deserve to be called her father.

A fierce anger rose in her chest at the idea that Genji might actually be her father. He wasn't her father. Her father was the man who'd taken care of her since she was born. Her father was the man she loved with all her heart—and was determined to find.

The crowd pushed into her from behind as the *Walk* sign lit. They were all heading towards Ōtemachi station a block away. Emiko went with the flow.

She had money now. She could take a train straight back to Kitayama. But she trembled at the memory of Genji's grip on her arms. He seemed unable to distinguish her from her mother in his crazed mind. His words "Hiroji isn't in our way any more" sounded like a threat or warning. He might come to Kitayama determined to satisfy by proxy his long-frustrated desire for her mother.

The only other place Emiko could think to go right now was back to the Sanya House. She hadn't given Genji the name. She'd be near Sergeant Oizumi's police box and able to check for news of her father if she stayed there.

The streets were less crowded when she got off in Kita-senju. She could walk a little slower and think. Although she could afford now to look for another place to stay, she was exhausted. She turned into the familiar lobby of the Sanya House to pay for the night.

"Miss Ozeki, is it?" The old man looked up from his table, sifting through some papers on a shelf and handing Emiko a note. It was from Mariko: *Yoshidama is furious. He's looking for you—says you cheated him.*

Emiko told the Sanya House man she'd be back by eight o'clock. She checked her map. Just one transfer and she could be at Shimbashi before Mariko left for work. She made it just in time.

"Emiko! I'm so glad you got my note." Mariko wore a worried frown. "Yoshidama does horrible things to people who owe him money. For some reason he seems especially crazy about that lately."

They sat face to face on the tatami. "That's why I came here," Emiko said. "I want to pay him for the clothes. And for the loss to his business that night."

"Oh. You have money now?" Mariko smiled. "From a man? From one of those customers in the Hi Crass Bar?"

"No, not from a man. Well, it was," she admitted with a sick feeling in her stomach. "But not what you think. From ... a friend of my mother's."

"Mm. Anyway." Mariko couldn't stop grinning.

Emiko opened her billfold and took out an envelope. "This is what I figure I owe Yoshidama. Would you give it to him?"

Mariko's face clouded. "Emiko, I can't. I already told him he could take it out of my pay, but he said he needs to get it directly from you." She covered her mouth with a trembling hand.

"Why?"

"I don't want to think about it. It's safest just to avoid him."

Emiko let this sink in. "You think he doesn't just want the money? He wants to ... punish me?"

"He's roughed up some of the girls for cheating." Mariko put her hands to her cheeks.

Emiko's blood boiled in anger. "Has he ever hurt you? Because—"

"Not much. We learn how to handle him."

"I can't believe you offered to pay for me, Mariko. You couldn't be sure you'd ever see me again." She put her hand on Mariko's. "I got you in trouble. I'm sorry."

Mariko smiled. "I didn't know your billfold would suddenly get so fat. So, yes, I thought you might need some help and I might see you again."

Emiko took her Hi Crass Bar blouse and skirt from her backpack and folded them on the mat. "I won't be needing these. You're about my size, so ...."

Mariko picked up the short white skirt, held it to her chest. "I love this."

"Except maybe you shouldn't wear it at the bar. Yoshidama will know you got it from me."

Mariko scoffed. "You think he'll remember you wearing it? No way. Men look at legs, not skirts."

She poured Emiko a cup of tea and frowned. "But, Emiko, I don't think you should stay at the Sanya House. Yoshidama knows you and I were staying there. He might go looking for you."

Emiko bit her lip.

"You can stay here with me. I only have one futon but lots of blankets. We'll just fold the table legs and stand it against the wall." Mariko giggled happily. "My first guest."

"I can stay? Really? Oh, Mariko. I mean, just until I find a place of my own."

"I won't be able to fix you dinner, though." She waved her hand across the room. A rice cooker sat on the mat in the corner, half a bag of rice next to it. On the wall over it, on a little shelf, there was a teapot, strainer, and a box of tea. Since there were no cabinets, that was clearly the sum total of her supplies.

"Let me take you out to dinner," Emiko offered.

"Really? He must be a rich man, that friend of your mother's."

The walls shook as a train rumbled by on the tracks below. Mariko's new yellow curtains were drawn open to let in the afternoon light, but the sun was setting. The blue light across the tracks flashed *Kirin Beer – Kirin Beer – Kirin Beer*.

"Getting dark. I'll close the curtains." Mariko got up.

"How about we go there?" Emiko suggested. "You must be curious what that Kirin beer restaurant is like."

"Actually, I am. I didn't want to go there alone."

It was teeming with men in dark suits and alcohol-reddened faces when the two women ducked under the dark blue *noren* curtain across the doorway. "*Irasshayimase*, a man in a white jacket called out from behind the counter. A few men looked up from their beer and snacks.

All the counter seats were taken. Emiko and Mariko found a table for two along the wall at the other side of the narrow shop. "Let's share a Kirin beer." Emiko chuckled. "I believe they have that here."

A woman in a gray kimono and white apron, probably the wife of the man behind the counter, came to take their order.

"Large bottle?" she asked. Emiko nodded. She looked around to see what the men—it was all men except one woman at the counter—were eating. Mostly, they were just drinking. One was slurping stir-fried noodles. "That looks good," Mariko trilled. They ordered two bowls.

Emiko lowered her voice. "Look at those men drinking, laughing, slurping noodles. They're having much more fun than the men at the Hi Crass Bar. They don't have to pretend. Neither do we."

"Pretend?"

"I mean like we're their girlfriends or something. I hated doing that at the Hi Crass Bar."

"Yeah. I don't enjoy it, Emiko. But they pay me to do it."

Loud laughter burst out at the counter. Emiko and Mariko finished their *yaki udon* and walked by the counter to leave. None of the men even glanced at them.

"*Arigato gozaimashita*," the counter man called out, the rumbling of a train drowning out his last word.

Mariko said, "Now when I see that sign flashing through my window, I'll think of you. Thanks."

Back in the room, Mariko got dressed for her night at the Hi Crass Bar while Emiko washed in the hall bath. After the beer and the noodles, and the excitement earlier that day, Emiko was exhausted. As soon as Mariko left, she rolled out a blanket on the floor and fell asleep.

The next morning, when Emiko woke up, Mariko was sound asleep beside her. Emiko left a note thanking her and quietly took the train back to Minami-senju. The police box, Sanya House, and Hi Crass Bar were all close by. Owing Yoshidama money was unacceptable. She breathed in some courage and marched into the dark bar.

The old janitor-slash-doorman was mopping the floor. "Not open yet. Nobody here. Come back in the evening."

Emiko approached him. "Is Yoshidama in his office?"

"No." The janitor straightened up with a groan. He recognized her now. "He's looking for you."

"Can I leave something in his office?"

"Nobody goes in there." He fixed her in a suspicious stare.

"Can you call him?"

He ignored the question. "Come back this evening."

She persisted. "I came to pay what I owe him. Can you call him and tell him that?"

The old man held out his mop handle like a *kendo* sword. "Come back this evening."

Emiko gave up and went to a newsstand on the station platform. She bought an *Asahi* newspaper and sat on a bench to check the Help Wanted section. Genji had given her an idea. Maybe she could get a job as a translator.

Fortunately, ads for translators didn't specify male or female. She found one for what identified itself simply as an "Advocacy Agency" and called the number from a pay phone beside the newsstand.

The voice on the answering end was curt. "It's newspaper editorials. Some other reports. Got to be fluent in English. We're looking for a university graduate."

Emiko wasn't a university graduate, but she saw a thread of a chance. She started talking in English. Fast. She'd developed a reasonable American accent by watching American TV shows. "What is your agency advocating for, by the way?" Her yakuza Rs, modified, came in handy when she spoke English.

"What? What?" the brusque voice stammered. "Never mind. Just come in this morning at 10:00."

The address was in Nerama-ku at the northwest end of Tokyo, three transfers and about forty-five minutes away, she figured. When she got to Ikebukuro, the last major transfer station, she went into the Tobu department store, thinking it best to buy some clean clothes. She left wearing a new black skirt and a white blouse with a big collar. She boarded the Tobu-Tojo railroad line for Narimasu, a place she'd never even heard of.

The man on the phone—he didn't give his name—had suggested taking a taxi from the Narimasu station. The roads were narrow and unnamed, and he didn't feel like bothering with detailed directions. "Just give the Asahi-cho address to the driver."

It looked more like Kitayama from the taxi window than central Tokyo. The shops and houses were low and made of wood, most with tile roofs. "This is it," the driver said. "Second house down that dead-end path. I can wait to make sure it's correct."

"Please."

It didn't seem right. It was an old two-story traditional house. Nothing like a business. She knocked on the thick cypress door, waited.

"Yes? Who is it?"

"I'm here for the interview."

When the door opened, a narrow-eyed man with an angular chin stood looking down at her. His hair was clipped short, military style. Emiko felt she'd seen him somewhere before.

"You're kind of young," he said. "But come in."

Emiko nodded to the taxi driver and stepped up onto the dark wooden hallway floor. "Back here," the man said, leading her down the hallway to a room at the end. Boxes full of papers were scattered on the tatami floor. The walls were spread with detailed maps of the areas surrounding the National Diet building and the Japan Self-Defense Forces headquarters. Wooden staves were stacked against one of the walls.

The powerfully-built man said to call him "Takashi." He sat in the only empty chair. "You can move those things and sit."

Emiko suddenly remembered where she'd seen him before. She decided to speak English. "I think we met in Hongo near the university when you came into the Beheiren office and talked to a student named Kasumi. I remember you said you were re-locating your office. You'd asked for—"

"Speak Japanese," Takashi barked. "That's enough. I get the idea you know English." He opened an English-language newspaper to an in-depth report on a recent business scandal. "See if you can translate this."

She figured he'd never know if she skipped something she didn't quite understand. She sat up straight and in her imitation of an NHK television anchor announced, "It is well known that Japan's Liberal Democratic Party relies heavily on donations from yakuza organizations. Now prominent members of the party have been found to have personal business ties with operations run by the yakuza. Recently—"

"Enough." He fingered his substantial chin. "The job comes with free housing, so the salary's not that high." He named a figure that was twice what she'd made in the Kitayama factory.

It seemed as if Takashi was waiting for her to accept the job. "You haven't told me anything about your organization," she said. "Are you connected with Beheiren?"

"We support Beheiren's opposition to the war in Vietnam."

"I wonder. Did you happen to know my father, Hiroji Ozeki? He did some work for Beheiren. That's why I ask."

Takashi squinted. "No. We don't tell everybody our names."

"I see." She persisted, "He had a slight limp."

Takashi stared at her. "I don't remember. The Beheiren people come and go."

Emiko didn't like Takashi, but working here might be a way to get some lead on what happened to her father. She stifled her distaste. "And what exactly would my job be?"

"Start by translating English-language news editorials. Then I assume you can work the other way, too. We've collected reports and research by Japanese supporters. They need to be translated into English and published."

"Into English? I guess I—"

"Do you want the job or not?"

It wouldn't be pleasant working for this man. That was for sure. But the income would allow her to stay in Tokyo while she looked for her father. And since this turned out to be an organization that had some connections with Beheiren, there was a chance she might come across someone who knew him.

"May I see the housing?"

"Follow me." He led her back down the echoing hallway.

"My quarters are upstairs," he said, pointing at the door to a stairway. "The only place we meet will be back in my office."

He led her to the end of the hallway and out the back door. There was small, walled garden, weeds mostly, and at the far edge of it a very small house. Inside was a bedroom/sitting room, a separate kitchen, and, amazingly, a bath room with a tub made of fragrant *hinoki* cedar. There were several closets with sliding *fusuma* doors of thick painted cardboard.

"It's furnished," Takashi said, "Refrigerator, stove, futon, sheets, towels, pots and pans, kerosene stove for the winter."

"Mm. It's fine. But I can't help wondering. This neighborhood, it's kind of an out-of-the way place. Why did you decide to locate here instead of central Tokyo?"

"It's cheaper here. And it's near the Grant Heights U.S. military housing base. I might have some activity there soon. Any other questions? Then let's go back, and I'll draw up a contract."

It was no more than an agreement that Takashi scratched out on a sheet of paper. "Includes free housing and utilities," he wrote. She signed it, and he handed her some newspapers with editorials for translation. "I'll give you a couple of days. I expect you to do your work in the back house. Bring the translations to my office here in the big house as you finish them. If I'm not here, there's a slot in the door."

So she was to live in "the back house." Living there had seemed more appealing before she heard it called that. Never mind. She emptied her backpack onto the table in the "back house" and went about making it her new home. Maybe she could invite Mariko to come visit her here.

12

Little America

Like the first whiff of burning incense, or like the taste of one's first cup of saké, there is in love that moment when all its power is felt.

—Sōseki Natsume, *Kokoro*

1900 hours. Juan finished his hamburger and French fries in the Grant Heights mess hall, or cafeteria, as they called it, trying to decide whether to go see Lieutenant Joss. He didn't know if Joss had been given a billet on the compound. That would be odd, considering Juan had been warned to avoid Joss. But logic wasn't the army's strong point, Juan had concluded long ago.

Why not go? Juan wanted a chance to tell Joss he hadn't given CID any information about him, had never made any complaint. Maybe he should have reported some things, but it was clear the army didn't want to hear about it now. And Juan was going to have to serve under Joss when they got back to Vietnam.

The Officers Club was a short walk from the cafeteria. Juan heard American country music as the drab, putty-colored building came into view. He saw a Japanese woman standing in front, apparently waiting for someone. Juan knew that some of the U.S. military stationed in the country had Japanese wives. She was probably waiting for her husband.

Then Juan saw Joss weaving unsteadily towards the Officers Club door. Joss lurched to a stop in front of the woman. Juan was close enough now to hear.

"Hey, Mama-san. Looking good. Here to have a good time?" Joss ran his hand over her behind and squeezed. The woman shrieked, a bewildered, uncomprehending look on her face.

Juan started forward to defend her, but another man who had jumped out of a car got there first. He grabbed Joss by the collar. "Go in and call the MPs," he told the woman, while he held Joss, who seemed too drunk to fight back.

"Wait till the MPs get here, would you?" the man asked Juan. "You witnessed this."

A van pulled up, and an MP jumped out and handcuffed Joss. Another took out a notebook and questioned the woman and the man who'd seized Joss. Juan started to walk away, but the MP taking notes stopped him. "Did you witness what happened here?"

Juan gave a brief description of what he'd seen. He was pretty sure Joss hadn't noticed him before being put into the van, but he was uneasy being on record as a witness. It would be another strike against him in Joss's eyes.

As soon as Juan got back to his billet house, he dropped onto the narrow, chilly bed. He hoped Joss wasn't staying at Grant Heights. Anyway, tonight at least Joss would be staying in the guardhouse. It wouldn't be the first time. Juan remembered a night in Saigon when the MPs picked Joss up off a barroom floor. He'd physically hurt a Vietnamese girl that time, but he was an officer, and they let him go without charges after he slept it off. It seemed likely he'd get off this time, too.

The next morning, when he first woke up, Juan was momentarily surprised to find himself alone in a furnished but vacant house. The total silence fell heavily on him. He was used to having people around—in the streets of San Juan, with his platoon in Vietnam, and even in the hospital. He opened the door onto a wide expanse of empty lawn.

Juan took a walk in hopes of finding somebody to talk to. He found a baseball field and lingered to watch American high schools boys at batting practice. They were arguing about the chances of the New York Mets and the Baltimore Orioles in the coming World Series. Juan felt like he was in the States. They asked him to pitch, and he threw a few, but his ribs hurt. He had to quit.

He walked to the post cafeteria to get a cup of coffee. The military who were off for the day were reading the *Stars and Stripes* for the latest word about what was going on "back home." The conversation was all about the Beatles and Woodstock and Jimi Hendrix. A group of dependent wives complained about the delay before first-run movies were shown in the Grant Heights theater. "We'll never keep up at this rate," one said. They were all living in Japan, but trying to make it as much like the States as possible.

Juan walked away over the mowed grass to get an idea of how big the base was. Eventually he saw up ahead a clearly-defined line of brown Japanese houses marking the edge of the compound—no fence, no wall, just the abrupt end of the U.S. grass and the start of Japanese civilization. It was like walking from a desolate grassland into a wall of humanity.

Juan followed the narrow road through the mass of cramped wooden houses that dead-ended at the edge of the base. The tiny homes of weathered wood pushed in against the road on both sides. Through some of the windows, Juan could clearly see people watching television or eating bowls of rice. Men bicycled by with pots of food balanced over the rear fender. Women in baggy pants and white aprons swept invisible dirt from spotless stone walkways and sprinkled them with water. Others hung clothes to dry on poles propped up wherever room would allow.

The road wound slightly uphill, other lanes branching off

on both sides. Back on one of these lanes, on a little rise, Juan saw a tree bursting with ripe orange persimmons. The roof of the house it belonged to was just visible behind the rows of other houses.

A miniature delivery truck beeped, and Juan stepped aside. Its flat bed was stacked with crates of vegetables Juan didn't recognize. A woman in a dress on a small Honda C 50 beeped as she passed the truck, an empty shopping basket tied to her handlebars. The houses on the road were sporadically interspersed with vegetable stands, ramen shops, a liquor store—all with their products displayed on the street.

The bacon and eggs Juan had cooked for breakfast was fine, but now that he had a stove, he wanted to try to cook some Puerto Rican food. He followed the road until it came to a larger intersection where the residences gave way completely to businesses specializing in specific items—blue jeans, men's suits, cloth for kimonos, shoes, tableware. Juan went into a supermarket. He wanted to make *bacalaitos* codfish fritters.

He was amazed by the neatly-stacked shelves of food that looked intriguing though he had no idea what it was. Behind each section was a man or woman who called out *Irasshay-imase* as he stopped to look. He pulled his phrase book from his hip pocket. OK, they were saying *Welcome*. A man with a blue and white headband standing behind a display of dried fish, some as small as toothpicks, said, "Hallo."

"Fish," Juan said. "I'm looking for fish."

"Fish. Yes, fish." The man pointed to his display.

"Cod fish," Juan clarified.

"Hah ...." The man scratched his head.

A young woman in a black skirt and white blouse stopped beside Juan. "May I help you?"

"Oh, you speak English?"

"A little."

The girl's pretty smile made Juan forget what he was looking for. "Great," he said. It came out louder than he expected.

The girl blushed. "So, is there something you're looking for?"

Several women shoppers, hearing English spoken, had slowed and were lingering near the dried fish, listening.

"Cod fish," Juan said. Not the ideal first thing to say to an attractive girl.

The girl's eyes widened. She pulled a dictionary from her shopping bag. "I think ... let me see. Yes. *Tara.*"

"Ah," the headband man exclaimed. "Tara." The women at his display nodded to each other, "Ah. Tara," as if a deep mystery had been solved.

The headband man waved his hand in front of his face. "No tara." He turned to the girl and said something in Japanese.

"I'll take you to the fish market, if you like," she offered. The women nodded their heads as if they'd understood.

The wide entrance to the fish market was open to the street. The smell was familiar to Juan from his childhood. Crowds of men and women jostled for position in front of racks of iced fish, some as small as sprat and some as large as bonito. White jacketed men in headbands shouted to others behind them at the cutting counters. There seemed to be competition to buy certain kinds of fish. A man delivering a plastic bin of ice accidentally brushed into the girl who'd led Juan here, causing her to trip. Juan caught her by the waist. He held her close as customers squeezed by on all sides. He knew it was longer than necessary. But her eyes were closed and her hand clung to his.

13

Codfish fritters

Autumn nights, it seems,
are long by repute alone:
scarcely had we met
when morning's first light appeared,
leaving everything unsaid.

—Ono no Komachi, *Kokinshū* No. 636

The first thing Emiko needed to do was get some food. She was excited that for the first time since she'd left Kitayama she was going to be able to cook her own meal. She found a gap in the fence behind her house where a dirt path led between tall bush clover and silver grass down to the main road. That meant she wouldn't have to walk past Takashi's house. He didn't need to be concerned with her comings and goings.

She headed up the road leading to the station, where the bigger shops were. She could buy some more clothes, too, since she now had some money and a place to keep them.

Halfway up the road, she noticed a dark-haired young foreigner staring with eyes that seemed to shift between green and blue at a passing truckload of Chinese cabbage. He was darker than most Americans she'd seen. More interesting. He looked lost, or lonely. She hung back, not wanting to pass ahead of him. When he started off again, it was at a halting pace much slower than hers. She wondered if he was hurt. To kill time she ducked into a little shop selling homemade items and picked out a shopping basket. When she came back out, the young man was halfway up the road.

She followed. Or it wasn't really following, was it? She did need to go shopping.

He seemed to be taking in the atmosphere or whatever of the neighborhood. He looked into every shop. When he turned into a supermarket, she did, too. She put a sack of rice and package of dried *nori* seaweed into her basket, keeping a short distance from him. He seemed to be looking at dried fish. Emiko was putting a tube of ketchup into her basket when she heard the dried-fish man sing out, "Hallo." It was soon clear that *hallo* and *fish* were the only English he knew. Emiko took a breath and approached.

Standing this close, she was amazed at his long, dark eyelashes. The women pausing to sift through packs of dried fish seemed intrigued by his appearance, too. "May I help you?" Emiko said in English. And in minutes she was guiding him out to the fish market.

The crowd of fish-buyers pressed them closer together than she would have dared. And then, as she stumbled, his hand was around her. She stood frozen for a moment, afraid to look at him. Then, to shake off her confusion, she led him to buy a piece of cod fish.

They left together. "My name's Juan," he introduced himself. "It's spelled with a J," he explained.

"I see. I'm Emiko."

Juan stopped again in front of the supermarket.

"Something else you need?"

"Flour, oil, baking powder, garlic, coriander."

Emiko laughed. "Now you're really stretching my vocabulary. But come on. We'll do our best." She swallowed before commenting, "Your wife must be a good cook."

"I'm not married."

"Ah."

"Are you?" he asked.

"No."

They found everything he needed. Emiko's basket was filling up. When they left the supermarket, Juan thanked her. "Here," he said. "Let me take out the stuff I bought. I'll bundle it in my jacket."

"I can carry it a while. I mean, which way are you going?"

"Down to the end of that narrow road."

"Really?" She wasn't actually surprised since she'd seen him walk up from there. "Me, too."

He seemed surprised. "Oh. Are you a military dependent?"

"No. I'm from up north. Kitayama. I'm sure you've never heard of it. I'm living here temporarily."

"I live on Grant Heights. Also temporarily."

"I see." So he was an American. "Are you in the military?"

Juan seemed reluctant to confirm it, but he nodded. He probably knew of the tarnished reputation some U.S. military had among Japanese women.

"You seem nice," Emiko said as if to assure him. "I wonder. What is it you're going to cook with this fish and the rest of these things?"

"Bacalaitos. It's Puerto Rican food."

"You must be a good cook."

"I've never cooked it before." They were moving at Juan's slow pace but getting towards the end of the road. He said, "You want to try it?"

"Oh! I don't think I'm allowed on the base."

Juan looked surprised. Emiko realized that's not what he meant. Maybe he just meant he'd give her the recipe.

Juan sighed. "Anybody can come on the base, but ...."

Emiko braced herself. "What?"

"There's somebody there who's *not* so nice. I wouldn't want him to cause me any trouble when you're there."

Emiko felt a chill. "Cause trouble?" She studied Juan's face. It was hard to believe anybody would want to cause him trouble. But now that they were nearing the base, it was true that he looked more and more concerned. She stopped. "This is the path I take to my house."

Juan looked up. "You live up there in the persimmon tree house?"

She chuckled. "Yes. But I haven't even slept there one night yet." *And there's also somebody on my compound who's not so nice,* she thought.

"I'll bring you some bacalaitos tomorrow if you want. If it's any good."

For the first time, the idea of returning to the little "back house" alone troubled Emiko. Even in the Sanya House there'd been other people nearby. Takashi would be nearby, but that was the problem. He was a little scary.

She'd only known Juan for a couple of hours at most, but somehow she felt sure about him. "Or we could cook it together," she suggested. "At my house."

Juan laid out all the ingredients on Emiko's kitchen counter in a precise order. He seemed intent on getting the meal perfect. "I hope you like cod," he said, grinding the fish with the only tool he found to use, a fork.

"Oh, yes," Emiko said. (She hated it.)

"Hm," Juan said. "I think my mom used to soak it in water overnight."

"No bowl. I just moved in."

"Anyway, we'll skip that part."

Soon Emiko's little house smelled like fried fish. Then the fish was re-fried in a batter with all the other ingredients. Now the house smelled also like garlic. Emiko opened a window. She'd never tasted garlic before.

In fact, the bacalaitos tasted much better than she expected. It reminded her just a little of her favorite octopus fritters.

It was dark already when they sat side-by-side on the tatami, leaning back against the wall, sipping green tea. Emiko wished Juan didn't have to go. She didn't want to stay here alone this first night. She asked, "Are you in the army or navy or what?"

"Army."

"You're assigned here?"

"No. Vietnam. I'll be going back in a month or so."

She felt her heart jump. "Oh. Is this Rest and Recreation?" She knew the term from her father.

"No. I'm waiting for my ribs to heal."

Emiko caught her breath. "Your ribs are broken? I knew you were walking slow."

"A couple of them. I'm getting better every day." He changed the subject. "I'm surprised to find a beautiful girl living in this little house all alone. I guess you came here for work?"

"You think I'm beautiful?"

He nodded.

She surprised herself by saying, "Well, I think you're handsome."

He smiled. Emiko couldn't take her eyes off the curve of his lips.

There was still his unanswered question. She drew a breath. It might be tricky to explain what her job was. She was working for a man who opposed the war Juan was part of. She didn't want to tell him that right now when he was recovering from a war wound. He didn't need somebody implying his sacrifice was purposeless.

"I'm a translator," she said. "Newspaper editorials."

The sound of a door slamming burst out from across the yard. They heard muffled voices shouting in Takashi's house. There was another slam. A dog barked outside, then let out a deep, pulsating growl.

Emiko instinctively seized Juan's hand.

"What's going on, Emiko? You're trembling."

"I don't know. It's the guy I work for. He's rude. And arguing with somebody, it seems."

"I'll go talk to him."

"No, Juan, please don't." She swallowed. "But …."

"What?"

"I wonder if you could …. No, never mind."

"You seem afraid. This is your first night here, you said."

"It's silly, but I'd feel better if …."

"I could stay here with you." He looked at the tatami floor, bare except for a low table and some mats. "I don't know where—"

"Could you possibly? I have two futons. I don't want to be here alone."

As they lay side by side later that night, more shouting broke out from the big house, and the dog barked again. Emiko pulled a blanket over both of them, snuggled next to Juan, put her arm around him. As she held on to him, he flinched.

"Sorry," Emiko whispered. "I didn't mean …." She was glad it was dark enough to hide her embarrassment.

"It's just my ribs," he explained.

"Oh, Juan. I forgot."

He turned on his side, wincing a little, and kissed her. It was just a light kiss, but her dread, her loneliness drifted away. She moved to pull him close again, then remembered his injury and lay still, holding his hand in both of hers.

"Juan, is this crazy? We hardly know each other."

"It's not crazy."

They kissed and touched, just that. But Emiko experienced a happiness she'd never felt before. She was sure Juan felt it, too.

14

Tadaima

> *Swift indeed has been*
> *the birth of my love for you—*
> *swift as the current*
> *where waves break high over rocks*
> *in the Yoshino River.*
>
> —Ki no Tsurayuki, *Kokinshū* No. 471

In the morning, Juan was already sitting by the low table when Emiko woke up. He was reading something in a newspaper.

She put her hand on his shoulder. "What's that you're reading?"

"Hmm. '… cruel, senseless war in Vietnam … putting men in harm's way for no purpose …' This is hard to read."

It was one of the English-language newspaper editorials she was supposed to translate.

Emiko felt her throat tighten. True enough, she'd always believed the world should be told about the tragedy of the Vietnam war. Her father believed the same. But she'd never imagined telling a young man directly to his face that he'd been wounded for no reason. "Juan, I'm sorry. Editorials like that—they're written against the people in charge, not the soldiers themselves."

"Yeah, I know how unpopular the war is." He dropped the newspaper back on the pile.

Emiko busied herself making rice and miso soup. Juan was quieter than the day before. He chuckled when she slurped her soup, but he was generally almost solemn. When he said he'd be going back to the base after breakfast, a knot formed in Emiko's stomach, and she couldn't finish eating. "You have to sign in or something?"

"Yeah. And there's something I want to check out."

"You said there was somebody there who might cause you trouble. Is that it?"

He nodded.

"You could come back tonight."

"I want to. I will if I can."

She walked down the path with him and watched him trek along the road towards the base. The image wouldn't leave her mind. He seemed to feel about her as she did about him. But when she asked if would come back, he'd only said, "I will if I can."

She sat at the table in her little house. For the first time since fleeing from Genji she was completely alone, with time to think about what had happened. She couldn't blame her mother for giving in to Genji when there was no longer hope her husband was alive. Emiko herself had come close to giving in to him, she admitted with a sick feeling in her stomach. She picked up the blue and white scarf her mother had made for ... her father, Hiroji Ozeki. That was who her mother loved. That was her true father.

Meeting Juan had made Emiko think of her father. Not her father the anti-war activist that she knew but her father the soldier as he must have been in Japan's last war. He never indicated whether he thought his country was right or wrong while he was fighting. He never talked much about it at all. When Emiko asked, he seemed to remember the actual war as trying to kill people who were trying to kill you. It was only afterwards that he came to question Japan's motives.

Until she met Juan, the current political situation was simple in her mind. Japan was wrongly supporting an American war that was based on that country's obsessive, irrational fear of communism. People in Vietnam were being killed as a result. She'd enthusiastically helped her father write some pamphlets he took to demonstrations. Of course she and her father knew that Americans were being killed in the war as well as Vietnamese. But since they were the foreign aggressors, they didn't get as much sympathy. Now she was starting to see from their point of view. She wished she could talk to her father about it.

Helping to oppose a cruel, senseless war would seem to be her ideal job. Then why was it that Takashi, the anti-war guy, seemed so heartless and aggressive, while Juan, the war-perpetrator, was kind and loving?

The vision of Juan walking back to the base wouldn't leave her. He seemed to feel about her as she did about him. But when she asked if would come back, he'd only said, "I will if I can."

She forced herself to stop worrying. It was time to get to work. The news editorials were piled in a corner and she took up the one Juan had been reading. It was an editorial in English from a foreign newspaper, written by a Japanese living abroad. It began: "Japan must stop relying for its protection on America as long as that protection is contingent on Japan's assistance in its unjust wars."

The editorial was mainly a call for Japan to revoke Article 9 of its Constitution, the one prohibiting Japan from maintaining armed forces. It condemned the American war in Vietnam, but that criticism was peripheral.

The translating went well. Emiko snickered to think Takashi wouldn't know whether it was flawless or not. Besides, she knew he didn't need literary masterpieces. He was just looking for basic propaganda. That made the work go faster.

She picked up another editorial, also from a foreign newspaper and written in English by a Japanese. This, too, criticized America's "illegal aggression" in Vietnam, but like the other it was primarily a call for Japan to revoke the Constitution that was forced on it after the war and return to being a world power under the emperor.

Emiko wondered how Takashi had come across these editorials. There were lots of articles like these written in Japanese. Someone or some organization must want people to read the ones that were written in English, too, most likely an ultranationalist far-right *uyoku dantai* group seeking to restore the country's imperial power.

She translated another editorial. It was much the same. This one didn't even mention Vietnam. It was a call for Japan to turn its Self-Defense Forces into a real military and revoke its disavowal of war. Emiko realized these weren't pro-peace editorials she was translating. They were pro-imperial Japan tracts advocating exactly what her father stood against. She thought of quitting the job. But she needed to stay in Tokyo longer—now more than ever.

In a couple of hours, Emiko echoed down the dark hallway of Takashi's house, gripping three translations in unsteady hands. A finger-smeared door marked the stairway to his private upstairs "quarters." Farther along the hall, from behind a sliding wooden door came the foul odor of a septic tank toilet. She knocked at the door at the end of the hall, Takashi's office.

"Just put the translations over there," he muttered without looking up from a magazine on his desk. In a full-page photo, the gorgeous young men in Mishima Yukio's private army paraded in the schoolboy-like uniforms he'd designed for them himself. Emiko tried to withhold a smirk.

"Something funny?"

A wave of her fingers failed to placate Takashi. "You think

patriotism is funny?"

Emiko grasped for a neutral comment. "Mishima's a very clever writer."

Takashi had his chin in her face now. "But his patriotism is comical? I see. You're just like the rest of the Westernized consumerists." His words rolled out like pent-up thunder. "I obviously made a mistake in hiring you."

"You hired me to translate, Mr. Takashi." Losing her job now would mean giving up her search for her father. And now there was Juan. "If you read what I've done, I think you'll see it's accurate."

He took a step back. "It better be. How long before you finish the rest of the English editorials? I have those Japanese reports for you when you're finished."

"I'll work as fast as I can."

He jutted out his jaw. "Good. I have other plans for you when the translating's done."

Emiko couldn't imagine what he meant by that. But she was beginning to think Takashi was not only scary but unhinged.

Emiko bought soap, toothpaste, shampoo, toilet paper, and a blue and white thin cotton *yukata* to wear in the evenings after taking a bath. And some more food. She was definitely moving in.

She hoped Juan would come back. If he didn't, maybe she would go looking for him. He was all she could think of now in her empty house. She put a double scoop in the rice cooker, prepared two breaded pork cutlets, and chopped twice as much cabbage as she could eat by herself. If Juan didn't come, she'd finish it tomorrow.

She filled the cedar bathtub and lit its gas heater. Soon the sweet smell of the wood and the steam from the rice cooker began to make the place feel more like a home. She washed and got into the hot tub for a long, relaxing soak. When she got out, steam rose from her reddened body as she dried. She put on her new yukata, then went to the kitchen and put on a kettle of water for tea.

There was a knock at the door. She opened it a crack and peeped out.

"*Tadaima*! I'm back." Juan stood there, grinning, his duffle bag in his hand.

"*Okaeri*. Welcome home." She clasped his arm. "You're speaking Japanese now! Come in."

"I memorized some phrases I thought might be useful."

"And the first one you used is the best one possible."

Juan stepped back a little. "You look beautiful in that. I ... really beautiful."

"It's called a yukata. Like a loose kimono." Her face was still warm from the bath, but she felt it grow warmer.

He lightly touched her cheeks and kissed her so gently it seemed he was afraid of breaking her. His hands traced her arms under the wide yukata sleeves. "Preciosa," he whispered. He kissed her again. "Te quiero."

Her eyes closed, she felt him pull her close against him. She was breathing too hard to talk. All she could do was hold onto him.

"Your hair's damp. Smells like flowers."

"Jasmine shampoo. I just got out of the bath."

A shrill whistle blared out from the kitchen.

"Sorry. That's the kettle." With an embarrassed laugh, she went to take it off the burner.

Juan followed. "The bath, is it Japanese style?"

"The only civilized style. Come on. I'll show you."

The room was still misty. Little currents of steam rose from the water in the tub. "You wash and rinse first, then get in."

He seemed intrigued.

"Want to try it?"

"I do, but ...."

"I'll help you. Here, take off your shirt. I'll hang it over there."

"It's just, the wound is healed. But—"

"Wound? Oh, Juan. I didn't know." She bit her lip. "I'm scared but I want to see it." She unbuttoned his shirt and gasped. A purplish red mark was spread out below his breast like a hand with its fingers extended. Emiko clasped her hands over her mouth.

"It doesn't hurt much any more."

"I thought you said it was your ribs."

"Yeah, those too." His face was flushed. "I still can't handle too much quick motion or strain. That's why last night—"

"Then how can you wash? I'll do it. You can keep your shorts on." She filled a plastic bucket with soapy water. "Sit here. I'll wash your back." After that, she moved to face him. She felt goose bumps as she softly dabbed soap over his wound. "Can you bend enough to wash your legs and feet?"

"I've mainly been rinsing them in the shower."

"I'll do it." When she washed his dark, muscular legs, it was a different feeling—she tried looking away, but it didn't leave her. She doused him with buckets of warm water to wash off the suds. "I'll wait in there. You can finish washing yourself, then get in. It'll feel good. Stay as long as you want." She draped a huge towel over a wooden chair. "I don't have another yukata, so you can wrap yourself in this."

In the kitchen she started frying the cutlets, then laughed out loud at herself. This wasn't the situation she'd expected to find herself in when she left Kitayama. It was more what she imagined for herself if she'd stayed. Were her classmates who got married soon after high school this excited to wash their husbands' backs and cook *tonkatsu* for them? It had always sounded boring to her.

But that's because she'd never imagined meeting Juan. She still felt his lips on hers. And his soapy legs in her hands. And ....

The pork cutlets started to smoke. She lifted the pan just in time and flipped them over.

"Emiko! Emiko, can you come in here?"

Juan was hugging his knees in the tub, a sheepish look on his face. "I can't get out."

Emiko bent over laughing. "Here," she said. "Put your arm on my shoulder."

Juan caught his breath in pain a couple of times stepping over the edge.

Emiko wondered, "You got in all right."

"I kind of slid in." He grabbed the towel. "I guess you've never had to help anybody get out of the tub before."

"I have."

"Really?"

"Yes. But nobody over two years old."

"Come here, you."

Emiko ran back to the kitchen.

After dinner, they crawled under the blanket like the night before. Juan had brought his gray hospital pajamas. She said, "Show me where your ribs hurt, Juan." He put her hand on his chest, and she stroked him there lightly. "Does that hurt?"

"No."

"I was touching you last night. Did I hurt you?"

"No."

"Because last night I didn't realize how bad you were wounded."

"I was thinking maybe I disappointed you."

"It was the most thrilling night of my life."

They kissed. They touched. "What did you call me, Juan? When you came in tonight."

He didn't seem to understand.

"*Pressy* something."

"Pressy? Ah, *preciosa*. Precious. Sometimes Spanish pops out. The language I spoke as a kid. I think I also said I love you."

Emiko had more questions, but she wanted to hear those last words in her head as she fell asleep.

15

Along for the ride

When I make myself imagine what it is like to be one of those women who live at home, faithfully serving their husbands—women who have not a single exciting prospect in life yet who believe that they are perfectly happy—I am filled with scorn.

—Sei Shōnagon, *The Pillow Book*

"Funny," Emiko said. "That dog barked the other night when we heard the shouting at Takashi's house. He didn't bark when you came last night."

Juan grinned. "I made sure he likes me. I brought him a piece of U.S. Grade A Choice sirloin steak from the PX."

"Crazy guy." Something else was still on her mind. "You said there was somebody on the base who might cause you trouble. You haven't mentioned him since then. How come? Did you throw him a piece of meat, too?"

Juan smiled but turned serious. "Actually, I got some bad news. He's staying on the base now. I'm going to be called as a witness to something he did there when he was drunk. The problem is he's my platoon leader. And he already hates me." Juan told Emiko more.

"So, your lieutenant puts his men in danger just because he likes to fight?"

"Yeah. He did other things, too, that the criminal investigators didn't seem to know about."

"Like what?"

Juan looked away. "Let's talk about something else."

He picked up an editorial from the top of Emiko's pile. "You're a translator. Is that why you came to Tokyo and are living here all by yourself?"

Emiko's throat swelled abruptly. "No," she said. "The real reason I'm here is to look for my father. He came to Tokyo for some ... business eight months ago and never returned."

Juan took her hand. "That's sad. I guess you've contacted the police?"

"It's been mostly a dead end. But before I moved here a police officer in Sanya told me he's working to get some more information. I'll be going back to check with him in a about a week."

"Can I go with you?"

Emiko laughed. "Um, sure."

"I mean, you know, just go along for the ride."

"You can come with me everywhere, Juan."

He flipped through his Japanese phrase book and read out something.

Emiko laughed again. The phrase—"I am much obliged to you"—was stilted and formal. But at least he was learning.

"I have to go somewhere myself today," Juan said. "As long as I'm on medical leave, I have to get drug tested at the hospital once a week."

Emiko didn't understand.

"To make sure I'm not taking illegal drugs."

"Really? Why would they suspect that?"

"Marijuana, cocaine, heroin—it's easy to get in Vietnam. Some of the guys seem to need it to keep them going."

"But here in Japan?"

"You wouldn't think so. But I heard some guys in the cafeteria at the base talking about it. They said G.I.s can get it here, too."

"So you're going today?"

"Yeah. It's in Oji."

"Where's that?" When he looked confused, she reminded him, "I'm new here like you." She wrinkled her nose at the stack of editorials to be translated. "Can I go, too?"

"To the hospital?"

"You know. Just go along for the ride?"

The sun warmed the September air, allowing patients at the Oji hospital to sit outside on the green lawn. As Emiko and Juan walked by, she saw young men with casts on their legs and arms. Some in neck braces. Some in wheelchairs with blankets draped over their laps. A few read magazines, some listened to music on transistor radios, but most gazed blankly as if seeing something in another place.

"So many!" Emiko whispered.

There was a visitors' room downstairs where Emiko had to wait. She was the only person there. She looked out through the window at the lawn. One boy looked barely eighteen. His whole torso was wrapped in white gauze. Another figure sat motionless beside him, his head completely bandaged except for slits at the eyes and mouth. She had to look away. Juan was so lucky compared to these.

A helicopter flapped overhead. Out on the lawn, one of the men ducked, holding his head in his arms. A nurse came to wheel him back into the hospital. The helicopter disappeared somewhere beyond Emiko's view. Trucks roared by in the road at the end of the lawn. She heard footsteps scraping up a stairway.

Juan came up behind her. "All done. Let's get out of here—what do you think?"

Emiko was ready.

"I'd like to see some more of Japan."

Emiko suggested the Meiji shrine. "My father took me

there once. It's beautiful." She checked her map. "Subway to Yamate line and get off at Shibuya."

She put her arm in his as they walked through the huge park along gardens of white, yellow, and pink chrysanthemums, then gardens of red and pink cosmos. There were lots of other couples in the park. Emiko couldn't stifle the pride she felt in being with a man as striking as Juan. She noticed other women glancing surreptitiously at him.

As they neared the shrine, a line of giant trees filtered the strong sunlight, casting speckled shadows on the stone pathway. Emiko stopped. "Look, Juan. *Komorebi.* I wonder if there's an English word for that. The sun shining through the trees."

They walked through the towering *torii* gateway into the courtyard and up to the majestic shrine. They poured water over their hands and dropped coins into the slots. Emiko was surprised that Juan seemed to know the routine. "I went to the shrine in Oji," he explained. "So, should we clap?"

"Oh, go ahead." Emiko was a little embarrassed. To tell the truth, she considered Shinto rituals nonsense. Or mostly nonsense. She wasn't completely sure.

"Tell me about *kami*," Juan said. "Are they spirits? Or what?"

"Yeah, spirits. That's about right. Spirits of trees and rocks and animals. But they can be spirits of people. They say the kami of the Meiji emperor and his wife live here."

"You clap to get their attention?"

"Uh-huh." Emiko suspected what was coming next.

"So if they're spirits, how can they hear you clap?"

"It's pretend, Juan. That's the best way to think about it. It's a religion."

Juan was peering into the *haiden* worship hall. "But I wonder if there *could* be spirits? My friend Walter believes in haints."

"I don't know that word."

"I guess they're sort of ghosts."

"You mean like people who died and come back to haunt you? We call them yūrei." She didn't really believe in yūrei, but in the hotel room with Genji, seeing the face in the mirror definitely felt like her mother coming back to tell her something.

On the train ride back, they managed to get seats. Juan lowered his voice. "You haven't told me about your mother. She must be worried about you living alone here in Tokyo."

"My mother passed away. I came here right after she died."

"Oh, Emiko." Juan put his arm around her.

A few passengers glanced at them. This wasn't done on a train in Japan. But it made Emiko feel better. She didn't care. She imagined Jun-oba clucking at her, and it almost made her laugh.

Juan said he'd take her to a restaurant, but she wanted to cook dinner. "Or maybe you're cramped in my house. Your place on the base is probably much better."

"It's bigger. Has American furniture. Has a big American stove and oven." He laughed. "And an American shower I can stand up in. But if I'm going to be in Japan, I want to live in Japan. Not America."

"Then you should stay with me."

They stopped in the Narimasu supermarket. Emiko kept holding up different things. "You like this?" His answer every time was he didn't know what it was. She didn't know the English words, so each time her answer was "It's *okazu*. A side dish to go with rice."

She lit the bath and started to get the dinner ready. Domestic Emiko. If her former classmates from high school could see her, they would laugh. Emiko, the girl who looked so bored when they talked about recipes and husbands and babies. The girl who'd always told them she wanted more in life than that.

16

Giving peas a chance

Tokyo people are complicated. They live in such noise and confusion that their feelings are broken to little bits.

—Kawabata Yasunari, *Snow Country*

"I have to check my mailbox every day," Juan said, "to see if I get a summons to witness that guy's assault. *Itekimasu.*"

It was another Japanese word that thrilled her to hear him use. *I'll be back.*

Juan moved and walked faster each day. Emiko thought of the wounded men she'd seen on the hospital grounds. Some of them might never walk again. Meeting Juan and seeing those men deepened and personalized her opposition to the war in Vietnam, to any war at all.

She translated more editorials. More of the same. She felt she'd been conscripted to work for the wrong cause. The words she wrote were hers, but the ideas weren't. Never mind. She couldn't quit. She wanted to stop using Genji's money. She was going to ask Takashi to pay her by the week instead of by the month.

She had to stop being intimidated by that man. Maybe it was best to be tough with the tough guy.

The smell from the indoor septic tank made her hold her nose. She knocked impatiently at the office door. "Your toilet stinks," she called out. "You need to call the vacuum truck now."

Takashi was reading her latest translation. "These are satisfactory," he allowed. He'd ignored the toilet comment.

"I'm glad you like them." She asked about the Japanese reports he wanted her to translate next.

"Investigative reports from Beheiren backers. I want to send them simultaneously to Japanese and foreign newspapers."

"From Japanese into English will be harder, you realize. I can do it, but I'm running low on cash. I'm going to need to be paid by the week, not the month."

"That's not in the contract."

"Then I'll have to find work somewhere else."

Takashi's face burned red as hibachi coals, but he gave in. She might be learning how to deal with this man.

Small packages the size of shoe boxes were stacked in a corner of the room.

"What are all these?" she asked. "They weren't here before."

"Important supplies for the cause." He sucked in a frustrated breath. "Our delivery guy quit the night you arrived. I need to get somebody else fast."

The job seemed simple enough. "How much does it pay?"

"Same as any delivery job. Or maybe less, I guess."

"I might know somebody," she told him. "Get that toilet cleaned out, and I'll see what I can do."

Takashi clenched his jaw but agreed.

This time when Emiko arrived at Shinjuku station she knew just where to go. Satoru wasn't down by the tracks, so she found him sleeping in the little park across the way. He sat up groggily when she shoved his legs off the bench.

"Huh? Ah, Emiko. Just thinking of you. Would you have any money you could lend me?"

She shook him by the shoulders. "I shouldn't bother with you. You know why I do? It's because you said you want to lead a 'purified life.'"

He gave her a mournful look. "Sorry about that bar incident."

"Look, throw that plastic bag away. And any glue you have. I found a job that you can do. You don't have to be a computer programmer. You can save money, go back to Nakakuni, and talk to that novice monk friend of yours. Maybe you're not good at memorizing prayers, but I bet he or the monk himself can put you on the right path."

He shrugged. "What's the job. I'm sure I wouldn't like to do it."

"Maybe you would. It's connected to the peace in Vietnam movement." At least there was a tenuous connection, she told herself.

Satoru blinked as if trying to come out of his fog. "They pay people?"

He had hit on something that had been bothering Emiko herself. Her father had never mentioned getting any pay from Beheiren. She had to assume Takashi got funding from the larger and more radical Zengakuren protest movement.

"They'll pay you to pick up and deliver packages," she said. "You'll be helping to stop the war."

Satoru studied her face for some time. Finally he pulled a plastic bag from his pocket and tossed it into the trash can next to the bench. A half-empty tube of glue followed. He ran fingers through his scraggly mane, now becoming dark at the roots, and stood up, brushing off his shirt. "All right, then. I'm ready."

Emiko bought him a sandwich in one of the station underground snack shops. On the way to Narimasu, he asked what was in the packages he would deliver.

"I don't know. Does it matter? You're just the delivery boy."

When they got back to Narimasu, the bad smell from the

toilet was gone. Takashi didn't seem pleased at the sight of Satoru. "*Chikushō*," he grumbled. "What the hell is this?"

"A very reliable delivery boy," Emiko lied. "Just look at his *Give Peas a Chance* shirt. He's one of us."

"I'll have to reduce his pay until he buys some kind of uniform."

"No way," Emiko objected. "Let's go, Satoru. Any other place will buy you a uniform." She glared at Takashi. "Reduce the pay! Get serious."

They turned, but Takashi stopped them. "Get back here. Regular pay, and if you do well the first month, we'll see about getting you a uniform."

Satoru said, "About the uniform, I don't—" But Emiko cut him off.

Takashi went on, "You deliver them by train and subway. I'll give you more instructions in private."

Emiko wanted to make sure Satoru didn't quit and go back to his Shinjuku life. She said, "Plus, he'll need a place to sleep."

"No problem. I like to keep tabs on my delivery boy. He can sleep in there." He pointed to a room off his office.

Emiko didn't ask any questions. She didn't need to see what the room was like. It was certainly better than the park in Shinjuku. And, besides, she didn't mind being able to keep tabs on him herself.

"Oh, and he'll need train fare or passes," she added. "And weekly pay, same as me."

He'd need some kind of pay advance, too, but she didn't want to press her luck. She followed the new delivery boy out the door and stopped him outside. He stood with two packages under his arm.

"Here's a little money until you get paid. Don't let me down, Satoru. Understand?"

He gave a half-hearted bow.

"Oh, and one more thing. I work for this man, too. Translator. I live in a house at the other end of the yard. You are *never* to go in there. Not even near there. I need my privacy. Do you understand that?"

Another half-hearted bow. He headed for the station.

Juan showed up with twinkling eyes. "No summons yet." His lips broadening into a smile, he presented Emiko with something wrapped neatly in white paper. "I bought you this. I went into one of those shops on the station road and this called out to me. I knew I had to buy it as soon as I touched it."

It was a ceramic bowl, brown with a heavy dripped glaze of white. Emiko's heart jumped into her throat. Unable to catch her breath, she fell to her knees on the tatami. She placed the bowl on the low table like an offering on a kamidana "spirit shelf." Bending her head over it, she froze, peering into its depth as if viewing a reflection floating in a well. The whispered word forced its way through her lips. "Mother!"

Juan knelt beside her, his eyes now sea-green and radiating concern. She felt his comforting hand on her back.

"This is her bowl—the very twin of her favorite bowl. The one my father gave her." Emiko couldn't hold back a sob. "I've never seen another one like this."

"I was just browsing." Juan's eyes widened. "There was something, I don't know what. Something made my buy it."

Her eyes closed, Emiko ran her fingers over the slippery-smooth ridges of glaze. Her mother's face wavered like a spirit before her.

Juan's warm lips on her cheek brought her back. She opened her eyes. "Juan, I can't believe you found this. Thank you." She raised it to her eyes with both hands, then centered it back on the table. "I know what I'm going to do."

She filled it with water and led Juan out to the yard. "I

saw these purple violas growing wild along the fence." She loaded her palms, then brought the blossoms in to float inside the bowl. Hands folded, she knelt again until the memory of her mother became one with the beauty of the flowers.

Juan fidgeted, grinned. "So. I guess we can use something else to soak cod fish in, huh?" This earned him a punch in the arm. "Oh, I brought something else," he remembered. "Not exactly a present." From his jacket he slid out a soft, red item in a plastic wrap, plopped it on the table.

Emiko's mouth dropped open. "What's that? It looks like a slab of—"

"Meat. I thought we could keep it in the fridge. I can cut off a piece for that dog any time he comes back. So he'll know me. So he'll think I belong here."

"You do belong here, Juan."

After dinner—not cod but a kind of fish Emiko liked much better—Emiko lit the bath. "Want me to wash your back again?"

His lips pursed sheepishly. "*Jama shitakunai*. I wouldn't want to inconvenience you."

"*Atsukamashī*. Look that one up in your phrase book. Impudent boy."

She not only washed him but sat on a stool in the room while he soaked wearing nothing but his dog tag.

Juan told her about meeting somebody on the road before he bought the bowl. "Skinny guy, weird orange and black hair and a little Ho Chi Minh beard. Doesn't anybody proofread the English words before they print them on shirts? Anyway, he dropped a package he was carrying, and I picked it up for him—heavier than I expected."

"I think I know him." She gave Juan a quick version of the Satoru story.

"So he's living right over there in the big house?"

"I told him I need my privacy here."

"You mean for ...."
"Yeah."

When Juan was away at the base, Emiko worked on her translations. She was finishing up the last of the newspaper editorials when shouts resounded from across the yard. Takashi was bawling abuse at somebody. Emiko made out the words "filthy" and "hold still." Meaning Satoru?

She hurried across the weedy lot in her socks, rushed down the hallway and into the office. The shouting had stopped. Naked to the waist, Satoru squatted on the floor submissively as Takashi shaved his head bare with a straight razor, flicking matted clumps of black and bleached hair onto the floor as if picking weevils out of rice.

"Don't move," Takashi growled when Satoru raised his face towards Emiko. A thin slit of blood appeared on the crown of the shaved head. "We're busy here," Takashi chided. "Cleaning up this slob you brought me."

Satoru said nothing, only closed his eyes. His lips moved almost as if mouthing a prayer. On the floor next to him, his Give Peas a Chance shirt lay under a heap of hair. Emiko pressed her hands together. "You all right, Satoru?"

"Be still," Takashi warned him, and Satoru swallowed his reply.

Emiko pointed to the cut on his head. "Let me find something to put on that."

Takashi aimed his razor at a shelf that held a rather substantial first aid kit, probably stowed for a future "offensive" that Takashi planned to lead. Emiko stopped the bleeding with styptic powder. Satoru hung his head, refusing to look at her. He seemed embarrassed. "I'm leaving now," she told him. "Come out to the yard when you're finished. I want to talk to you."

She sat on her doorstep in the warm autumn sun, making final word changes to her last translation. When the big house door opened, her jaw dropped to see a bald, clean shaven young man in a dark blue collarless jacket and matching pants. His eyes studied the ground as he stopped midway in the garden. "He offered me money. That's why I let him do this." He fingered the neckline of his new white shirt.

"Satoru! You look ...." *Much better*. But she stopped herself from saying it.

"Stupid, right? I look ridiculous."

"I wouldn't say that. With the hair gone, you look like a monk. I like it."

He slid a palm over his naked head.

"And the new clothes—very smart."

"My delivery uniform, Takashi calls it."

Emiko realized what the outfit looked like—the uniforms worn by Mishima's *Tatenokai* private defense force, the Shield Society. Just like those pictured in the magazine Takashi had been reading.

"See? You're laughing." His face was red.

"I am not. Anyway, at first Takashi wanted to make you buy a uniform. Remember? But now he gave you one. And he's paying you to wear it. So you're getting by, it seems?"

"It's a job I don't mind doing."

"You're not lonely staying in that little room off Takashi's office?"

"Takashi-san talks to me a lot. He wants Japan to stop helping America in its war."

"I'd agree with that."

"He hates the way people nowadays just think about buying things and making money. They forget about traditional values. They forget about the glory of Japan's past."

"Hm. I see."

"He says by working for him I'm helping to make the country better."

Emiko sensed danger in Satoru taking everything Takashi said as unquestionable truth. This was a new, spirited Satoru, though. He hadn't had anything like this confidence before. She asked, "Those boxes you pick up and deliver—what's in them?"

"I don't know. It's secret."

"Hm. Where do you take them?"

"I'm not supposed to tell."

Emiko saw this was going nowhere and changed course. "Have you called your parents, told them you're all right?"

"Tell them I'm a delivery boy? It's not what they want to hear."

In a voice surprisingly throaty, Emiko pleaded, "Call them, Satoru. I'm sure they'd want to hear you're safe."

She wished she could call her own parents. The only person she could call was Jun-oba, who, she had to admit, must be worried about her. Especially considering her warnings about Genji. But Emiko didn't want to talk to her and decided to write a letter instead.

She told Jun-oba she'd found a job as translator at a place called the "Advocacy Agency." She said the weather was getting cooler and asked her to send the rest of her clothes to her in Narimasu. "I'm enclosing a little money," she wrote. "I wonder if you could cancel the house rental and store the rest of our things in your spare room for a while. My mother would want you to have any of her clothes that fit." Which was none of them except maybe a kimono or yukata. "I'm doing fine. I'll be staying here for the time being, trying to find Dad. There's still another lead to follow up on."

On the way to mail the letter, she took her translations to Takashi's office. Satoru wasn't there. "He's always in his room listening to some crazy Zen lecture on the radio," Takashi told her. "Finished with the editorials? Now you can get to work on those." He pointed a thick finger at a box of reports in Japanese.

"I'll pick them up when I get back from the post office. By the way, I can't help wondering. How come you don't just use Black Cat Transport for those packages Satoru picks up and delivers? Wouldn't that be cheaper?"

"That's my business," he shot back. "Your business is translating. At least for now. Then there's something else I want you to do later."

"What's that?"

"I'll let you know in good time."

17

Mono no awaré

The ephemerality of worldly things is like springtime blossoms scattering in the breeze; the brevity of man's existence is like the autumn moon disappearing behind a cloud.

—*The Tale of the Heike*

Emiko and Juan slept together every night. As his body healed, his agility increased. So did Emiko's ardor. Before long she found the full meaning of being "lovers." Her previous life faded to a dim, meaningless blur compared to this.

She would rest her head in the curve of his arm, lying awake for a time after he'd fallen asleep. She'd never known such pleasure—and, at the same time, such sadness in realizing this couldn't last. It was the sadness they called *mono no awaré*, the consciousness of the ephemeral nature of beauty or bliss.

Juan's sleep was deep but often disturbed by nightmares. At first Emiko was frightened, then sad as she listened to his muttering and sometimes louder cries. She wondered what memories, fears, or perhaps regrets lay inside him. There existed a part of him hidden from her, only to be glimpsed through his sleeping words. "*Yūrei*," he whispered more than once. "Haints." And, one night, "All dead."

His body was nearly healed, but his mind had also been hurt. Emiko pressed her hands together whenever Juan had these dreams, wishing there were some way she could help. In the mornings she told him what she'd heard him murmuring.

His usual response was an evasive, “Sorry. Did I wake you?”

“Do you still think about fighting in the war,” she pursued one morning.

“Sometimes,” he answered. “Not so much these days.”

“Last night you called out, ‘Haints.’ That word your friend Walter used.”

“Oh. I was dreaming about a field in Vietnam. Sorry.”

“Do you really have to go back there, Juan?”

“Two years’ tour of duty. I have half a year left.”

“What if you quit?”

Juan’s lips closed, stifling a laugh. “Quit the army?”

“It doesn’t seem fair. You’ve given them enough. Too much.”

Juan’s greenish eyes slowly became a darkened sea.

“I mean, aren’t you afraid you’ll be killed?”

His eyes refused to meet hers. “By the Viet Cong? A little. But they’re the enemy. You can keep them on the other side.” He clenched his fist. “It’s one of our own I’m more afraid of.”

“Lieutenant Joss?”

“I told you he’s facing assault charges at the base. I guess he found out I was listed as a witness. He came to my house. Banged on the door. I wouldn’t open it. But he wrote something right on the door.”

“What?”

“Just some nonsense.”

“What?”

“You really want to know? It’s nothing to worry about. He wrote, *If I don’t get you here I’ll get you in Nam. You’ll see what happens to disloyal pukes.*”

“Pukes?”

Juan grinned. “It’s what they call enlisted men.”

“Just stay here with me, Juan.”

His cheeks widened into a smile. “You’ll protect me?”

“Yes. I will.”

One day blended into another when they were together. Juan's medical leave was only thirty-five days, and the first week was gone already. In the mornings, he went back to the base to check in and see if they'd announced the time and date of Lieutenant Joss's hearing. Sometimes he had to wait hours before he could get this information. But as soon as he could, he came back to Emiko.

The violas at the edges of the walled garden were now in full bloom. In another two weeks they'd be gone. Somehow Emiko found herself trying to hold back tears—at the fleeting beauty of the flowers, of happiness, of love. *Mono no awaré.*

Juan's return to the war got nearer and nearer like the edge of a precipice, yet they seldom mentioned it. When they talked, it was Juan telling her how beautiful she was, or her gushing over the color of his eyes. The few times Emiko forced out any words about their future, she'd broken off before finishing what she wanted to say, often as they began again to make love.

She was in the garden pulling weeds from around the violas when Juan came up the path.

"Look!" He was holding an empty brown cardboard box labeled *Sugar Pops*.

"What's that for?"

"I thought we could pick some of those persimmons before they go bad."

She held the box while he picked up a few of the best ones from the ground. Then he held the box while she climbed part way up the tree, not wanting to chance Juan re-injuring himself.

Emiko set the box on her table next to the bowl of viola blossoms. "What are Sugar Pops?"

"I'll bring you some." He raised an eyebrow at all the persimmons. "We should bake a pie."

"No oven."

"I have one on base."

"Also, I don't know how to make a pie. Do you?"

"Not really." Juan studied the box of persimmons again. "Makes you think. Who planted that tree? The people who built the house? It's old. Are they still alive? Whether they are or not, do they mind us eating their fruit?"

"Same with the violas along the fence. The people who planted them don't get to see them any more. We do, but just for a short while. Then they're gone, like the persimmons."

"I guess we should just enjoy them while they last."

"Yes. But it makes me sad."

"One thing won't change, Emi. I'll always love you."

"But what if you got hurt or killed? Juan, I don't want you to go back." She'd finally said it.

He had no answer other than to pull her close in his arms. Emiko's heart pounded with a bliss that appeared destined to end. *Mono no awaré*. The kind of sadness she was sure there was no English word for.

18

The dark pond

"I've just come from a place at the lake bottom!"
—the look on the little duck's face.

—Jōsō, *haiku*

"Remember I told you about Police Sergeant Oizumi promising me some information on my dad? It's time to go see him." Emiko shifted her eyes sideways at Juan. "You said you might—"

"I want to go with you."

On the way to Sanya, she thought she needed to tell Juan more about her father. Even though she spoke English, she lowered her voice on the train. "It's actually arrest reports—that's the information the policeman's going to give me. My dad took part in some anti-Vietnam war demonstrations. I know the police arrested lots of demonstrators at the time he disappeared."

She glanced sideways at Juan for a reaction, then went on. "My dad had various fake names he might have used. They're checking them all." Another glance at Juan. His brow was furrowed. She didn't know if it was disapproval of her father's activities or something else.

"That's so sad, Emi. I know you and your dad were close." He looked out the train window as the blur of concrete and glass passed by. He was holding his chin.

She said, "My dad didn't dislike Americans, just so you know. It's the government he had a problem with. I hope you can—"

"Sure. I understand. I wish I was close to my own dad. And mom. We used to be, but then …." He told her about their re-marriages and the distance that had followed. "I haven't gotten a letter from either of them since I've been in the service."

"Have you written to them?"

"No. My father got angry when I joined the army." Juan looked away. "He thought I joined because of the divorce."

"Did you?"

His lips pursed. "I don't know. It wasn't just that. After two years at a community college, I wanted to go to the university, but I couldn't afford it unless I got a veteran's benefit."

"You should write to them, Juan. You're lucky you can."

Juan agreed to wait in a nearby coffee shop while Emiko went to the police box. She was wearing her formal white blouse and black skirt. She hoped Sergeant Oizumi would recognize her. The last time he'd seen her was when Yoshida-ma kicked her out of the Hi Crass Bar—wearing that ridiculously short skirt, blouse pulled out, hair messed up.

Sergeant Oizumi looked up, beaming. "Miss Ozeki. Emiko. You look … very nice." He drew out a chair. "Please."

When she sat, his face showed half a frown. "Nothing wrong, I hope? Nothing new, I mean."

"Thank you for your helpful concern." The formal phrase felt alien on Emiko's lips, but in this case it expressed exactly what she meant. "I have a proper job now. And a decent place to live." In case he'd forgotten, she added, "While I'm trying to find my father."

Sergeant Oizumi pulled open a drawer, slipped out a green folder, opened it on his desk. He sucked air in through his teeth.

Emiko's heart jumped.

"I don't know whether it's good news or bad news. You

see here?" He turned the paper to face her. "Arrest records were checked for all of these names. Nobody with any of these names has been arrested."

It had been her last hope of finding him.

Sergeant Oizumi poured her a cup of tea, stealing a look at her—a look that brought out tears she'd been determined to hold back.

"I'm sorry, Emiko. If we'd found that your father was arrested, there's a good chance you could have arranged his release."

Emiko bowed her head in a nod.

"Our Records Department head says—you probably know this—that people often disappear without a trace." Oizumi unsnapped the flap of his pocket and diffidently took out a business card. "Sometimes when we work on cases involving people in mourning, or I shouldn't say only mourning but feeling sad or depressed, we find it helpful to recommend counseling." He twisted his jaw to the side, staring at the card in his hands. "I hope you don't find it out of line if I give you the name of a professional who has been helpful to people who've talked to her."

Emiko took the card. Her vision too blurry to read it, she looked up at Sergeant Oizumi. A numb sadness rose from her chest. Not only was the search for her father over. Was she now expected to get over her grief at losing him?

Oizumi put his palms together, "Please ignore the idea if it's intrusive. I just thought—"

"Not at all, Sergeant Oizumi." Emiko stood and gave a deep bow. In a husky voice, she told him, "I can't thank you enough for all you've done."

The numbness engulfed her as she ambled along the sidewalk, pedestrians brushing by her on either side. The reality was she was not going to find her father. She had to face a future without him. The only reason for staying in Tokyo now was Juan. And she wouldn't have him for long. He didn't want to leave her and go back to the war. That was obvious. But he was going. Even the alternative, desertion, which she never dared to bring up, might result in their living in different countries.

If her mother were alive, Emiko could imagine what she'd say. "Wait like I did. If he loves you, he'll come back." Emiko now knew too much about war to have faith in that easy advice. And what might her father say? He wouldn't be resigned or philosophical. He would try to solve the problem. He'd try to help her devise some sort of plan.

But her father was gone. She envied Juan having both parents. His reasons for breaking off with them seemed superficial. The closer she got to the coffee shop where he was waiting for her, the more she gritted her teeth at his stubbornness.

The sharp grip of a hand on her arm jerked her to a stop. Yoshidama. He dragged her towards the coffee shop window. "Caught you, you bold tramp."

She kicked his shin and twisted away. But he grabbed both wrists. "I hear you came looking for me."

"Let me go."

Most passers-by ignored the disturbance—not their business—but a few stopped to look. Emiko trembled to think Sergeant Oizumi might be called and find her causing trouble on the street again.

"Come with me." Yoshidama's sneer bared his gold teeth. "I'm going to teach you something about damaging a business's reputation. And you'll pay me for my loss."

"Let me go. I don't need any business lecture, but I'll pay you." As soon as she said this, she realized she'd left almost all of her savings hidden in her house. She hadn't expected to run into Yoshidama when the Hi Crass Bar was closed during the day.

Yoshidama freed one arm at her offer to pay.

"I don't have it with me. I can bring it—"

Yoshidama's head suddenly jerked back, an arm around his neck. It was Juan, growling into his ear, "What the hell!"

Hearing English seemed to frighten Yoshidama more than the arm lock. "A foreigner's attacking me. Help!" More people stopped to look, although none approached closely. The last thing Emiko wanted was for somebody to run for the police.

"He'll let you go," Emiko said, "and I'll pay you. Be quiet and listen." When Juan cautiously loosened his arm, Yoshidama stepped back, rubbing his neck.

"Pay me, then. And call off your goon."

Emiko told Juan she didn't have the money.

"*Ikura desu ka*?" Juan asked Yoshidama. He'd learned to ask how much something cost. He gave the man what he asked for—twice as much as Emiko thought was fair—and Yoshidama took off down the street.

"It's all right," Emiko announced to the onlookers. "Just your friendly neighborhood yakuza collecting on a debt." She and Juan rushed to the station.

It felt good to be lost in the anonymous crowd rushing down the stairs to the platform. She clung to Juan's arm. Back in Kitayama it would have drawn attention to be walking with a foreigner, but in the Tokyo throngs, people seemed to have other things to be concerned with. Which was mainly getting from one place to another as fast as possible.

Emiko held to a pole on the subway, and Juan to an overhead strap, their bodies, along with everybody else's, lurching back and forth into one another as the train sped up and slowed down. Emiko gripped Juan's jacket. "I guess you're wondering what that was about?"

"You can tell me later."

"Let's get off at Ueno," Emiko urged. "I want to sit in the park and clear my head." They walked along the Ueno Park paths in a light breeze towards Shinobazu Pond. Emiko put her arm through Juan's.

Juan was silent, patient, as if giving her time to sort out her thoughts. Emiko took in a stuttering breath. "I never told you about a job I had before I met you. I was a bar girl. At the Hi Crass Bar. Working for that man you paid my debt to."

Juan's mouth gaped. "I can't picture that. It doesn't seem you'd like that kind of work."

"I got fired the second night. That's why I owed him money. You were wonderful, Juan. I'll pay you back. I promise." She moved her hands to her face.

Juan stared ahead, his lips pursed. It was impossible to tell what he was thinking.

Along the edge of the pond, huge chrysanthemums waved their white and yellow heads aimlessly in the breeze. Ducks paddled in circles, now and then plunging their heads into the dark water, never coming up with a single thing. Emiko sighed. "Let's sit on this bench."

Juan took her hand. "Bad news about your father, I guess. You haven't said anything."

"Yes, bad news." Emiko's eyes ranged across the pond, its dark surface obscuring what lay in its depths.

"So finding your dad isn't going to be as easy as you hoped. But that doesn't mean you have to give up."

She met his blue-green eyes. "I think it does. I think I do have to give up."

Juan took two blue envelopes from his jacket. "Give up? Just when you convinced me to try again?"

"What do you mean? What are those?"

"Letters to my parents. I wrote them in the coffee shop. I told them all about you."

19

Korareta

Yet few were the nights
we had slept together
before we parted
like crawling vines unfurled.

—Kakinomoto Hitomaro, *Man'yōshū*

As soon as they got home, Juan showed Emiko the letters he'd written to his parents on aerogrammes, still unsealed. They were largely a catalogue of places he'd been in the States and in Vietnam, guys in his platoon, and things he'd seen in Japan. His injuries were covered in the phrases "got hurt" and "feeling better." In the letter to his mother, he asked for a recipe for persimmon pie. The final part of the letters was all about Emiko. She was the most beautiful, wonderful, amazing girl he'd ever met. Yet Emiko found no reference to the future with this *maravillosa niña*, which she assumed meant marvelous girl.

That night, Emiko's mind chased itself in circles. If she really had to give up on finding her father, then Juan was the sole reason to stay in Tokyo. But he wouldn't be here for long. Then what? She couldn't imagine staying alone in this house where the two of them had been together. So maybe she'd go back to Kitayama. But she didn't want to do that. Tokyo was starting to offer her a freedom she could never have there.

She tossed and turned while Juan quickly fell asleep. She touched him to see if he'd awaken. He moaned, turned on his side, muttered something she couldn't make out.

The next morning, Emiko awoke to the smell of cooking. Juan was dressed and stirring something in the skillet. "American breakfast. Ham and eggs."

She rubbed her eyes. "Good morning."

"I hope you like it. Miso soup and rice every morning is fine, but—"

"We eat *hamegu*, too, I'd like to inform you." What she'd meant as a light-hearted quip somehow came out flatter, sounding more like a reproach.

"You waking up in a bad mood?"

"No. Just teasing you." But she couldn't help adding, "I guess I should act like everything is fine just as it is. Like you do."

Juan shut off the burner and knelt beside her. But Emiko had already said as much as she dared. She wasn't going to complain that thinking about their coming separation saddened her more than him. What would be the point?

Juan took her hand. "Fine? Everything's finer now than it ever has been for me, Emi. I don't want to ruin it by worrying about the future."

Emiko had a vision of the Chinese poet Li Po writing a poem on a piece of paper, then folding it, setting it adrift in a river, and watching it float away. The momentary pleasure that the poem had brought was the point. Securing its permanence—meaningless.

"Juan Li Po," she murmured. "Spelled with a J."

"Huh?"

She climbed onto his lap and kissed him. "I said I'm not hungry." She kissed him again. "Make me feel right now that everything's fine."

Hours went by before they stirred from the futon. They'd skipped lunch. It was dinner time, but Emiko still wasn't hungry. She had a slight ache behind her forehead and went to get a glass of water. Juan sat up, contentedly leaning back against the wall reading a tourist brochure he'd picked up at the base.

He had never questioned her about the Yoshidama incident. It was hard to imagine how he could let that whole episode slide without wanting to know more. Emiko had dealings with a yakuza? She'd been fired? Owed him money?

But Juan didn't ask. Was it because he didn't care, because he assumed they were only together for a brief time anyway? She had to know.

"Juan, can you put that travel brochure down for a minute?"

"Sure. I was just reading about this Shinto shrine that—"

"Juan, you have to tell me. Aren't you disappointed to find out I was a bar girl working for a yakuza?"

"I don't know, Emi. I never pictured you doing that, I admit. But it could be worse."

As he said that, there was a rap at the door. "*Gomen kudasai.*"

"*Korareta,*" Emiko gasped. No. It couldn't be. She opened the door to see Jun-oba in her mother's blue kimono standing next to a large package tied in brown paper. Beside it was a bulging furoshiki bundle. "Emiko-chan, I brought you these things myself. I needed to see how you're doing."

Juan took a timid stand behind Emiko.

"Oh, my!" Jun-oba covered her mouth with a plump hand. She stood rigid as a startled deer.

"Come in, Jun-oba. This is my colleague. His name is Juan."

"Chinese?"

"He's American."

"Oh, my!"

"Helping with my translations."

There was some stiff back-and-forth bowing between Jun-oba and Juan.

"He'll get your things." Emiko nodded to Juan. "Jun-oba, I insist you stay the night."

"The night?" Jun-oba waved her hand towards the hefty bundle. I've brought what I need for a week. We're on holiday until after the autumn Higan equinox."

"I see."

Juan's glance at the bundle, then at Emiko, showed he got the idea Jun-oba was staying for a while. "*Ocha*?" he offered. Tea? He was going to get a chance to test out some phrases Emiko had taught him.

"You shouldn't let a man make the tea," Jun-oba scolded. But while Juan was busy making it, she freely voiced her observations on his appearance. "He doesn't understand Japanese, does he? Very handsome. Oh, my. Those eyes. Those eyelashes! And so sturdy. This man could be on television doing commercials." Jun-oba normally didn't take much stock in foreigners, but apparently an exception could be made for a good-looking foreigner. "He's so much better looking than that Genji-san. Don't you think?"

Without waiting for a reply, Jun-oba rattled on. "I was a little afraid Genji-san might have ensnared you."

"I'd rather not talk about Genji."

"Well, I'm glad you listened to me and stayed away from him. Genji-san was still obsessed with your mother up until she died. You don't know this, but he came to the factory looking for her back in January, about the time your 'father' had gone missing. What she told him I don't know. But he went right back to Tokyo. He wasn't seen again until your mother's funeral."

Emiko's mouth dropped. "He came back then? Did he know Dad was missing?"

"It would seem so."

Before Emiko had a chance to digest this, Juan came over to serve the tea. Emiko raised an eyebrow at Jun-oba. "He cooks, too."

"Nonsense! Shameful. You can't be serious."

Juan sat smiling at Jun-oba as if she'd made a flattering comment.

She spoke behind her teacup. "You have to be careful of these foreigners, though."

Juan knew the word "foreigner." His cheeks flushed. He offered to refill her cup.

Jun-oba turned to Emiko. "It was such a long trip. You don't have any *shōchū*, do you?" Women Jun-oba's age considered this drink more healthy than saké, although its alcohol content was actually higher.

In English, Emiko asked Juan if he'd go up the road to the liquor store. "It's called *shōchū*. And maybe get some otsumami snacks." She walked out to the yard with him.

"Who's Genji?" he asked.

"Huh?"

"You and Jun-oba were talking a lot about 'Genji-san.'"

"Just ... maybe you better get going before the liquor store closes."

Long before Juan got back, Jun-oba was installed. Bundle unpacked and clothes folded in the closet, Kitayama crackers and sweets she'd brought on the kitchen shelf, and she was stir-frying vegetables. "I'm glad you have a second futon," she clucked, adding soy sauce to the pan. "I was a little worried."

"*Tadaima*." Juan held up a huge brown bottle with a wide grin. "The guy said Satsuma is the best brand. *Ichi ban ii no*," he told Jun-oba.

Jun-oba turned off the burner. "We'll have some before we eat."

Emiko found three small glasses. She signaled for Juan to pour for Jun-oba—straight—and for her—diluted with water, then raised the heavy bottle in two hands and poured for him. *Kampai*. They raised their glasses in a toast, Emiko half-heartedly.

"*Oishii*," the woman said, and Juan nodded. He knew the word for delicious.

Emiko sipped and choked. Juan made a face like he'd swallowed dirt. In two long drafts, Jun-oba drained her glass. Juan refilled it.

Jun-oba opened the package she'd brought of Emiko's things. "I brought your portable radio. We should have music." She switched it on, and a popular song by Miyako Harumi rang out. "Does your colleague like *enka* singing?" She launched into a vibrating, guttural hum to accompany the singer.

"That song—I heard it in the coffee shop," Juan broke in. "I love it. What is it, Emiko?"

"It's called something like *The budding camellia is the flower of love*. I don't know how to put it in English."

"What's it about?"

Emiko fought down the lump in her throat. "It's about a young island girl watching a ship sail away without delivering a letter from the man she loves."

"Oh."

Juan studied Emiko's face, then Jun-oba's. He took a substantial gulp of Number-One Best Satsuma shōchū and bit off a piece of the dried squid the liquor store man had insisted was the best otsumami to go with it. He chewed and chewed. "Interesting."

"The song or the squid, Juan?"

"Both." He was bobbing his head along with the music. "I mean, it's sad, I guess, but what a voice!"

Jun-oba started singing—droning?—along with Miyako Harumi. She stood up and did some dance steps beside the table. "Ask him, Emiko. Americans don't dance?"

"Puerto Ricans do." Juan got up, and imitated her. "Different music, though. How's this, Jun-oba? *Dō desu ka*?"

The woman giggled like a young girl. "I like this man, Emiko." She turned off the radio and started singing a Japanese folk song, showing Juan how to dance to it.

"What does *yoi-yoi-yoi-* mean?" Juan asked, a little too loud.

"It means *yoi-yoi-yoi*." Emiko wasn't having as much fun as they were.

"*Yoi-yoi-yoi, YOI, yoi-yoi-yoi*!" Juan and Jun-oba sang out together in the chorus. Emiko had to steady her glass when they bumped against the table.

Rather abruptly, Jun-oba sat down. "I'm hungry."

"Let me warm up the vegetables," Juan suggested. "The rice is ready."

Emiko pushed the broccoli and snow peas to one side of her plate, then to the other. Jun-oba's arrival didn't seem to faze Juan. He was having a great time with this old lady.

Later, when Emiko heated the bath for Jun-oba, just putting her hand in to test the temperature made her think of the first nights with Juan. While Jun-oba was in the bath, Emiko had a chance to sit down beside Juan. She gave him a long kiss, and he responded with a heat that took her breath away.

"We're not going to be able to do this while Jun-oba's here, Juan."

"I guess not. I'll sleep at the base."

"You're taking it pretty well. You seem to be having a great time with Jun-oba."

Juan sighed, "Yeah. She reminds me of my grandmother. Back in San Juan when I was young, Granny always came to our house on weekends. I loved it."

"Jun-oba's staying for a whole week."

Juan twisted his jaw. "That long?"

"She's staying seven of the twenty-four days we have left."

His only response was to give her another kiss.

Water splashed on the bath room floor. Jun-oba was definitely making herself at home. Juan sighed, "Guess I should go. Still want me to come back tomorrow and help you with those translations into English?"

She nodded. "I'll walk down the path with you."

"What was that word you said when Jun-oba knocked on the door? *Korareta.*"

Emiko smiled. "I don't think there's such a word in English. The passive voice of *to come.*"

"Huh?"

"We have been *comed*. Something like that. An unwelcome visitor has come."

"I kind of liked her."

"But now we can't sleep together."

A nearly full moon lit the pink clover of the shrubs and the purple buds of the silver grass along the path. Tea olive trees perfumed the air with the citrus smell of their yellow blossoms. Halfway down the path, Emiko and Juan slowed, then Emiko stopped him. "You never talk about when you have to leave Japan. Tell me what's in your head."

"Emi, when I climb this path, it's like I'm going to an enchanted place only I know about, where a beautiful girl in a blue and white yukata is waiting for me. Then, when I walk back down to the base, I feel like I'm returning to the colorless real world, alone. It's like whatever happens on top of the hill is a dream."

Emiko's eyes misted over. A dream? Maybe it was.

On the way home, she glanced back once at Juan plodding down the hill, but the image was blurred by her tears.

20

Tea for three

As firmly cemented clam-shells
Fall apart in autumn,
So I must take to the road again,
Farewell, my friends.

—Bashō Matsuo, *The Narrow Road to the Deep North*

Emiko had never heard such loud snoring. She poked Jun-oba on the futon next to her several times, but after a sharp snort, the woman soon began the deep nasal drum roll again. Juan seemed to enjoy this woman's company, but he didn't have to endure this.

She imagined Juan sleeping in his bed on the base. Probably a bed like in the movies, high off the floor, maybe with a lacy cover. She wondered what it would be like to sleep in a bed like that, what it would be like to make love in it with Juan. What would keep you from falling onto the floor?

Emiko awoke still groggy from lack of sleep. Jun-oba awoke refreshed and ready for action. She'd found a picture of a *sadō* tea ceremony in Juan's travel brochure. "What does this say, Emiko? It looks like something I'd like."

"Let me see. It's a lesson. To learn about the sadō ritual."

"Where? When? Let's go."

"Sure, but Juan-san's coming to help me with the translations today."

"Can't you take off one Saturday? Maybe Juan-san will want to come, too."

When Juan came back, he was frowning. He bowed to Jun-oba. He even gave a mini-bow to Emiko. "There's a message taped to your door," he told her with worried eyebrows.

She re-opened the door and brought in an official-looking notice on U.S. Army, Grant Heights, Japan, letterhead.

"Let me see that," Jun-oba demanded. "Are you in trouble?" She took the letter from Emiko. "Ugh, it's English."

Emiko read it, then translated: "Neighbors have complained about loud music and singing coming from this house at night. The Advocacy Agency provides free housing for a single employee. No one who is not an Advocacy Agency employee is permitted to stay in the agency's housing. An inspector will come tomorrow at noon to verify that only one person is living in this house. Thank you for your cooperation."

"Heh …."Jun-oba scoffed. "Inspector?"

Juan took the letter, skimmed over it, and sank to the floor, pulling at his hair with both hands. "No, no, no. This is terrible."

Jun-oba knelt before him, hands of consolation on his knees. "There, there. It looks like I'll have to go back to Kitayama, but you can come visit me. Isn't that so, Emiko? Tell him not to worry."

Emiko told Juan, "It looks like she fell for it."

"But I have the rest of this day," Jun-oba calculated. She brought the travel brochure to Juan, tapping the tea ceremony picture. She spoke Japanese to him as if he were hard of hearing: "*Sadō*. DO-YOU-WANT-TO-GO?"

Juan saw the picture and understood GO. He nodded enthusiastically. "*Hai. Iku.* Yes. Go."

Jun-oba took at least an hour to get ready. Emiko had to tie and re-tie the pink flowered obi she'd brought along until she got it to Jun-oba's satisfaction. "I don't want people to think I don't know how things are done," she scolded. "Aren't you wearing a kimono?"

"You didn't bring mine." To placate the woman, Emiko changed from jeans to her white blouse and black skirt. As for Juan, she didn't think she'd ever seen him wearing anything other than a sport shirt and gray pants.

On Saturday it was easy to get a seat on the Tobu-Tojo line to Ikebukuro. Juan sat between Emiko and Jun-oba, who had decided he understood Japanese if you spoke loud enough. "SADŌ IS VERY OLD," she told him. "YOU WILL LIKE IT." When she started asking him at the top of her voice about his family and where he came from, a few passengers got up and changed their seats. Somehow Juan guessed what her questions meant. "Puerto Rico," he said. He pointed to himself and held up one finger.

"Is that so?" Jun-oba turned to inform Emiko. "An only child."

At Ikebukuro, Emiko was pleased to see that squeezing into the subway brought Jun-oba's conversation to a halt as they all struggled to keep their balance. But when they got off at Ochanomizu to find where the tea ceremony lesson was held, Juan started trying out his Japanese phrases again. "*Doko?*" he asked. Where?

"*Soko*," she pointed. There.

Emiko hoped this wouldn't go on throughout the tea ceremony. When they found the door to the studio and started up the stairs, she tapped Juan on the shoulder. "I should warn you. You might be the only man in the group. And the two of us might be the youngest."

"What?" Jun-oba complained. "Let's speak Japanese. No secrets. Right, Juan-san?"

The room was formidably stark. Tatami floor, neutral tan walls. The only furniture was a low tea table of gleaming rosewood and a matching low, narrow table against the wall below a hanging scroll. Emiko recognized the charcoal brazier, iron kettle, bamboo whisk, and large tea bowl from magazines and movies. Ever since she was a child this had all seemed so boring. But she was happy to send Jun-oba off with an experience she could talk about back at the factory.

A woman in a formal black kimono with white chrysanthemums ushered them in. The three of you are our only guests," she explained. This was to be instruction in how to perform the basics of the ritual. "Please." She laid down dark blue mats for them to kneel on *seiza* style, with feet folded beneath the haunches. Jun-oba, the oldest, would sit in the first position, then, probably because he was a foreigner, Juan would be next to her, then Emiko. A momentary grimace flashed on Juan's face as he got into position.

The hostess laid out a small white *chakin* napkin in front of each guest. Then she put *matcha* powdered green tea into the bowl, added hot water, and whisked it to a froth. With both hands, she presented the bowl to Jun-oba, who bowed and accepted it in both hands. She sipped—her puckered lips signaling aversion to the raw taste. Then, following the hostess's instructions, she wiped the rim of the bowl with her chakin, turned the bowl away from where she'd drunk, and passed it to Juan, who took it with trembling fingers.

"Relax," Emiko whispered.

The procedure was straightforward, but Jun-oba seemed to think she needed to repeat the hostess's instructions loudly for Juan. "BOW, DRINK, WIPE—"

Emiko put a hand on Jun-oba's knee. "It's all right. He gets it."

If Jun-oba's mouth was puckered, Juan's was fully contorted when he took a sip. Emiko coughed over a laugh and only pretended to sip.

The guests, starting with Jun-oba, followed the hostess's instructions to hold up and admire the rustic light brown bowl. "*Shino* ware. Very elegant," Jun-oba declared.

"Actually, it's *karatsu*," the hostess corrected her. "Shino bowls are white."

Juan took it next. He whispered to Emiko, "Do I have to say something? I don't want to ruin the ritual."

"No. Just look at it and pass it to me."

The lesson over, the hostess rose, but Jun-oba reached into her handbag and withdrew a camera. "Take a picture, would you?"

The picture of the three of them together didn't satisfy her. "Now take a picture of just me and Juan-san, please." She posed kneeling next to him, posed passing the bowl to him, then got a picture standing beside him. "Wait till the ladies at the factory see these."

Afterwards, Juan suggested they take Jun-oba to a restaurant. His brochure identified a "typical old-style Japanese" place.

"We have those in Kitayama," Jun-oba objected.

"How about this?" Juan showed her a picture of a restaurant on the top floor of the Seibu department store in Ikebukuro.

"Yes!" She said this in English, patting Juan on the arm.

The restaurant was directly connected to the station, so they found it easily. As they walked in, five waitresses in white dresses with red sashes chimed *Irasshayimase* in unison. Jun-oba gave Juan a congratulatory nod—he'd chosen the right place.

They were led to a table by the window, where all three stood silently gazing before they sat down. In the autumn air, the city lay spread out below them as clear as a woodblock print, the setting sun painting the windows of the tallest buildings red. Jun-oba clucked with satisfaction. Emiko sighed and wondered what Juan was thinking.

A popular song played in the background:

"Somewhere in the city a lonely person on the verge of tears is playing the guitar ...."

Emiko tried not to listen. "Shall we eat?"

Jun-oba ordered the "Western extravaganza," which contained more meat than she or Emiko had ever seen on a single plate. Juan ate what she couldn't finish, which was most of it. He also ordered saké for Jun-oba and beer for Emiko and himself. And then they had more saké and beer. "What a wonderful place Tokyo is," Jun-oba proclaimed. "I think I should move here."

"Heh ...?"

"You don't believe me, Emiko? Just wait."

The air chilled their cheeks the next morning but sun poured through the clear sky to warm them. After buying omiyage gifts for Jun-oba's friends and for some of Emiko's high school friends, they saw Jun-oba off at the Narimasu station. It had been Emiko's second night sleeping with Jun-oba instead of Juan. She clenched her teeth to stifle the giggle that wanted to break out as she watched the woman board the train.

"Farewell," Jun-oba called from the train step. "I'm so sorry I have to leave. I know you were hoping I could stay longer."

"Good-bye, Jun-oba. Good-bye."

With a jerk, the train pulled away, and Jun-oba waved from the window until she was out of sight.

Juan turned to Emiko. "What should we do now?"

"Hmm. Any ideas?"

Juan's ribs no longer seemed to hurt, or at least he was managing to ignore the pain. She could hardly keep pace with him along the road back to her house and was panting when they collapsed on the bare tatami. She pulled Juan's head to her breast, her fingers tracing the waves of his hair. Her whole past life, any thoughts of the future—all evaporated like banished ghosts. Nothing remained but the desire of the moment.

21

The unspoken word

A woman who had become the wife of a soldier should know and resolutely accept that her husband's death might come at any moment.

—Mishima Yukio, *Patriotism*

The sun was lower in the sky when Emiko opened her eyes. The room was cold. They had fallen asleep in each other's arms unclothed on the mat. Emiko felt the chill air on her bare chest. She didn't dare to break the spell by moving or speaking. She wanted to halt time at this moment, side by side with Juan. But she knew it was impossible. As fear for the future relentlessly returned, a cold wave rushed over her body, wiping away the thrill of their recent pleasure like surf on a sandy beach.

Juan was silent, too, eyes fixed on the low ceiling. She wanted to know his thoughts but feared to ask. Goosebumps prickled her arms and neck. What lay ahead for him was too horrific to think about. She closed her eyes. Maybe sleep would return, and the future she dreaded would fade to nothing more than a dream.

But she didn't sleep. She lay thinking of a famous story, by Takashi's favorite writer in fact, that she and most people thought excessive. A story ending in *seppuku* suicide. She'd found it disgusting, contrived. Yet the part about a woman wondering if her husband would be killed in war—that was real. Her mother had gone through that before Emiko was born. Now it seemed to be Emiko's turn.

She couldn't have feared losing Juan more if he'd actually been her husband. Maybe it was time to speak aloud the word she hadn't dared to utter yet. Desertion.

Before, when Emiko had told Juan she'd protect him, he'd grinned. But it might be possible. Within Beheiren there was a group devoted to helping U.S. soldiers in Japan on medical or recreational leave to escape the horrors of Vietnam—by deserting. Just thinking about it brought a tightness to Emiko's chest. Her father hadn't supported this effort, or even talked about it. His goal was to end the war. But now the prospect of getting Juan safely to another country appeared before her like a previously hidden road.

To another country. That wasn't what Emiko wanted. Her throat constricted and she gasped for breath at the thought of maybe never seeing him again. But letting him be plunged back into the war if she could prevent it was wrong.

How would he react if she mentioned desertion? She was sure the idea had never occurred to him. The way he talked, going back to the war was just doing his job. Emiko was afraid that even uttering the word would diminish her in his eyes.

She took a breath for courage. "Juan?"

"Hmm?"

"You don't have to go back."

She waited for his response, but none came. "I know of an organization that can help soldiers ... escape."

He turned to warm her body with his. "I know. I've heard of it. There was talk about it even in Vietnam. And lots of talk about it here on the base. Don't think I haven't thought about it."

"You never mentioned it."

"You haven't either. Could you leave Japan and live in a strange country, Emi?"

Emiko's heart pounded. "You mean you'd take me with you?" This was the closest they'd ever come to talking about their future.

"I shouldn't have mentioned it. I know you couldn't tear up your whole life in Japan."

It was true. Her stomach ached at the thought of leaving Japan. To go to what country? What would she do there? What would he do? They'd be all alone.

But none of that mattered. She swallowed hard. "With you, Juan? I think I could do it."

He held her tight. "I ... didn't think you—"

"I *know* I could do it, Juan." She felt her fear and uncertainty fading away. Yes, she would join him ... wherever. "Can *you* do it?"

He tightened his hold. "Yes. I'll just close my eyes and jump, holding your hand."

"We'll give each other courage. We'll make a new world together."

Neither spoke for a while. Emiko wondered if he'd heard the stories she had. Of deserters being taken by fishing boat at night from a small port in northern Hokkaido and picked up by a Soviet patrol boat that took them to Nakhodka. The Beheiren newsletter described them going on to Leningrad and finally Stockholm—never to be welcome in their own country again. She needed to be sure he really wanted this. "Juan, Sweden. That's where we might end up." She described the desertions she'd read about.

"I know, Emi. I've heard all that. But we'd be together."

Takashi was reading a newspaper when Emiko walked in. He looked up, squinting. "Well, Miss. This should make you happy. The *Tokyo Daily* printed one of your translations of the English editorials."

"What? How did they get it?"

"I sent it to them, of course."

"Without asking me?"

"Don't worry. I made up a pen name for you. Ushirouchi Nagako."

Nagako Back-house. Emiko didn't know whether to laugh or curse.

"I'm sending your other translations to the *Daily*, too. If readers like them, Ushirouchi Nagako might make a name for herself."

"You should have gotten my permission. It advocates abrogating the Japanese constitution."

"You're just the translator."

This wasn't a time to argue with Takashi. She needed something from him. "I want to get in touch with the Beheiren group that helps GIs escape."

He glared at her over his square chin.

She breathed in. "I suppose you know how I can do that?"

"Well, well. Miss Back-house is a closet activist?"

"Can you just answer the question?"

Takashi lit a cigarette, eyeing her under the smoke. "I'll tell you, but you have to do something for me later." It was the second time he'd mentioned an additional job. Emiko waved smoke away from her face, giving him a noncommittal stare.

"I'll take that as a yes." He leaned back in his chair. "You've been there, you told me yourself. It operates out of the Hongō office of Beheiren."

"Where Kasumi works?" Emiko remembered the student saying they weren't organizing protests these days. They were doing something else.

"Girl who coughs a lot? Yeah, you could contact her." He lifted his chin, blew out a thin stream of smoke. "Just don't get so involved it affects your work for me. I thought you were bringing me some translations into English."

"I surely will, Sir. Very soon, Sir." Of course, Takashi didn't get the sarcasm. He growled, "*Yosh.*" All right, then.

In cryptic, guarded tones on the train and crammed subway to Hongō, bodies of stone-faced commuters in dark suits pressing them on all sides, Emiko and Juan shared their fears.

"It's going to be scary," Emiko muttered under her breath. In Tokyo lots of people knew English, and even though they didn't seem to be listening, she knew they were.

"Mm." Juan's eyes shifted over the other passengers.

"Wonder if we can get jobs."

"Mm. Guess it depends on what country we end up in."

"I hope we can leave together."

"That's not certain?"

"No."

She led Juan past used book shops, newsstands, and street vendors towards the dark lane off Hongō-dōri. A woman at the corner eyed them closely across her display of exam cramming booklets as they turned into the narrow alleyway. A man in the alley squatting on a wooden crate looked up from his abacus and followed them with his eyes.

The weathered cedar door she'd gone through with Kasumi was towards the end of the alley. Footsteps scraped towards them from behind. Emiko took Juan's arm, pulled him to a stop. The footsteps also stopped. She sneaked a look over her shoulder. A young man in jeans, his height exaggerated by the high clogs on his bare feet, stood fixing Juan in his stare.

Her hair tingling, Emiko clenched her teeth and nudged Juan on towards the unmarked Beheiren door. The clogs followed.

They stopped at the door. The man following them stopped only a couple of meters away. Emiko knocked. No answer.

"You have business here?" The clog man moved between them and the door.

Emiko glared at him, saying nothing.

As if replying to her scowl, the young man said, "I see" and banged hard on the door. "Kasumi," he called out, "a customer, it looks like."

At first, Kasumi didn't recognize Emiko. She closed the door behind them, turned to the man in the clogs. "Did anybody see them coming?"

"No." He gave a bow no deeper than a nod and left.

Kasumi gave Juan a look and led them down the unlit hallway to the Beheiren room at the back. The placards, helmets, and megaphones still leaned against the walls. The desk, however, looked neater than when Emiko had been there before. Emiko re-introduced herself, introduced Juan.

"Ah, you were looking for your father. I remember." She coughed. "I hope you …."

"No."

"I'm so sorry." Kasumi sat with them on the vinyl couch. Juan still hadn't said anything but the *Hajimemashite* introductory greeting Emiko had taught him. Kasumi began, "I wonder, would you be here to ask about options for U.S. soldiers?"

Emiko nodded.

"I don't mean to be impolite, but may I ask how long you've known each other?"

"Only a couple of weeks, but, uh…."

"Yes?"

"… we're very close."

"I can see that. We have to take certain precautions, though. I wonder if both of you would show me your identification?"

Emiko had her health insurance card, and Juan had his military ID. Kasumi studied them, put them on the desk. "Would you mind waiting here a minute?" She left and came back with the young man in clogs, who had apparently been standing in the alley outside the door.

"This is embarrassing," Kasumi said. "U.S. army and navy

intelligence have tried to infiltrate us in the past. Taro will have to search your friend for a recording device."

When Emiko translated, Juan said, "Maybe we should search them, too." He was serious.

"Except we're the ones who are desperate. They're not."

While Taro took Juan out into the hall, Kasumi said she'd have to search Emiko, too. "Would you mind taking off your jacket?" Kasumi examined the pockets. "And—I'm very sorry—would you pull up your shirt for a second? It's something we have to do. Thank you."

Taro brought Juan back in. "Nothing but his dog tag. He's definitely a wounded soldier."

Kasumi spoke English to Juan. "So. We can try to help you."

Juan told her he'd heard of the fishing boat to Soviet border patrol boat escape method.

"We don't do that any more. The Soviet Union stopped working with us after a U.S. informant infiltrated our group and a G.I. was arrested trying to escape. We're left with creating false identities and just flying people out on commercial flights."

"To where?"

"We're working on contacts in Switzerland now."

"Not Canada?"

Kasumi coughed. "Too expensive. We operate on volunteer donations."

Taro took a camera from the desk. Kasumi asked Juan to stand against the wall for passport and Canadian driver's license photos.

"Just me? Not Emiko?"

"Japanese citizens are on their own. There's nothing to stop her from flying to Switzerland, but of course our Beheiren group can't pay for it." She asked Emiko if she had a passport. She didn't. "What about your Family Registry?" Emiko had brought a copy to help in finding her father. "You'll need that to apply."

After taking the photos of Juan, Taro left with the camera. Kasumi warned, "It takes time. How long do you have before you're considered AWOL, Juan?"

Juan stared at the floor. Emiko saw pain clouding his eyes. She knew he'd never thought AWOL would be mentioned in the same breath as his name. "Juan," she coaxed when he didn't seem willing to answer.

"I have to report back at the Oji hospital on October 13."

Kasumi checked a calendar. "That will give us time. It's going to be close to the thirteenth, though. Here's what we'll do: Juan, you don't come here any more. Emiko, could you check with us early in October to see if we have Juan's documents and airline reservation ready? Don't call. Just come in person."

They stopped in the Ikebukuro passport office on the way back. There was a place downstairs to get a photo. The clerk upstairs said they'd mail it to her in five to ten days. Japanese didn't need a tourist visa for Switzerland. She was both surprised and scared to find out how easy this was.

The ride back to Narimasu was quite different from the ride to the Beheiren office. Juan peered out the train window as if scrutinizing something invisible to anyone else. Emiko read again and again the *My Home* ad for washing machines posted behind the train strap she clung to. The happy couple's faces in the ad showed no doubt they knew exactly where their home would always be.

On the road home from the station, Juan stopped at the liquor store and bought two large bottles of Sapporo beer and some *edamame* beans. They sat at Emiko's table stripping beans from their shells and drinking beer. Juan finally broke the silence. "A flight to Switzerland must be expensive." He drained his glass and opened another bottle.

"I know."

Juan filled her glass. She filled his. He said, "And we'll need money after we arrive in Europe. You can't be making very much working for Takashi. I'll give you some."

"No." Emiko's cheeks warmed—partly from the beer, but she knew it was also because the topic of money had come up. She probably *did* have enough money for her flight. Not from what she earned by her translations but from what Genji had given her, most of which lay unspent in the post office bank. She drank more beer, seeking courage to tell Juan about Genji.

Juan shelled some beans onto her plate, refilled her glass, stirred the now-dying violas floating in the bowl.

"Before I met you," Emiko began, "there was a man—"

"Genji?"

So Juan hadn't forgotten Jun-oba talking about him. It must have been on his mind ever since, even though he'd said nothing.

"Yes." Emiko told him the story, trying to avoid his sad, intent eyes focused on her as woefully as a patient listening to a doctor's diagnosis. "I might have let him," she confessed. "I almost did."

Juan stiffened, ready for the worst.

"And then he pronounced my mother's name. I felt something. Like my mother was there."

"Her spirit? I thought you didn't believe in that."

Emiko shrugged. "It gave me chills. And then I asked him."

"What?"

Emiko swallowed more beer. She never wanted to give away this secret, but Juan needed to know. "I asked him if he'd ever slept ...."

Juan's eyes flashed aquamarine. He took her hands. "You can tell me."

"... with my mother. He said yes. It was before my father came back from the war."

"What are you saying? You mean you could be his daughter?"

She gave a single nod. "So I guess all this changes your opinion of me. I wouldn't blame you if—"

"You're the victim, Emi. Come here." He leaned and kissed her. They lay together on the tatami. She'd made her confession, and he sympathized with her. Emiko's heart raced with love.

22

Wabi-sabi

His purity was as brittle as a new moon.

—Mishima Yukio, *The Sailor Who Fell from Grace with the Sea*

The morning sun streamed through Emiko's window onto the box of reports Takashi was waiting for her to translate. The night of love was over. After breakfast, Emiko asked Juan for help. "Could you proofread for me, Juan? I need to keep Takashi off my back for a while." She showed him the box.

"Sure. Who wrote all these?"

"Japanese free-lance researchers. For Beheiren. Takashi wants to send English versions to the *Japan Times* and American newspapers." Lips pursed, Emiko met Juan's eyes. "Just to warn you. I'm sure some are against the American presence in Vietnam and in Japan."

Juan only sighed.

She pulled the top report from the box. It was by a writer in Okinawa who'd witnessed the rape of a local girl by a U.S. soldier who went unpunished. "This ... I don't know." She put it aside.

"I can handle it." He arched his eyebrows. "You don't have to hide anything from me. I'm pretty sure we proved that last night. Don't you think?"

"*Atsukamashī.*" Brazen boy. "Let's get to work."

Juan kept busy studying his phrase book while she translated.

"All right," she chuckled when she finished with the article by the Okinawan writer. "You can put in all the missing plurals and articles."

The next report, by a Socialist Party member, accused the yakuza of importing handguns into Japan from California. While Emiko translated it, Juan proofread the first one. "This is terrible," he mumbled. "The poor girl. People need to know about this."

When both reports were proofread, Juan left, saying he'd be back after six. "I have to talk to some people on the base. About Lieutenant Joss."

"Any chance we'll be out of the country before his hearing even comes up?"

"That's what I'm hoping for."

When Juan left to check in at the base, Emiko took the reports to Takashi. He didn't answer her knock, but the door was unlocked. She went in and dropped the translations on his desk.

The door to Satoru's room was cracked open. Martial music and exhortations from some ultranationalist group shrieked from a radio. "Restore Japan's imperial glory. We must honor *all* our wartime martyrs. End our dependence on America. Bring back our military power." Emiko peeped into the room.

Satoru sat cross-legged on a futon in front of a portable radio, his back to the doorway. The only other items in the room were a litter of magazines in one corner and a heap of clothes in another. An exposed lightbulb dangling from the ceiling lit the windowless room. Satoru was living alone, like a hermit, remote from the struggles of the city, in a room reflecting his disdain for worldly possessions. His life was an expression of the rustic simplicity and stark beauty of the *wabi-sabi* aesthetic. But wasn't *wabi-sabi* an aspiration for older people? Satoru was only eighteen.

As the radio polemic blared on, a jolt of guilt choked

Emiko. She was the one who'd put Satoru in touch with Takashi, and Takashi seemed to be converting the young man from a proponent of peace into champion of nationalistic militarism. Satoru, sitting stiff in his blue "delivery" uniform, was being indoctrinated into what Emiko considered an old man's heartless dream. She knocked and went in.

Satoru didn't hear her over the radio. Her cough made him jump.

"Sorry. The door was open. How are you doing?"

He stood up, smoothing hair that no longer existed. Gave a nodding bow.

"Mind switching off that political harangue?"

He jabbed the button with his toe. "It's a program Takashi-san recommended."

"I kind of thought so. You thinking of bringing back the whole feudal system? Or just the Japanese Empire?"

"We need to respect our heritage."

"I guess." Emiko sent her eyes around the room. "You told me you wanted a pure life like a monk. It's definitely *wabi-sabi* in here."

"I'm keeping my mind on what's important, turning away from things that aren't."

"You think people are too attached to material things? I agree."

"We should break our attachment to the world."

"All right, that sounds a little extreme. Anyway, I don't see the connection between that and wanting to build up Japan's military."

"There's a connection."

Emiko waited for an explanation, but it didn't come. She widened her eyes at the uniform. "You look spiffy in that, but I think I liked your Give Peas a Chance shirt better after all. Still have it? I'll wash it for you if you want."

Satoru blushed. Emiko took the shirt.

"Because you look like one of Mishima's Shield Society private army crazies."

"They pledge to lay down their lives for the cause."

"And Mishima tells them what the cause is. Does Takashi tell you what his cause is?"

No response. He seemed confused, and Emiko decided to let it go. His face looked drawn. She asked, "I know Takashi lets you use the bath and kitchen down the hall. You cooking your own food?"

A nod.

"Any time you run out, you can let me know."

"I'm all right. Thanks."

Emiko gestured out to Takashi's office. "Those packages—where do you pick them up from? Just wondering."

"Yokohama."

"You go all the way there? What, to the post office?"

"No. It's a special place. I'm not supposed to talk about it."

"Why? Nothing illegal in them, is there?"

He seemed surprised at the question. "No. I told you. I don't know what's in them."

He'd also told her he couldn't say where he took them. It seemed too mysterious. She tried to sound casual. "When's your next job?"

"I should leave now. Pickup from Yokohama."

Emiko had time to go and put on the knit wool hat and dark coat Jun-oba had brought her before Satoru left for the nine o'clock train. She watched from the shadow of an old pine for him to come out, her collar turned up and the hat pulled down over her forehead. When he left the house, she followed him at a distance, stopping briefly in a drugstore to buy a white medical face mask. At the station, she hung back and didn't go through the turnstile until she'd seen him enter the forward door of the coach. She managed to slip through the rear door just as it was closing.

She stood hidden in the crowd but watched Satoru from the corner of her eye. When he exited at Ikebukuro, she slipped out behind him, pushing sideways between slower commuters to keep up. Satoru entered the Yamate platform with a pass. Emiko had to buy a ticket and was afraid she'd lose him, but there he was, standing erect at the front of a line in his blue uniform. She waited at the end of a different line for the same car.

It was hot inside the train. A bead of sweat trickled down Emiko's cheek, but she kept her hat on—even though the car was so packed it would be hard for anyone to recognize his own mother. She lost sight of Satoru, but it didn't matter. He would certainly get off at Shibuya and take the Tōkyū Tōyoko line to Yokohama.

From Shibuya, she managed to ride for half an hour in the same car as Satoru, unrecognized. As the train stopped at one station along the way, a large group of Chinese passengers got on, talking loudly. When they reached the Yokohama station, Emiko stepped onto the platform, but Satoru didn't get off. She jumped back on before the door closed. In two more stops, at the end of the line, everyone got off. She kept as many people as possible between her and Satoru. He was walking towards the port and the massive gray ships.

Once across a small bridge, the Chinese-speaking people began turning off into one street after another until there were only a few people, dressed like laborers, between Emiko and Satoru. She had to drop back farther behind as Satoru headed for a longer bridge. A vague fishy odor mixed with a smell of diesel exhaust crept through her medical mask. She followed him across, keeping her distance.

The sudden blare of a ship's horn brought her to a breathless stop. It took a moment to recover her composure. A man with a white sweatband pushing a two-wheeled cart came across the bridge towards her. Emiko had to back up against the railing to let him pass. When she looked again towards the old red brick buildings on the other side of the bridge, she had lost sight of Satoru.

He'd been heading towards one of the huge, seemingly abandoned warehouses when she last saw him. There was nothing to do but go and walk along its brick wall, ready to duck into one of the empty doorways if she spotted him.

A rat shot out from one of the doorways just in front of her. She thought of turning back. But she closed her eyes, sucked in a breath, and crept on in the shadow of the long warehouse. Peering into the musty darkness of each barred, glassless window as she passed by, she reached the corner of the building. He had to be behind it.

She peeped around the corner. Satoru stood in front of a man in a shiny floral-design blazer with white pants and shoes. Emiko saw Satoru take an envelope from his pocket and give it to the man, who picked up a bundle of boxes taped together. Satoru took it by a bamboo handle tied on with a string. Without bowing or saying good-bye, the man disappeared back into the rear doorway. As Satoru fumbled with the package, Emiko ran back to the nearest side doorway and slipped inside.

She almost bumped into a guard in a shabby brown uniform.

"No admittance." The guard looked as surprised as she was. She heard the rasping of a saw far back in the dim hallway. Some repair or rebuilding must be going on.

She stepped past the guard and turned, putting him between her and the open doorway. She needed to watch for Satoru to pass by. She needed to stall.

"What are you doing here?"

Emiko held her hands over her ears. She whispered, "Please. I have a condition. Can you lower your voice?"

The guard took a step back. "What are you doing here?" he repeated in a near-whisper. "You have to leave."

Satoru still hadn't passed by the doorway. "I was hoping to find a public toilet," Emiko improvised, still holding her ears.

"No toilet," the guard whispered. "There's one out along the wharf."

"Can you give me more exact—?" She saw Satoru dashing by with the package held on his shoulder.

The guard walked her to the doorway. He pointed in the direction Satoru was walking. "Just on the other side of that bridge."

She bowed and thanked him at length in language that would have made Jun-oba proud until Satoru was far enough away, then left.

Following Satoru now, she noticed he seemed more circumspect, and she let him get even farther ahead. Now and then he looked from side to side and even glanced behind him, but Emiko had left an even bigger buffer of pedestrians between him and her. At the station, she boarded the car behind his. It wouldn't be hard to notice a person with that large a package get off.

As she suspected, Satoru was retracing his route. When she saw him board the train to Narimasu, she waited and took the next train. She knew where he was taking the package and wanted to make sure he didn't know she'd followed him.

"Charges against Joss were dismissed. I didn't have to testify." Juan didn't look as relieved as Emiko expected. She said, "That's great, right?"

"Yeah. He already hates me enough."

"And you won't have to worry about meeting up with him in Vietnam any more. Before long we'll be in Switzerland."

Juan frowned. "I do worry about the other guys in our platoon when he's shipped back. He told me a bunch of us are on borrowed time."

Emiko gave him a hug. "I have an idea. To take your mind off it, before we eat dinner, let's do something else." She slid the door latch shut.

It wasn't until after an extended "something else" that Juan noticed the medical mask on the floor next to them. "You sick?"

"No." Emiko told him about Satoru while they ate a late dinner.

Juan remembered, "When I picked one of the boxes up for him on the street that time, it was heavier than I expected. Then that article you translated—Takashi couldn't be piling up guns and distributing them, could he?"

"That's what I'm wondering."

23

Dead souls

In the dim light of a hanging lantern he busily recited sutras before the altar of the dead, while hemp sticks burned away in the fire of welcome for the ghosts.

—Ihara Saikaku, *Five Women Who Loved Love*

The voice on Emiko's radio announced it was the first day of the Higan autumnal equinox in Tokyo. Emiko's heart sank. She wanted to put red higanbana spider lilies on her mother's grave. But her mother didn't have a grave. Emiko had left Kitayama before removing her ashes from the temple. She'd hoped to bring her father back so he could decide what to do.

It was the same for the memorials she should have held every seven days for seven weeks. She'd planned on having her father help with those. But she'd already missed the first three.

"What's wrong, Emi?" Juan sat down beside her.

"Thinking about my mother. We have these customs of honoring the dead. It's hard to explain."

"Incense? Chanting prayers?"

"Silly. I know. They say it's to bring peace to dead people's souls."

"It sounds good. You're saying it doesn't work?"

"It works, but for us, not the dead. We can only bring peace to our own minds."

"I wish there really was a way to bring peace to dead people's souls. I've lost a lot of buddies. Vietnam is filled with ghosts from both armies. Ghosts of civilians, too. I wish there was some way to put them to rest." He looked at Emiko as if she might know the answer.

Emiko had an idea. "We have a shrine you might want to see. It's for putting Japanese war dead to rest."

On the way to the Yasukuni Shrine, Emiko felt she had to warn Juan. "A lot of the 'spirits' enshrined there are soldiers and sailors who fought against the United States."

This only increased his curiosity.

The long tree-lined walkway led under a towering steel torii gateway, past a gigantic statue of a Meiji-period Minister of War, under another torii—and Juan stopped.

"Something wrong?"

"Over there. People are rinsing their hands."

Emiko giggled. "Sure. All right. You want to do it properly. We'll perform the cleansing ritual."

They still had to go through a lower wooden pagoda-style entrance, then under a third torii before approaching the main hall, identified by a wide white curtain featuring four chrysanthemum crests of the imperial family. The double curved roof inlaid with gold designs seemed to reach up into the sky. Emiko took Juan's hand, impressed despite her cynicism.

They stood looking in below the high curtain at a stark, basically empty room. "No gold Buddhas or fancy stuff in a Shinto shrine," Emiko told Juan.

"Yeah, like the Meiji shrine we went to. Should we clap?"

"Maybe just bow. Do you really want to get the attention of two and a half million spirits who died in one war or another?"

Juan looked like maybe he did. Like maybe he had something to say to them. Emiko became more serious. They walked until they found a bench.

Juan asked, "What does it mean: their spirits are 'enshrined' here?"

"Supposedly their spirits actually live here. At least you could say the dead are honored here. Their names are written down."

"Are they at peace?"

"Supposed to be. The priests keep praying over them."

"But you don't believe it?"

"I believe the real purpose is to give ourselves peace of mind. The shrine is actually for us, the living, not for the dead. You imagine they hear your prayers, and it makes you feel better."

Juan nodded solemnly. "And if it's your fault they died, do the prayers keep them from coming back and blaming you?"

"That's definitely part of it." She put her arm through Juan's. "Aren't we all to blame for the people who die in war? At least partly?"

Juan pursed his lips but said nothing.

"And they're not all heroes, either," she added. "My dad told me there are a few war criminals enshrined here. Meaning people America convicted as war criminals after World War II."

"Really?"

"A lot of Japanese don't like it. My father didn't."

Juan gave a half-smile. "I guess they could benefit from the prayers more than the rest. We wouldn't want them to come back and haunt us." He seemed to be teasing, but she couldn't tell.

She gave him an elbow nudge. But Juan looked somber again. She had an idea. "Want to send the dead souls a message of your own?"

She took him to buy a wooden *ema* votive tablet. "You can write your wish in English. I'll put it in Japanese, too, just to be sure."

Juan seemed to love the idea. He wrote: "I wish all souls

who died in all wars to be at peace." Emiko's hand moistened as she wrote that in Japanese. "What a wonderful wish, Juan. Let's go hang it on the rack with the other tablets." She showed him how to loop the string over one of the hooks.

Juan's mouth dropped. "There must be thousands of these tablets."

"Yeah. But *your* wish is the best. Most are just to find a husband or make lots of money—stuff like that."

"Thanks for bringing me here, Emi."

She hugged him. "Want to get something to eat?"

"Yakitori. There's a place in Shinjuku where Walter took me. I don't think I could find it, though. We had shiro … I forget the rest."

"*Shiro*? Ew. Chicken's insides? Sounds like something my father would eat. Let's head towards home. We're sure to find real meat yakitori being sold on the street."

They didn't have to go far before they found a vendor's smoking stand. They ate leaning back against a trading company wall. Then Juan wanted to go back for more.

"So is it just as good as Walter's soul-food yakitori?"

"I'm not really a yakitori connoisseur."

"Huh?"

"Expert."

"Oh. Don't feel bad. You're a connoisseur of codfish."

By the time they got to the Takadanobaba transfer station, they were in a sea of dark-suited salarymen rushing to get home from work. The crowd was so thick Emiko and Juan couldn't walk side by side. She went ahead holding onto him with one hand behind her back. They were swept up the stairs unable to see where their feet were landing. In the middle of a corridor where stairs converged onto one platform, a ragged man with tangled gray hair down to his shoulders sat cross-legged, drinking saké from a can, which he raised up to toast the flood of dark suits and shiny black shoes that flowed around him on both sides. Not a single person gave the slightest indication of surprise, disgust, or concern.

"Did you see that guy?" Juan asked on the train. "Smiling up at all of us. I think he was laughing at us."

"Definitely. Fools, he was implying. Look at yourselves. You're all the same. You've lost your humanity. I'm the normal one. Wake up."

"You think the salarymen got the message?"

"No. All they were thinking was *Hurry into line to get a seat on the train.*"

Emiko and Juan stood all the way back to Narimasu.

A large manila envelope with Emiko's name on it lay against her door. She brought it in and saw it was stuffed with leaflets and a note. She dumped the leaflets onto the table—and gasped. Pictures of dead Vietnamese mothers, children, babies. Bodies scorched by napalm. She held both hands over her face.

Juan looked through the leaflets, shaking his head. "Why did Takashi give you these?"

"The note says to put them up at Grant Heights where people will see them." This was probably part of the "other job" Takashi said he had for her. It might explain why he chose to live near Grant Heights.

Juan said, "I guess he thinks the military families need to know about innocent civilians being killed and wounded. But the truth is they already know. We all have a way of putting things out of our minds."

"Those poor babies. Those poor kids." Emiko was sobbing.

"That ema prayer tablet we wrote? I included them on it, too."

She put her hand on his back. "Maybe it'll work. Maybe they'll find peace, too."

He nodded slowly. "Anyway, I wouldn't advise going to

Grant Heights and posting these pictures."

Emiko stood up. "Of course I won't. I'm going to take these leaflets back and shove them through Takashi's door slot. Light the bath, would you? I feel like I need a good soak after this."

"Me too."

"Yeah. Tonight we'll help each other put this out of our minds."

24

A fanatical cause

An obstacle which would frighten discreet men is nothing to determined women. They dare what men avoid, and sometimes they achieve an unusual success.

—Ōgai Mori, *The Wild Goose*

Juan warned Emiko that getting involved with Takashi and the secret packages Satoru was delivering might be dangerous. "We only have a little time left before we leave the country. I think it's best to let it go."

But when he left to check in at Grant Heights, she told him she just had to know what was in those packages and where they were going. "If Satoru's making a delivery today, I'm going to follow him."

He was. She found out after listening to Takashi scold her for refusing to post the leaflets at Grant Heights.

Again she hid under the pine tree. She knew when Satoru was leaving, but this time she had no idea where he was going. When he came out with the bundle on his shoulder, she followed, hat and medical mask hiding most of her face.

She followed him all the way to Waseda station with no difficulty. Waseda University students, mostly wearing dark jackets and lighter pants, rushed from building to building, making it easy to follow Satoru without being seen. He went through a bamboo gate to a picturesque little park near the station and sat on a bench at the edge of a pond lined by shrubs, setting his package beside him. Emiko stood behind a tall row of trimmed bushes, watching.

Satoru tapped his leg up and down nervously, looking around. He fidgeted, massaging the shoulder he'd been carrying the package on. A white bird swooped down with a cry to snatch a small fish out of the pond. Emiko was watching that and didn't see the muscular young man with a Japanese Red Sun headband cross the path behind her. He sat on the bench next to Satoru. They exchanged a few words—Emiko couldn't hear—and the headband man left with the package.

Satoru walked to the pond, tossed in a pebble, and stood transfixed by the ever-widening circle of ripples. Emiko hoped the sight might make him consider the repercussions of blindly following Takashi.

She followed the Red Sun headband towards the bamboo fence at the park entrance, where she paused to take off her hat and mask and fluff out her hair. She trailed the man with the package into a maze of narrow streets that bordered the park.

As he stopped for a car to pass, she approached him. "Pardon. I wonder if you could help me?" When he spun towards her, his piercing eyes sent a chill down her back.

"I'm looking for the office of a journal called *New Empire.*" It had published a right-wing article Takashi had given her to translate.

"Heh …." He jerked his head forward as if he hadn't heard correctly.

"I want to write for them."

"Heh …. Seriously?" His eyes gave her a closer look, softened. "Is that right?" He introduced himself. "Morita."

"Sachiko." She wasn't going to give her real name.

"Are you a Waseda student?"

"Uh, not yet. I guess you are?"

Morita nodded. Then squinted. "Haven't I seen you before?"

Emiko's heart skipped. "No. You couldn't have."

"Ah, I know. It was a TV commercial. For skin cream, I think."

"No, that wasn't me."

He scratched his head with his free hand. "Right. I see my mistake. You're even prettier."

This wasn't going the way Emiko anticipated. "Well, if you don't know—"

"I'm going to the *New Empire* office myself, actually. I'll take you there."

He heaved the package onto his shoulder Satoru-style, and they wound through streets jammed with small houses, two-story apartments buildings, bookshops, and soba, ramen, and coffee shops. Morita led her into a photocopy shop. "It's upstairs."

A round-faced student with round frameless glasses looked up at Morita from a desk that slanted to one side. "How many?"

"Twelve."

"Automatic?"

"Semi."

"Rounds?"

"Next shipment."

"Put them in the back with the others." The round face acknowledged Emiko for the first time. "You new?"

"I'd like to write for your journal." She threw in some buzz words she'd learned from Takashi's literature and finished by slipping in her "admiration" for Mishima's Tatenokai Shield Society.

"We don't pay for articles, but we'd like somebody to do research on Katsumata Seiichi, head of the Japanese Socialist Party. We want to know his daily routine—where he goes, what meetings he has, how he gets there. His complete schedule. Do you think you can get that?"

"Like call his office and ask? Would those details make a news story?"

"It's what we need. Can you do it?"

"Yes, Sir." She gave a mock salute, Tatenokai pretend-army style, and whisked down the stairs. The only information she was interested in getting she already had.

Juan came back with a disappointed droop to his lips. "I thought you weren't going to post those leaflets."

"I didn't. What do you mean?"

"They were all over the base. People are furious. MPs are questioning everybody. Teachers say the school kids were crying."

"Takashi must have sent Satoru to post them. It seems Satoru will do anything Takashi asks these days. I'm sorry this happened, Juan. I guess they took them all down?"

"Yeah. I helped."

Emiko studied his sea-green eyes for signs of disgust with Beheiren, war protestors, her. Maybe going to a neutral country is what they needed. Japan was the only country she knew and she hated to leave it. But it would be good to escape the political and social battles here that seemed to consume the few who cared. And good to give up the struggle for economic success that consumed everybody else. Of course, she was no better than any of them. She wanted to tell Juan she would quit working for Takashi. But she also wanted the extra weeks of pay.

Over green tea and rice crackers, she gave Juan the details of following Satoru. The frown never cleared from his face. "Semi-automatic? Rounds?" he said. "It sounds like they're serious weapons, for sure. Have you told the police?"

"Not yet. I don't want to get Satoru in trouble."

Juan's frown deepened. "What's the deal with you and him, anyway?"

Emiko's face warmed. She didn't know how to answer. If Satoru were a wayward brother, that would be easy to explain. What was he, really? Just some young man she'd met on a train, a recent high school graduate going to the big city to escape the debilitating expectations of conformity heaped upon him. In that, he was like a slightly younger version of herself. Except he tended to follow whatever guru's theory provided quick, easy answers. "I hate to see him taken advantage of. That's all, Juan."

"OK, but I don't want you to get in trouble yourself. There's probably a law you have to report something like gun smuggling. If it comes out you didn't, the police might accuse you as an accessory and keep you from leaving the country."

"I'd like to help him get another job first. Or, better yet, go back to Nakakuni and become a monk or something. That's what he really wanted to do."

"How about just telling him he's working for a militaristic movement, not one that favors peace?"

"I will. But this kind of person, you can't talk them out of a fanatical cause. You have to replace it with a different cause."

Somehow Satoru's idea of living a simple and pure life had merged with nationalistic calls for re-establishing the Japanese empire. Over the next few days Emiko tried to reason with him. Finally, she convinced him to come and meet Kasumi at the Beheiren office.

Satoru listened to Kasumi's description of the right-wing group that Takashi was now supporting as "bellicose, tyrannical, cruel." She told him that the needless slaughter in Vietnam would be compounded around the world if that group came to power. "Also, it worries me that you and Emiko live so close to Takashi. I've worked with him in the past. He's dangerous."

Emiko bit her lip, and Kasumi told Satoru, "You could

come work for us instead. We'll never ask you to do anything against the law."

"Takashi-san doesn't ask that, either. He's against the war, too."

"Maybe," Kasumi said. "But when Takashi worked here, we realized he has long-term political ambitions. He's anti-war only because he wants anti-American support. He'll make use of any group he thinks could back his bid to power."

"You think I should quit?" Satoru asked.

"We need somebody to make deliveries, too," Kasumi told him. "We could find you room and board somewhere, but we can't afford to pay you."

"Take it," Emiko urged. "You can find a second part-time job somewhere."

Satoru frowned, glanced down at the uniform he was wearing. "I'll have to ask Takashi first."

And Emiko realized it wasn't going to happen.

Each time Juan returned from the base, he seemed careful not to bring up Satoru again. Emiko didn't either. There were only a couple of weeks before they had to leave the little house where she had spent the happiest days of her life. If she didn't want to diminish the glow of these days, she would have to let Satoru choose his own path.

25

Time to go

"We can then steal away from here, go anywhere you please, and pass the rest of our years together."

—Ihara Saikaku, *Five Women Who Loved Love*

Juan came back from the base lugging an enormous shopping bag. "From the PX. Winter clothes for Switzerland." He seemed quite pleased with himself.

He pulled a few things from the bulging bag. The theme seemed to be warmer clothes.

"Nice," Emiko said, trying to keep a straight face. "Two new pairs of pants. Same color. The exact color you're wearing now. Two shirts—heavier, but the same color as the one you have on now."

Juan only gave a happy nod. "And look. I got this for you. He held up a thick parka with a white fur-lined hood. "I don't know if you—"

"It's beautiful." She put it on, pulled up the hood. "I never want to take it off."

"And gloves. I noticed Jun-oba didn't bring you any. So … and this sweater. The lady said it was made in Ireland."

She held it to her face. "So soft. I don't know what to say. Thank you, Juan."

She gave him a long kiss. And then—it was happening a lot recently—they postponed dinner to "do something else" first.

These days, even though the time to pick up Juan's papers

from Kasumi was drawing near, they never talked about it. Emiko, at least, put it out of her mind as if they had settled permanently here in her little house. As if this was where they were destined to play out the rest of their lives.

When Juan was at the base, she continued with her translation, and he proofread when he came back. And when he finished, they did … something else. A week went by when they hardly ever left the house. Some days they didn't even bother to fold the futon back into the closet.

"What if I go to Europe and you can't come with me?" Juan worried.

"I already got my passport. I can't buy my ticket until I see what flight Kasumi got you on. Then I'll buy a ticket on the same plane."

"But if you can't? Or what if you have second thoughts and change your mind?"

She hooked her little finger in his with a promise.

"But what happens if … maybe you get there and you can't find me?"

"I. Will. Find. You." Maybe it was how she said it. Juan's smile and arched eyebrows conveyed complete satisfaction with that answer.

He began to bring her more things from Grant Heights. One day it was a box of Sugar Pops with a bottle of milk. "Told you I'd let you try them." Another day it was a bottle of Chanel N° 5. "The PX lady said Japanese women love it." He brought a cross-stitched blouse ("From Greece"), a leather belt with a lone star buckle ("From Texas"), and finally something in a box marked *Budweiser* covered with a white dish cloth.

"What's this? Smells delicious."

"A persimmon pie." He couldn't stop grinning.

"How did you—?"

"I got a letter from my mother. She sent the recipe. I baked it in my oven on the base."

"A letter from your mother! That's great."

"From my father, too. Both letters arrived today. They were both glad to hear from me."

"Of course they were. I told you. What did they say?"

"My mother mainly asked questions about you. My dad said he'd like to visit me in Japan."

"But—"

"I know. We'll be gone in less than a week."

"Maybe he'd like to visit Switzerland."

"Hm."

It was past time for Emiko to go back to the Beheiren office to pick up Juan's passport and ticket. Kasumi had told her to come alone. Was there really a danger that American agents watched and kept track of people coming to her office? Emiko felt foolish but just in case put on her hat and medical mask before walking past the woman selling booklets on the corner and the man—still there—making calculations on his abacus. He might have been there the very first time she followed Kasumi to the office, but she hadn't noticed.

No Taro in clogs haunting the alley this time. Maybe he only showed up if word was passed that a foreigner was coming. Emiko's hand trembled as she knocked on the door. What Kasumi had actually said was come back to "see if" the papers were ready. If they weren't, if Juan had to wait until after he was due back at the hospital, he'd be AWOL.

Kasumi was smiling. "We got the papers just this morning. Passport with visa, Ontario driver's license, airline ticket to Geneva, and, thanks to our sympathizers there, an affidavit of support if he needs to stay in Switzerland after the tourist visa expires." She flipped open the passport to the photo. "Good-looking guy."

Emiko's knees were weak. She had to sit down.

"I'll pour you some tea. Take a deep breath." Kasumi mimicked doing it and ended up coughing. "Now this is important. 'Jose Alvarez'—that's what we called him—will have to memorize the home address and all the information here. He'll need to be quick in answering questions. The last thing he needs to do is arouse any suspicions. And here's the guest house he's to go to on arrival. The purpose of his visit is tourism."

"What if they do suspect?"

Kasumi frowned. "That's why we asked you to get your ticket separately. Don't stand in line with him, and don't sit next to him on the plane. If anything happens, you won't be involved."

On the way back, Emiko stopped at the Japan Airlines office near the Tokyo station. There was a seat on the same plane Juan was scheduled to take. She bought it. The die was cast.

On the station platform, she stood wondering if she could really go through with this. If she and Juan could leave their countries forever. From habit, she picked up a newspaper from a trash can instead of buying a copy. Also from habit, she looked first for her father's name in the arrest and death notices. Then she scanned the reports on the Vietnam War.

In America the peace movement was growing dramatically, it seemed. A series of demonstrations across the country billed as a Moratorium to End the War was planned for just a couple of days after she and Juan were flying to Switzerland. President Nixon had withdrawn some U.S. troops, and the army catchphrases now seemed to be "Vietnamization" and "pacification" rather than the long-favored "body count."

Still there were pictures of wounded and dead soldiers on both sides. They were still killing each other. And there were pictures of dead and captive villagers. Those terrified faces—it was hard to believe the claims that they were clandestine combatants. Any misgivings she'd had about running away with Juan to a foreign country were swept away again by the urge to protect him from all this. And from the criminally violent Lieutenant Joss, who'd declared he'd be there waiting for him.

She bought a large deep-purple suitcase in a shop near the Narimasu station and lugged it all the way home and up the back path without passing Takashi's big house.

"What's that?" Juan asked, as if he'd forgotten they were going somewhere.

"It's called a suitcase."

"Oh, right." He put it in a corner.

She held out the bogus documents, forcing a smile. "Here you go, Jose Alvarez. I got your passport and papers." Juan stared for a moment before reaching to take them.

"And my ticket. We're on the same flight. The day you're due to report back for duty."

Juan took a breath. "Only a few more days."

"Yeah." Emiko swallowed the lump in her throat.

Neither said much as they ate dinner. Emiko remembered how excited a high school friend had been days before taking a trip to Ōshima Island in the south of Japan. Her friend couldn't stop chattering about it. The girls who went off to college were the same. Emiko was going much farther away, to a country known for its beautiful lakes and glaciers. She should have been jumping with excitement. But there was a difference. She wasn't coming back.

"Did you write to Jun-oba?" Juan asked.

"I just said I'm taking a short trip abroad. I didn't mention you."

"Did you tell Takashi?"

"No. I'll write to him after we're safe in Switzerland."

Juan didn't ask if she'd told Satoru. She hadn't. She'd wait before writing to him, too. Luckily he and Takashi still knew nothing about Juan. She'd managed to keep that part of her life private—which wasn't hard since Satoru and Takashi were too wrapped up in their own worlds to care.

Juan's deep blue-green eyes were focused on her. "I wonder what kind of bath they have in Switzerland?"

She grinned. "Not as good as ours, I'm sure."

They stayed in the steamy little room washing each other's backs, taking turns soaking in the hot wooden tub until their bodies were deep pink. Emiko ran her wrinkled fingers over the scars on Juan's chest. "All better, it seems. Just a few battle scars. Kind of 'turns me on'—is that the right expression?"

Juan opened his mouth, but no answer came out.

In seconds, they were embracing on the futon. Emiko wondered what she'd been worrying about. It wouldn't matter what country they were in. They would always have each other.

Only two days were left before they would leave Narimasu. Emiko took one more translation in to Takashi. Until they were safely abroad, she wanted him to think she was still in the "back house" working.

"I signed out at the base," Juan told her when he came back with his duffle bag. "Somebody told me Joss already went back to Camp Zama."

"The big U.S. base?"

"Yeah. Where I'd be going after checking in at the hospital. Yokota Air Base is nearby. They'll probably fly him back to Vietnam from there."

"I'm so glad you won't be going back. Come on, let's go shopping."

They bought socks, underwear, jeans, and bags of toiletries. They looked for a tour book of Switzerland but couldn't find one anywhere in Narimasu. They put off packing for another day while Emiko talked about TV documentaries she'd seen on Switzerland. Juan mostly listened.

That night Emiko was startled awake when Juan began tossing on the futon. She heard him mutter, "Spirits, no, no" in his sleep. She rubbed his back, and he soon calmed down. But it took her a while to fall asleep again.

When she awoke, Juan was sitting with his elbows on the table, his face in his hands. Piled neatly in front of him were the passport, airline ticket, and some cash. She put her arm on his back, and his eyes sought hers.

"I can't do it, Emi."

"You can't do what?"

"I can't go. I can't desert." It was the first time he'd used the word.

"Please forgive me. I love you, but I can't do it."

The room started to spin and she sank to the floor, sobbing into her hands. The tatami seemed to waver under her. His broad hand touched her shoulder. "Emi, Emi, I'm sorry. Tomorrow I'm going to report back for duty." He knelt beside her. "Six months. That's all. Can you wait for me?"

He helped her sit up, but she couldn't face him. She knew it would be impossible to change his mind.

"Will you?" he repeated. "Will you wait for me?"

She gripped his shirt. "You know I will."

"Think about it, Emi. In six months the violas will be blooming again. That's when I'll be back."

Somehow this only deepened her sobs. Juan wanted to go out for a walk.

They walked holding hands without talking, and Emiko began to recover her composure a little. An airplane roared low overhead, possibly heading overseas somewhere, she imagined. Juan stopped. "So. I hate to mention this. But about the ticket you bought ...."

Emiko closed her eyes and nodded. "I'll call today and cancel it."

Their whole plan had turned to nothing.

On their last night together, she hoped love would overcome their sadness, but her tears got in the way.

In the morning, they walked together to the station. Juan carried his duffle bag with ease now. Emiko remembered following him up the road the first time she saw him. He'd walked so slowly. She hadn't realized he was hurt. Now it was Emiko who was dragging her feet. For six months she would have to worry whether he was alive or dead.

"I'll write you letters," Juan promised. "You can write back."

"I will."

"I left some money on the table in case you need it. And you could give the documents back to Kasumi. Maybe Beheiren can use them for somebody else."

A three-wheeled cart carrying giant brown bottles of saké swerved around them with a little *beep*. Emiko realized they'd stopped in the middle of the road. Still unwilling to move on towards the station, she held tightly to Juan. A bicycle *dinged* its complaint as it veered around them.

She took Juan's hand. "I noticed a little shrine down this side street the other day. I wonder ...." She led him there. The shrine was no bigger than a ticket booth and looked neglected or forgotten. "You can definitely clap for the spirits' attention here," she teased. She clapped, too.

As if in answer, they heard a loud rattle. Emiko jumped and looked around. A bent old woman in a drab kimono was just rolling open the metal door to her shop next to the shrine. She bowed greetings, and Emiko saw a display of bright red, blue, gold, and orange *omamori* amulets on her shelf. She bought a red one, and asked for a string to hang it with.

"This is for you," Emiko told Juan. "To keep you safe." When she hung it around his neck, the woman applauded.

Emiko rode with him all the way to the Oji station. On the train, men in suits sat and stood reading—newspapers mostly, but some read thick comic books or graphic novels. Emiko sneaked a look at the *manga* the man next to her was absorbed in—a story of a man spying on a high school girl as she put on and took off her uniform. A sour taste rose in her mouth as she recalled her two nights at the Hi Crass Bar. And then her experience with Genji. Loving Juan had driven all that from her mind. She'd learned what love actually is. And now she was in danger of having it taken away forever.

"I won't go all the way to the hospital," she told Juan at the taxi stand outside Oji station. Her heart couldn't take the sight of those wounded men now. She ignored the sideways glances of strangers and hugged him, trembling, until the next taxi pulled up.

"Just six months," Juan whispered in her ear. He kissed her good-bye. As the taxi drove away, he was holding his head in his hands.

Unwilling to make her grief public, Emiko hurried into the station, found the restroom, and rinsed her face with cold water. Six months. Six months Juan would have to survive in a world gone mad.

26

An unwelcome passenger

Clouds come from time to time—
forcing men to break
from looking at the moon.
—Bashō Matsuo, *haiku*

The doctor at the Oji hospital didn't remember Juan. "Ribs? Let me see. Does that hurt? You walking OK? All right. Back to your unit you go. Keep your head down."

The bus to Camp Zama was full—all American servicemen, all about the age of eighteen to twenty-four, but they didn't talk to one another. Like Juan, they gazed out the windows as the scenery became less cement gray and more green. Like Juan, most were probably going back to duty after being rehabilitated. He wondered if any of them were leaving a girl behind.

He wished he hadn't waited until the last minute to decide he couldn't desert. Emiko wanted so much to keep him safe he'd convinced himself he could do it. It would have been better to insist from the start he could never be a deserter. Then they could have made other plans.

He hated the idea of leaving Emiko in that little house working for a man who had a radical, possibly violent agenda. He should have insisted she tell the police about the guns that boy was delivering. But when he learned about it, he was still thinking they would be going away to Switzerland.

Camp Zama was a sprawling, ugly slab of America stamped onto the verdant Japanese countryside. It was huge.

It made Grant Heights look like a toy village. Juan showed his papers at the Commandant's office. He had one night there, then he'd be bussed to Yokota for the flight back.

The barracks was about the same as at the hospital. Again, he had the top bunk. But this time he could easily make the climb. No Walter to talk to. In fact, he didn't feel like talking to anybody. He lay awake starting to write a letter on a pad he'd bought at the PX.

The mood on the bus to Yokota Air Base was even gloomier than the day before. The sky was heavy with clouds. Everybody was going back to Vietnam. A couple guys joked loudly with each other to cover up their apprehension. One boy about eighteen bit at the stubs of fingernails that had already been bitten away. Several had transistor radios that emitted the tinny sounds of Creedence Clearwater Revival's *Fortunate Son* or John Lennon's *Give Peace a Chance*. The tall, skinny boy in front of Juan kept rocking back and forth in his seat as if trying to change the bus's course.

One empty bus had already parked on the tarmac. An army sergeant bellowed through Juan's bus door when it stopped. "Our deepest apologies, ladies. The charter planes are all booked up. We're going to have to squeeze you into our luxurious dual prop C-7 Caribou cargo plane. Bring something to sit on."

A busload of GIs were already aboard. Juan found a place where he could sit on the metal floor and lean back against the outer wall. There was no chatter, only the scraping of boots along the aisle. After unidentifiable screeching and clanking, the plane started down the runway. There were no windows to look out. The plane took off so steeply that the soldiers fell back into each other like dominoes. An icy chill from the floor froze Juan's bottom. He yanked a jacket from his duffle bag to sit on.

The rumble of the plane made it impossible to talk. Besides, it was too dim to see each others' faces. Juan kept thinking, "Six more months. That's all." He reached under his shirt to clutch the omamori safe-keeping talisman Emiko had given him.

The drone of the plane eventually put him to sleep. For how long he couldn't tell. A sudden drop as the plane hit some turbulence woke him up. His hand was still clutching the omamori. He'd been dreaming that Emiko was trying to tell him something.

The visibility in the plane was still quite low, but his eyes were adjusting. The row of GIs leaning against the opposite side of the fuselage gradually came into focus. Directly opposite him, staring at him with dark, intense eyes, was Lieutenant Joss.

27

Another good-bye

For clearly it is impossible to touch eternity with one hand and life with the other.
—Mishima Yukio, *The Temple of the Golden Pavilion*

Emiko had never slept alone in the little "back house." She didn't want to go back without Juan. But she had to.

The pile of forged documents and money he'd left on the table was still there. She moved it to a shelf in the closet, the shelf where her father's blue and white scarf was neatly folded. She collapsed on the floor by the table—and there was the bowl Juan had given her, the bowl so much like her mother's bowl. This was going to be hard. She forced herself to get up and make some tea. There on the kitchen shelf was the last piece persimmon pie.

Was there really any reason to keep living here? She'd given up the search for her father. Takashi scared her, and even Kasumi in the Beheiren office had warned that he was dangerous. She could take Mariko's offer to stay with her in Shimbashi. It was a tiny apartment, but at least she wouldn't be alone. Or she could go back to Kitayama and stay with Jun-oba. Go back to assembling parts in the factory. But the fact was she had found a kind of work she actually liked. She was starting to think of herself as a translator. Maybe with a little more experience she could find a job somewhere else. She took a deep breath. For a while at least, she'd have to take her chances with Takashi.

Before going to bed that night, Emiko opened her door

for a breath of fresh air. It was a dense, black night, only the last sliver of the moon's waning edge flickering occasionally behind clouds that hid all the stars. She heard a rustle at the edge of the path. Two glowing eyes moved towards her. She inhaled for a scream, then checked it. It was the black dog they had named Kuro coming for the little piece of meat Juan gave him every night he appeared.

She ran to the refrigerator. There was still some left. She cut off a piece, opened the door again. The dog sat up, ears perked. He whimpered faintly, probably expecting to see Juan, not Emiko. She held up the meat, and the dog's tail raked across the ground. "Here you go, Kuro." She tossed, and he caught it in mid-air. "Good boy," she sang out. "I'm afraid it's just me now. Juan's gone."

The futon spread, she crawled under the quilt and lay her head on the long pillow that they had both used. Juan's smell was still on it.

The persimmon pie was several days old, but Emiko wanted to eat the last slice. She sniffed. It still smelled good, so she had it with tea for breakfast. If she and Juan had gone to Europe, she was planning to encourage him to get back on good terms with his mother and father. Now that would have to wait. She'd even had hopes of traveling to Puerto Rico to meet them. That would have to wait, too.

A chill air blew through a crack in the door and made her shiver. She might have to start lighting the kerosene heater soon. For now she wrapped herself in a blanket and started in on the next translation—a report describing yakuza contributions to the ruling conservative Liberal Democratic Party. Focusing on the details of the exposé helped keep her mind off her personal troubles.

She was translating into English without Juan's proofreading help. And without hearing his reaction to the content.

Instead, she imagined what he would say, replying to him under her breath.

After checking it over several times, she took the report over to Takashi's office.

"Well, well. Miss Ushirouchi. The *Tokyo Daily* published another editorial you translated into Japanese."

"Maybe you should raise my salary."

"No way. And I don't want you to contact them directly. Remember, you work for me."

The door to Satoru's room was closed and no right-wing harangues could be heard. Emiko asked if he was there.

"He's on a special mission." Takashi's lips curled more sharply than usual. "I'm telling you to stay out of his business."

The sooner Emiko could find another employer, the better. She walked towards the station and browsed through the Narimasu department store stationery section. A box of letter paper and envelopes embossed with pictures of violas seemed perfect. She hoped the violas would remind Juan of the day she floated petals in the bowl he gave her.

While Emiko sat at the table about to start her first letter to Juan, her radio played the song he liked so much.

Carrying letters three days old,
The ship surges out from Habu port.
No matter how much I love you,
you're so far away—
Vanished to the other side of the waves.
Anko girl's letter? Anko girl's letter?
Ah, no response.

Emiko put down her pen, dropped her head onto the table. All her pain at the loss of Juan distilled at once into tears that she felt rolling down her arm.

As she lifted her head to change the station, the song was

interrupted by a news alert:

"Tokyo police report that a terrorist attack planned in the vicinity of the Japan Socialist Party headquarters in Nagatacho has been prevented by the accidental triggering of a chemical bomb. Several bystanders have been rushed to Saint Luke's hospital, where they are being treated for exposure to poisonous gas.

"Police suspect the target of the attack to be Katsumata Seiichi, head of the JSP, who was due to leave the building at the time of the incident."

Emiko turned up the radio:

"Witnesses say they saw a young man in a blue uniform place a brown package near the Social and Cultural Center steps. They say he appeared to be opening it when it exploded. The young man is also being treated in Saint Luke Hospital and, unlike the bystanders, is reported to be in critical condition. Police have not released his name, but a source at the hospital reports it as Suzuki Satoru of Nakakuni City."

Emiko slipped behind reporters talking to hospital staff and stopped a nurse in the hallway. "My brother, my poor brother. I have to see him. Can you help me?" Her tears were real, and the nurse believed her. She took Emiko to a room where she dressed her in a chemical-proof gown and mask. Outfitted like this, Emiko walked right past the policeman guarding Satoru's room.

A cadenced hissing from the other side of the curtain gave the room an unworldly aura. Satoru's eyes were lifted towards the ceiling as if in a trance. Emiko stepped close to the bed. "Satoru, can you hear me? It's Emiko."

Without moving his head, he mouthed something that sounded like "Ooom." She leaned into his line of vision, but he seemed focused on something far away.

"Satoru, I should have warned you. You don't deserve this."

He slowly pressed his palms together as if in prayer. "Ooom ... Em ...Emi ...."

She touched his cheek through her latex glove. His eyes widened and made contact with hers. He seemed to be reaching towards her but the effort was too great. His hands collapsed together in a soundless clap.

The lights in the room buzzed and flickered. Satoru's eyes rolled up into his head. In the weak light, his skin became a golden yellow. He was gone.

The nurse helped Emiko out into the hallway. A man and woman in protective gowns and masks stopped in front of the policeman. They had to be his parents.

"What has my boy done?" his mother cried. "Where is he?"

The policeman, also wearing a mask, pointed to the nurse. "He didn't make it," the nurse said. "We're so sorry."

"Oh, my son," his father mumbled through his mask. He sighed. "At least we won't suffer the shame of him going to prison."

Emiko stepped up. "Satoru was a good boy. He thought he was doing something good."

"No, no," his mother said. "We were very disappointed in him." His father nodded agreement.

Emiko felt the same hurt in their attitude that Satoru had. She felt compelled to lift him up in their eyes. And she was sure there was only one quick way to do it. "It's too bad," she lied. "Satoru had just been accepted into the Nippon Senmon Denshi Keisanki computer school." She made up the important-sounding name.

"Heh ...," his father breathed out. Emiko couldn't see the smile through his mask, but she heard it. Satoru's mother crossed her hands on her breast.

28

Destroying evidence

But there are gods and there is retribution. Every secret will be made known.

—Ihara Saikaku, *Five Women Who Loved Love*

A man standing outside the door to Satoru's hospital room in a lumpy brown suit pulled out a badge. "Tokyo Metropolitan Police, Public Safety. It seems you know the perpetrator. I'd like to ask you some questions."

"Actually I hardly know him at all."

"Still, I heard your conversation with his parents. I'm afraid you'll need to come with me to the station." He led her to a car parked at a back entrance to the hospital, a uniformed policeman behind the wheel. Its red flashing lights and siren squawks helped them get through press cars and heavy traffic to the police headquarters in Kasumigaseki before Emiko had time to organize her thoughts.

It was going to be awkward explaining that she and Satoru both worked for the same person. Or that she was the one who got Satoru a job with Takashi. And then there was the fact that she knew about the weapons delivery and hadn't notified the police.

The detective took her up an elevator and into his stuffy office. Emiko noted the nameplate on his desk. Inspector Fujiwara. He called into the office a woman wearing horn rimmed glasses to sit across from Emiko and take notes. Emiko gave her name, address, and the place of birth where her Family Registry was kept.

"Where do you work?"

"I'm a translator for the Advocacy Agency." She gave him Takashi's name. "I don't know his family name."

"You work for him and don't know his full name?" The inspector put down his pen and nodded to the note taker, who whisked out of the room. "Just a minute, please."

The woman returned with a file, placed it on Fujiwara's desk. He ran his finger down a list. "Could it be Nakamura? You don't know?" He flipped through the folder and held up a picture. "Is this him?"

It was.

"A Beheiren supporter."

Emiko nodded.

The inspector turned again to the woman taking notes. "Would you bring the Beheiren files, please?"

Before Emiko could calm herself down, he was holding up another photo. "Is that you? Going into a Beheiren office with a foreigner?"

She swallowed. "Yes." It wasn't illegal for Japanese to help American servicemen desert. But Japanese police were obliged to arrest the deserters themselves and turn them over to the Americans.

"Where is this young man now? Are you hiding him?"

"He went back to Vietnam."

"We'll check on that before we search your house. Don't move without notifying us first."

Emiko's heart was racing. She hadn't had time to return Juan's fake passport and papers to Kasumi yet. It wasn't illegal to assist deserters, but it was definitely illegal to possess forged documents.

The inspector closed the file. "How do you know Suzuki Satoru? I understand you told the nurse you're his sister. Now you say you hardly know him."

"I met him on a train."

"Your boyfriend?"

"No. He needed a job and I …."

The inspector and his note taker both stared at her, waiting for her to finish.

"… I found him a job."

"Go on. Where?"

"As a delivery boy. With the same man I work for."

"With Nakamura Takashi?"

"Yes."

Fujiwara scratched his head with his pen. "Help me understand this. The chemical bomb Suzuki Satoru set off was in front of the Japanese Socialist Party headquarters, just before lunchtime when lots of officials would be walking out. Including Katsumata Seiichi, the party head. What is Beheiren doing trying to attack a party that backs its cause?"

Emiko shrugged. "I never understood politics." This would have been the time to tell the police about Takashi's right-wing extremism—and about the gun deliveries—but she didn't want them to assume she was part of it.

"All right," the inspector said. "We'll bring Nakamura Takashi in for questioning."

There were two things Emiko had to get rid of right away before the police decided to search her house. First, any right-wing subversive material she was scheduled to translate. She spread the reports on her floor to sort into two piles: one for subversive imperialist propaganda and another for everything else. She would put the anti-government papers back in Takashi's office and keep the rest to continue working on. After all, she'd told the police she was a translator.

Takashi's office door was open. The first thing she noticed was that the maps had been taken down from the walls. The wooden staves stored along one wall were gone. And there were no packages on the floor. Takashi's desktop was clear and spotless. She dropped the stack of reports she didn't want to be associated with on a chair.

The door to Satoru's room was also open. She sucked in a breath and stepped in. There was his futon. And his radio. And his little pile of magazines. Everything here was as it was the last time she'd seen it. Except Satoru was gone.

She dropped onto her knees, cupping her face. Would Satoru have listened if she had demanded he find a different job? Should she have put everything aside until she found him one? It was too late now. She dried her eyes on her arm and looked up. There in a corner of the room, neatly folded, was the shirt she had washed for him. *Give Peas a Chance*. She picked it up and left.

Next, she had to get rid of Juan's fake documents. She retrieved them from her closet. Beheiren's voluntary contributions had paid for them, and it would be good if they could be used for somebody else. But she realized it wasn't a good idea to take them back to Kasumi now. Obviously, the police were watching that place. The safest thing would be to destroy them.

She took them with a box of matches into Takashi's toilet, which was deeper than hers. She squatted and tore out page after page of the passport, lit them, and dropped them into the stinking hole in the floor. Then the letter of financial support, then Juan's ticket to Switzerland and the Ontario driver's license. Finally she burned her own canceled ticket to Switzerland.

Just as she came out of the toilet, two police cars pulled up in front of Takashi's house. Emiko tried to slip down the hallway and out the back door to her little house, but a uniformed policeman saw and stopped her. "Miss. Are you Miss Ozeki? We'd like to talk to you."

Two other policemen were already searching Takashi's office, pulling papers out of drawers, taking pictures. Emiko noticed one of them wrapping up the stack of reports she'd just put on a chair. The policeman who stopped her asked, "Where is Nakamura Takashi, your boss?"

"Um, upstairs, maybe?" She knew he'd almost certainly run off somewhere.

"We already checked."

The shortest policeman waved her to a corner and spoke softly. "Be reasonable, Miss Ozeki. If you're not one of his terrorists, you'll tell us where he is."

Once again, she had the chance to tell about the guns, and about her visit to the office of the radical journal where they were stored. At the moment, though, it seemed safest to imply she knew nothing about Takashi's business except that he had hired her to do some translating.

"I don't know where he is."

"We may be contacting you later," the policeman in charge said. He watched her walk down the hall and out to her little house.

Emiko nibbled at some leftovers from her refrigerator but wasn't hungry. She listened to the police car doors slam as they drove away. Juan was gone. Takashi's house was empty. Emiko opened her door and looked out to see if Kuro the black dog would come by for his piece of meat. He didn't.

She lay on the futon, but it wasn't going to be easy falling sleep. In her mind she heard Satoru lying in the hospital bed trying to say her name. She sat up and noticed his *Give Peas a Chance* shirt. She held it to her face, then pulled it on to sleep in.

When she woke up the next morning, the total silence of the room overwhelmed her. The day before seemed like a nightmare. She was alone and had to decide what to do.

With Takashi gone and sought by the police, she didn't seem to have a job any more. She'd never seen Takashi's landlord and had no idea when the rent was due—or how much it was. Mariko would probably let her stay in her room a little while. But it was really too small. She could go back to Kitayama and stay with Jun-oba, but that would have to be a last resort.

Maybe she could get by for a while and find other work. She still had most of Genji's funeral offering in the post office bank. She'd saved some money from what Takashi paid her. And Juan had left more than she expected. She was probably being stubborn, but she wanted to try for a career as a translator, and the best place to do that was in Tokyo. It was going to be lonely without Juan, but she would stay here as long as she could.

With a sigh, she picked up a report from the top of the pile on her floor. It was an exposé of drug and weapons smuggling run by yakuza gangs. Guns were being shipped from California suppliers to yakuza gangs for sale in Japan. Heroin and other drugs were being shipped from Thailand for distribution to U.S. military here in Japan.

Emiko felt a chill as she remembered Satoru picking up packages in Yokohama. That was where the article said weapons and drugs were entering the country. She read on. The report was detailed, citing direct evidence. It was a Japanese trading company that was behind the drug smuggling—the Gen-Sa Trading Company. Genji's company.

At the end of the report, Emiko saw the name of its writer. Hiroji Ozeki. Her father.

29

Killed in action

"Ah, his deeds have come home to roost,"
people whispered in the city ....
—The Tale of the Heike

The C-7 Caribou bounced onto the runway, giving Juan a jolt that made him realize his ribs weren't perfectly healed. Pleiku Air Base in the central highlands. He was right back where he'd started. Squinting in the light, he looked out from the plane door. The rainy season was drawing to an end, and the acres and acres of deforested mud surrounding the airstrip were drying to a light brown dirt. Squat white-roofed barracks and supply sheds fanned out as far as he could see.

Lieutenant Joss grabbed Juan's shirt as he stepped off the ramp. "Hold up, Gomez. When you get to your barracks, here's a suggestion. Ask the men left in your squad what happens to troublemakers."

The ride through the camp took them past men sitting on truck bumpers drinking cans of Budweiser or playing cards in the shade of stacks of loading platforms. Loud protest songs from the States blared from the quonset barracks everywhere. For the first time, Juan noticed some soldiers wearing peace insignias on their uniforms. He'd been at the base just a few weeks before he was wounded, but the mood had changed since then.

Blake sprung up from his cot. "Hey, Juan, am I glad to see you! We thought you might be dead, or sent home." He looked Juan over as if checking for any missing body part.

"What about Alan? He was evacuated along with you."

"Bad news." Juan knew Alan had been Blake's best friend. "He didn't make it."

Blake slumped back onto his cot. "Fucking Joss. He's stupid, but worse than that. He's mean-stupid."

Sergeant Johnson heard them and came over. "Good to see you back, Gomez. Heard what you said about Alan Riggs. Damn shame. We lost another in the squad, too. Will Hughes." Sergeant Johnson rubbed his graying sideburns, started to go on, but didn't.

Blake said, "Hughes complained to the captain about Joss. He was shot in a point-man search operation before the captain could look into it. Joss made sure of that."

A young draftee assigned to Johnson's squad just before the Bighorn fiasco walked up to the group. "I can't believe you're back, Juan. I was hoping you'd been discharged and sent home."

"Looks like this is my home for a while, Riley."

"Until our government throws in the towel for good. Nixon withdrew 35,000 troops while you were recovering. The papers say that's just the beginning. We're starting to face facts: we've lost the war."

Sergeant Johnson disagreed. "It's a new phase, that's all. Pacification and Vietnamization. Our Search and Clear operations make it so the villages can be pacified and ARVN can take over."

Blake scoffed. "Tell that to Lieutenant Joss. He thinks every villager is Viet Cong. When somebody like Alan Riggs tries to talk some sense into him, you see what happens. Friendly fire."

"Which is not going to happen again on our watch," Sergeant Johnson promised. "Any order he gives that violates the army code of ethics, you come to me right away. From now on, I swear we're going to keep our lieutenant in line."

The squad took Juan to the mess hall and pumped him full of Budweiser. Sergeant Johnson had heard the CID was investigating Joss. He cursed when Juan said the case was dropped. "Too soon after the Calley charges," Johnson growled. "The army couldn't handle another scandal."

"Maybe we'll take care of it ourselves." Blake was drunk.

"Enough of that talk," Johnson barked. But then he bought everyone another round of beer. "Change of subject. Juan, how did you like Japanese women?"

The whole squad fell silent, as if the Previews were over and the Feature film was about to begin. Juan knew they longed for stories of sexual escapades with one woman after another. It wasn't a situation in which he wanted even to mention Emiko's name. "Well," he deflected. "Since I was wounded ...."

Lieutenant Joss tromped into the mess hall, wavered unsteadily towards Juan's squad. He was known to like mixing hashish with beer. "Ladies," he slurred. "Tomorrow at 0600 a covered utility truck will pick you up in front of your barracks. Have a hundred-pound bag of confiscated gook rice from the dispensary ready to load."

Sergeant Johnson saluted. "Yes, Sir. Search and Clear patrol, Sir?"

"Something like that. Get an interpreter. Captain says gooks in a pacified village report hearing an explosion."

"I'll pass the word to the platoon, Sir."

"We won't need the whole platoon. Your squad can handle it."

"With Riggs and Hughes gone, we're down to just me and three men, Sir."

"Three men or three pussies? 0600, Sergeant."

The green M715 covered utility truck stopped by the barracks door. Blake and Riley opened the tailgate, heaved in the large bag of rice and a rocket launcher, then climbed in with Ve, the short Vietnamese interpreter. Sergeant Johnson drove, Lieutenant Joss rode shotgun, and Juan balanced on a box of ammo between the two seats. At the west gate of the base, a guard looked into the cab and the bed, his dog sniffing everywhere. "Long-Ho Village security check," Joss told him. The guard checked his clipboard and saluted.

Away from the scraped land of the base, elephant grass and trees grew right up to the dirt road the army engineers had carved through the jungle. Juan had been out here before when his platoon had driven the VC almost to the Cambodian border. The air was so humid it felt like you could drink it. Sweat trickled down Juan's face, and the ammo case hurt his butt as the truck slammed through ruts and holes.

"Good to be back?" Johnson joked.

"Sure is," Juan answered dryly. In fact, he liked being back with his squad. And going out on patrol brought a nervous high he'd never truly hated.

In some places, they had to swerve around fallen trees. In others, Juan had to hop out and measure the depth of puddles. There were only a few they had to drive around. It was noon before they saw the muddy path that led to Long-Ho. "Drive through it," Joss ordered. He checked his map. "It's less than a click from here."

The truck slipped and moaned through the mud until it reached a clearing. Men, women, and children were lined up in front of their thatched-roof houses. They must have heard the truck coming for some time. "Yowee," Joss sang out.

Johnson stopped the truck. "What, Sir?"

"Nothing you'd be interested in," Joss snapped. "A beautiful girl. Keep driving."

The villagers stood in line in front of their houses when the men got out of the truck. Some of them bowed. Blake and Riley unloaded the rice and carried it into a shed behind the houses that some villagers led them to. "Courtesy of the US of A," Joss called out, even though the bag, Ve told Juan, had a North Vietnamese label painted on it. Johnson told Juan, the only one carrying his rifle, to stand on watch.

Ve approached the oldest man to ask about the explosion they'd reported. Johnson brought a map, but the man didn't look at it. He pointed back down the mud path, then waved his hand to indicate farther west along the dirt road.

"About three kilometers farther up the road," Ve translated. "A loud sound like booby trap. Not big like a bomb or rocket. Three days ago."

"Three kilometers." Johnson rubbed his chin. "That's about as far west as we cleared. We didn't lay any mines or traps. Anybody hurt?"

"No," Ve translated. "He says this is the last village before the border. Nobody's hurt or missing. He says it could have been an animal."

"We'll have to see." Johnson studied the map. "We already cleared that whole area. Bombed it to hell. Maybe we missed a trip wire, though. Face it: people are going to be stepping on booby traps and land mines for years to come."

The piercing scream of a girl shot out from one of the village houses. Joss was dragging a girl who couldn't have been more than thirteen by the arm. Her long black hair waved over her light blue dress as she struggled to get free. Joss was pulling her towards the tailgate of the truck.

Juan saw Joss trying to lift the screaming girl into the truck bed. Johnson and Ve seemed frozen in disbelief. "Lieutenant, back off," Johnson yelled. Juan ran towards the truck. But a man, probably the girl's father, beat him to it. In an instant, he slashed Joss's neck with a butcher knife. Joss slid to the ground.

Johnson and Ve rushed to help Joss. The girl had run back into her house. The father stood stiffly in the clearing, his bloody knife dropped by his feet, ready to die. Juan aimed his rifle. Their eyes met. Both stood frozen, looking at each other. Juan slowly lowered his rifle.

"He's dead," Johnson called. He turned to look at the girl's father, still standing as if at attention before a firing squad. "Gomez, watch that guy. Where the hell are Blake and Riley?"

They came running from a shed behind the row of houses. "We heard screaming."

"Joss is dead," Johnson told them. "You two, help me lift him into the truck." He turned for another look at the girl's father, who stood motionless as a statue of Buddha. "Ve, tell that man to go in and check on his daughter. And never ever mention this to anybody. In the truck, everybody. We're out of here."

Blake sat in the front with Juan. "You didn't shoot that guy? Or even arrest him?"

Juan shook his head. "Joss was about to rape his daughter. You missed that."

"Shiiiit."

"And, Sergeant," Juan said, "I hope we're not going to report that guy. Colonel Chadwell will send choppers in to bomb the whole village in revenge."

Johnson nodded. "Uh-huh. And send us back to count the bodies."

Juan said, "Still, I guess they're going to see Joss was knifed."

"No, they're not," Johnson said grimly, and neither Juan nor Blake asked any more questions.

They drove to the end of the road where the villager said they'd heard an explosion. Johnson gathered the men by the tailgate. "Everybody, listen up. If we take Joss back with his throat slit, that village will be burned to the ground. So Lieutenant Joss is going to have an accident looking for booby traps. Understand? Ve, you in on this?"

Ve nodded, ran a finger across his lips.

Juan, Blake, and Riley carried Joss's body into a deep ditch in the tall grass beyond the road. Johnson called them back to the truck, drove a short distance away, and stopped. "Stay in the truck," he told them all. "Be right back." He put on his helmet and jogged back towards the ditch.

In moments they saw Johnson running full speed towards them. Just as he reached the truck, there was a loud explosion from the ditch. Johnson leaned on the truck, out of breath. "OK, boys. Let's go see what's left of him. Blake, call in the medivac chopper."

"First time I've heard of fragging a dead body," Riley said.

The official report was that Lieutenant Joss died when accidentally setting off a booby trap.

30

Confronting the enemy

For Genji life had become an unbroken succession of reverses and afflictions.

—Murasaki Shikibu, *The Tale of Genji*

Emiko had a copy made of her father's exposé of the Gen-Sa Trading Company's criminal activities, locked it in a post office box in Narimasu, then pushed her way into a commuter-packed train to Ikebukuro. The subway to Genji's office was even more crammed. Clinging to the overhead strap, she caught glimpses of her reflection in a lighted window. She'd left in a hurry, and her hair had a wild, tangled look. She didn't care.

The date on her father's report was just a few days before their last letter from him—a few days before he disappeared. The implication was frightening. The report was connected with his disappearance.

Emiko bobbed along in the stream of gray and dark blue suits gushing out of the station and onto the sidewalk towards the tall buildings of the business district. At the glass doors of the Gen-Sa Trading Company, she paused for a breath. She knew the routine for getting to see Genji himself. "It's not business," she told the perky woman in a gray uniform behind the lobby desk. "Please tell him it's Ozeki Emiko, a personal friend."

A series of smiling, gray-jacketed young women led her up the elevator, into Genji's waiting room, and finally into his office. He came out from behind his desk. "What a wonderful surprise." He signaled for the gray-jacket in the doorway to bring some tea.

"No tea, thanks."

Genji waved the woman from the room. His face was more worn and wrinkled than Emiko remembered. It hadn't been that long since she'd seen him, but his hair seemed more gray. She had read in the newspaper that his company was being investigated for money laundering.

She unzipped her backpack and smacked her father's report onto Genji's desk.

He picked it up. His mouth gaped. "What's this? I thought I had the only copy."

"I guess not."

"Sit with me over there." He leaned towards her on the soft maroon couch. "I was hoping you'd come to me because you'd changed your mind about ...." He tossed the report onto the rug. "I don't know where you got that, but if you need money, you don't have to threaten me. All you have to do is ask."

She shifted her hand out of his reach. The naïve excitement she'd admittedly felt previously in his presence was replaced now by pure anger. "Mr. Sato, my father sent us a letter just after writing that report. He hasn't been heard from since. You say you have a copy. I assume he brought it to you?"

Genji stared down at the report, breathing hard. Several times he started to speak but stopped. Finally he faced Emiko. "Yes, he brought me the report. He was giving me a chance to deny it." Genji gripped his hands together. "Of course, I couldn't. The evidence was all there."

Emiko waited. Genji seemed to be painfully reliving the scene. He held his face in his hands. "Exposing our drug smuggling would have brought down the company. I offered your father money, a position in the company. He said he'd give me two days to turn myself in. After that, he was going to take his report to the police."

Emiko could hardly get the words out. "And? What did you do?"

"I couldn't let him do that. I called my contacts. They said they'd take care of it."

Emiko gasped. "And that's when my father disappeared. What did they do? Tell me."

"I didn't ask. All they said was he was no longer a threat."

Emiko remembered Jun-oba saying Genji had come to see her mother at about that time. "So you came and told Mom ... what? That Dad was never coming back? You were hoping to get back together with her with my father out of the way?"

"I told her I still loved her. But all I could see in her eyes was anger. I saw it was hopeless and came back to Tokyo." He turned his head away and muttered, "It wasn't until then that I asked what they'd done to your father."

Emiko bit her lip, held her breath.

"I've been tortured with guilt ever since."

"Tell me. Is he dead?"

"He's alive. He's in a fenced compound in northern Thailand. My contacts are holding them there."

"Thailand! And you were never going to tell me? Or anybody? You planned to keep him there forever?"

"No. Every day I regret what I did. But I don't know what to do."

She waved the report in his face. "I'll tell you what to do. Get him out. Bring him back."

"You don't understand. These aren't ordinary businessmen we're talking about. They're yakuza. If I tell them to let your father go, they know he can expose their whole operation."

"*Your* whole operation. And here's what's going to happen if you *don't* get my father back right away. The police and all the newspapers in the country are going to find out Genji Sato is a drug smuggler."

He stiffened. "I see. But if I do get him freed?"

"You have my word I'll destroy this report. I just want my father back."

"What's to keep *him* from reporting me?"

"I'll ask him not to."

"That's all you can offer?"

"You'll have to trust us."

There was a silence. Finally, Genji said, "Call me back tomorrow. I'll see if I can convince my contacts it's safe to let him go."

"All right. But you're running out of time, Mr. Sato. If my father isn't brought back soon, if anything happens to him or me, my friend will have a copy of the report. She'll send it to the police."

Pushing hair from her face, Mariko opened the door to her one-room apartment. "Emiko! Come in. I just got up. I'm a mess." She folded away her futon and leaned the little table back onto the floor. "I've been thinking of you. I have so much news. I don't work at the Hi Crass Bar any more. It's closed down."

Emiko had come with news of her own, but this was intriguing. "What happened?"

"Yoshidama was arrested for gambling. Remember how determined he was to get back the money you owed him? He was like that with everybody, no matter how little they owed him. We found out he had a lot of gambling debts and really needed money. He was going crazy."

"And he got arrested?"

"It seems the local police-box cop had been keeping an eye on him ever since that night Yoshidama kicked you out of the bar. He caught Yoshidama threatening somebody else who owed him money."

Emiko smiled. "Sergeant Oizumi."

"Pardon?"

"That's the policeman's name."

"Ah. Anyway, guess where I'm working now. The Kirin Beer restaurant." Mariko laughed. "I wear a white apron instead of a silky skirt. It's half the money, and I'm on my feet all evening, but I like it." She grinned. "I met a guy there. Masa. We've gone on two dates. He's a junior-level advertising illustrator. Very shy. I do most of the talking."

"Oh, really?"

"He lives with his mother. Tonight after I get off I'm going to ask him here for the first time."

"How exciting." Emiko was happy for Mariko, but she'd begun to think it would be nice to sleep at her place that night instead of going back to her empty house and worrying about the police returning with more questions. She put these thoughts aside by telling Mariko about Juan.

"He sounds perfect for you." Mariko asked question after question, and, skipping over only a few details, Emiko was pleased to answer them all. But finally she got to the part where Juan had gone back to fight in a war for six more months.

"You should go to a temple and get a fortune paper."

"I did. Back when I was leaving home. It just said *Uncertain Luck*."

Mariko avoided her eyes a second, then turned back. "At least it's not *bad* luck. Right?"

"Mm."

"Don't be sad. Stay here tonight. I'll tell Masa not tonight, I have a visitor."

"No, no. I can see how much you've been looking forward to this. I'll come and stay another night." Emiko took her hand. "I do have a favor to ask, though." She slipped a key from her pocket. "This is to a post office box in Narimasu. There's an addressed envelope in it. I'm going ... back home," she lied. "It can't be mailed right away. But I don't know how long I'll be stuck in Kitayama. If I don't come back within three weeks, would you mind mailing it for me?"

The mid October sky was beginning to darken when Emiko walked down the road towards her house. She stopped to eat curry rice at a restaurant that had only four tables. The waitress smiled as if she recognized her. "Alone tonight? I see you and your husband walking past here often."

"Oh. Yes. He's ... working."

When Emiko got up to leave, the waitress brought a covered plastic dish of curry rice from behind the counter. "For your husband. When he comes home. *Sabisu.*" A gift.

On her way home, she noticed a light on in Takashi's house. Was it possible Takashi had come back? She hoped not. But before she went to sleep in her own house she wanted to know for sure. She walked towards Takashi's door.

It was open. "Anyone here?" she called. No answer. She crept in. The office door was also open. It seemed the police had left Takashi's desk drawers scattered empty on the floor when they searched his place the night before. She tiptoed into Satoru's room. There was nothing in it at all, just a bare floor. The police had probably carried everything of his away. Going down the hallway towards the back door that opened to her yard, she saw where the light was coming from. The stairway door up to Takashi's room was open. The light was on at the top of the stairs.

"Takashi," she called. "Are you up there?" She called again. "Anybody up there?"

There was a heavy thumping sound. Emiko stepped back. Then a scratching across a tatami floor. Emiko grasped the door post, trembling. Something black rushed down the stairs towards her. Her scream came out a squeak.

Then she saw the dog. "Oh, Kuro! Hello, boy. Were you

asleep up there?" She gave him a pat.

She'd never been upstairs. Since the light was on, she thought she'd better check. "Come on, boy. Let's go take a look and turn the light out."

She found herself in a room that, like Takashi's office, had been completely emptied out. If he had left anything behind when he vanished, the police had taken it. She turned out the light and closed every door of the house.

Kuro followed her to her own house. The door was shut as she'd left it. She turned the key, slowly opened it, turned on the light. Her own house hadn't been disturbed. The police had probably verified that Juan returned to his unit in Vietnam.

So. No worries. Time to get a good night's sleep. Then why were her hands shaking?

Kuro whined, giving Emiko an idea. "Here, boy. Some meat like Juan gave you. And since you don't seem to have any particular owner, why don't you sleep in the genkan just inside my door tonight? I'll put down a cushion."

It took a while, but she finally settled down enough to write.

Oct. 15, 1969

Dear Juan,

I love you. I hope this letter gets to you. I really wish you were here. I think about you all the time.

I worry so much about you getting hurt. Please take care of yourself.

There are so many things to tell you. I can't put them all in this letter. I hope I'll have some good news about my father soon.

Love,

Emiko

31

Traveling alone

Did you come to me
because I dropped off to sleep
tormented by love?
If I had known I dreamed,
I would not have awakened.

—Ono no Komachi, *Kokinshū* No. 552

Emiko listened to news reports of the chemical bombing. They said the police were still trying to locate Nakamura Takashi, the man Suzuki Satoru worked for. Without naming Emiko, the reports said that "another employee of Takashi, apparently not connected with his terrorist activities, claimed to have no knowledge of his whereabouts."

Genji had had twenty-four hours to contact his yakuza gang. Emiko went to a phone near the Narimasu station and called him on the direct number he'd given her.

His voice was throaty. "They laughed. They threatened to find and kill you if the report gets out. Both you and your father. Believe me, they can do that."

Emiko took a breath. "All right. I'm taking the report to the police and the *Asahi* newspaper right now. Then we'll be dead and you'll be in prison. Is that what you want?"

Genji's voice quivered. "No. Of course not. They cut me off before I could explain the situation."

"Then listen, Mr. Sato. Call them back. When you talk to them this time, also remind them that if you're arrested, you'll be under a lot of police pressure to reveal their names and locations." She clenched her teeth. "And you *will* be arrested. The report and evidence is in an envelope already addressed to the police. Another copy will go to the press."

Genji's panicked breathing came through the phone. "No. You can't do that. Give me another chance to tell these yakuza why we have to let him go. Call me back in an hour."

Emiko waited in the Narimasu Kissaten coffee shop. A few young women and men sat alone at the polished tables. They were almost certainly waiting for their dates to arrive. Like them, Emiko stretched out the time by taking tiny, infrequent sips of her coffee. Unlike them, unfortunately, she wasn't waiting for a date.

She realized the tightening of her throat was from anger as much as fear. That was good. It gave her the courage she needed. Maybe the coffee helped. She wasn't used to the strong caffeine. By the time an hour had passed, she was gritting her teeth.

Outside the shop, she dialed Genji again.

"It took some convincing," he said, "but I've arranged the release. But I have to warn you. I had to give them your name and address in Kitayama. If the report is published, they know where to find you and your father."

"I'll keep my word."

"They'll send your father back on a ship going to Okinawa with certain goods we sell to some Americans there. Not Naha. It's a little port we use on one of Okinawa's northern islands."

"But Okinawa is American territory. My father won't be able to enter."

"Just listen. The Japanese territory nearest to Okinawa is Yoron island, only about twenty-five kilometers away from the port we use. They'll take him there by launch at night. Once he goes ashore, he's on his own."

"When is this going to happen?"

"The ship leaves Bangkok the day after tomorrow. They'll have just enough time to get him there and on board. It takes a week to get to our Okinawan port."

"I'll be on Yoron waiting for him."

"No, Emiko, I wouldn't advise that."

"You told them what happens if we disappear, didn't you?"

"I did."

The phone felt slippery in her hand. "So where exactly will they take him?"

"They said they'll drop him ashore at a deep-water beach."

"Where is it? Does the beach have a name?"

"I don't know. It's on the south coast of the island, they said. The only beach with water deep enough for a boat to get near the shore. That's all I know."

"Are they sure when that will be?"

"Yes. Nine days from now. The boat's always on time."

Emiko hung up.

At the station, she picked up a map of the complete national railroad system and took it back to her house to study. You could get to Kagoshima in the south of Japan by train, and the schedule showed a boat from Kagoshima to Yoron. All told, she'd need about three days to get there from Tokyo. That meant she'd need to leave in less than a week.

To occupy her mind, she re-read the original copy of her father's report. There were two different yakuza gangs he'd written about. One brought guns to an ultranationalist group. It might have been Takashi's although he wasn't named. The other brought drugs to Genji.

Emiko's heart ached as she set off without Juan all the way across Japan, past the clear view of Mount Fuji, past the green islands in the sparkling Seto Inland Sea, past the tropical palms of Kyushu, and on to the southern port city of Kagoshima. All the beauty felt wasted since she couldn't share it with Juan.

She transferred from train to train without stopping off anywhere to sleep. At first she couldn't sleep in her seat even when there was nothing but black night outside the train windows. But eventually her mind became numbed by the monotonous whirring of the wheels on the tracks, and daytime or nighttime didn't matter. She slept off and on at random times during the whole day and a half to Kagoshima.

The city was covered in a thin coat of white dust from a recent small eruption of Mount Sakurajima. The locals didn't seem to be bothered by it, but Emiko covered her face with her father's scarf. She was dazed by lack of sleep but had to hurry to catch the boat. She was the last one to buy a ticket and get on board.

When the departing blast of the horn sounded, the boat silently slipped away from the pier, and Emiko felt she could relax at last. She'd been on very short ferry rides before with her father, but this trip would go on for twenty-four hours. She stood at the rail watching Mount Sakurajima recede in the distance. Ahead was nothing but a flat, pastel blue sea. For the first time, it occurred to her that Genji might be sending her on a wild goose chase.

She watched from the deck until she saw the pink sun dissolve completely into a baby blue sea. On the glassy water, the ship seemed not to be moving at all. It wasn't like the train, with scenery flashing by the windows at breakneck speed. That had made her feel she was rushing towards her father. But this? It was hard to believe they'd ever get there. If she was late, she'd miss seeing her father put ashore.

She went below and found her little bunk. She hadn't eaten anything since noon on the train, but she fell asleep immediately in her clothes. It seemed like no time had passed when an announcement came over the loudspeaker for everybody to get up. Just at sunrise, the ship pulled into the Amami

Oshima dock. And stayed there. And stayed there.

Emiko felt like she was the only person on board anxious to get on with the trip. Cranes lifted wooden crates of saké, beer, vegetables, blankets—one at a time, slowly lowering them to the pier. Barrels of kerosene and gasoline followed. And then Emiko heard a loud squeal. A huge hog tied in a rope sling was being lifted high in the air to be lowered onto the pier. More hogs followed, one at a time. It was hard to believe all this unloading wasn't going to put the ship behind schedule. She found herself pacing the deck.

Rice balls covered in seaweed were for sale in the "commissary." She ate some with green tea while studying a brochure of the Amami islands. Yoron was the smallest by far, only five or six kilometers across. The brochure didn't have a map of the island. It showed the port, a campsite, and only one guest house.

The ship horn finally sounded the departure. Emiko looked at the clock hanging conspicuously on the bulkhead. Eight more hours to go. She went up on the deck and sat staring at the horizon, which never got any closer. Some young men sat talking across from her. They seemed to be recently out of high school, like Satoru, and like Satoru they were probably rebelling against the heavy load of expectations now laid on them by society. They were outfitted like hippies—headbands, tie-dye shirts, bead necklaces. But the items all looked brand new, as if they had all been bought recently at the same store. She heard them say they were heading for the campsite on Yoron.

The ship stopped at two more islands before approaching Yoron just as a huge red sun burned through streaks of clouds and balanced on the edge of the motionless blue water, painting a pink path towards the ship. Emiko heard passengers rumbling below towards the gangplank, but she stayed up on deck until the last minute, enthralled by the view. In the distance, American-occupied Okinawa and its islands overshadowed the tiny Yoron island where the ship docked.

Most of the passengers piled into a waiting bus, and Emiko followed. The young men masquerading as hippies in their last fling before assuming the yoke of societal conformity told the driver they were going to the campsite. An old man with salt and pepper whiskers and no teeth got on, leading a goat. He told the driver he lived across the road from the guest house.

The bus wound through sweet potato and soybean fields, past groves of laurel trees, and stopped at the guest house. Emiko got out, followed by the goat and the old man. She turned to watch him cross the road and tie his goat to a tree in front of a low wooden cabin with a dome-shaped thatched roof. He bent to light a fire under an outdoor bath tub. She noticed his toothbrush hanging from a tree limb.

"Welcome, Miss."

Startled, Emiko turned back to the guest house. The proprietor smiled in the doorway beside his wife. "We have an indoor bath here in the guest house, in case you were wondering."

Emiko was the only guest. The rooms were on the second floor, and there were two tables and chairs that made up the "Gold Coast Restaurant" at the foot of the stairs. The owner's wife brought Emiko rice, fish, and some pickled side dishes, then sat with her while she ate.

"Coming from far away, Miss?"

"From Snow Country. It never gets this warm there."

"You should feel what it's like in the summer. Going to the beach tomorrow?"

"I wanted to ask you about that. I might go to the beach by the campsite, but a friend told me about another beach on the south coast. Do you know it?"

"Heh .... Tourists don't usually go there. Boats use it to

come ashore. The beach drops off fast into deep water. Not a good place for swimming."

"I just want to take some pictures. Can you tell me how to get there?"

She pointed. "Down that road, first right, quick left, and follow the path all the way down to the beach. It's about one kilometer away." She met Emiko's eyes with a grin. "You have to pass between two graveyards to get there. Not afraid of ghosts, are you?"

The guest house owner had been drinking local sweet potato shōchū and Emiko could hear him snoring in the room below hers. A full moon hid behind dark clouds in the dusk outside her window. If she was to get to the beach before her father was put ashore, it was time to go.

The road in front of the guest house was gravel, but the paths leading from there were packed dirt passages cutting between fields of crops at first, then through overgrown expanses of grass and scrappy bushes higher than her head. No houses. No people. No lights—only the moonlight. She felt like an insect crawling in a darkening maze.

She picked up her pace to make sure she'd be at the beach watching before the launch put her father ashore. The path made a final turn, and crowded grave markers appeared against the deep blue twilight sky on each side. The ashes of the dead lay buried beneath slabs of stone set so close they almost touched—a square stone at the bottom, a smaller rectangular stone on top of that, and a tall, thinner stone on that with the chiseled name of the deceased. Beyond the cemeteries, the moon spread a soft glow on the dark water lapping the sandy shore. In the distance, the lights on Okinawa flickered in the crepuscular light.

Emiko read the name on the nearest grave marker. It was a woman who'd died young. Dizzied by the thought of her own mother's death, she slumped to the ground, whispering her mother's spirit name. "Mom," she gasped. "I know you can't be at rest yet. As soon as I find Dad, we'll give you a proper burial. I promise."

She stood and peered over the shoulder-high cemetery wall down onto the beach, shadowed now by a single gray cloud creeping across the moon. Far out in the ocean she could see one dim light and one twinkling light on a small Okinawan island. Slowly the dim light separated from the flashing light, growing larger as it moved towards the beach. A faint hum gradually became a whining drone until she saw the distant shape of a launch heading her way. She started for the slope to the beach but stopped. It might be safer to watch from behind the cemetery wall.

The whining of the engine stopped short. She could make out the launch gliding silently in towards the shore. Three men in wide cone-shaped hats sat alert as the boat drifted to a stop near the beach. All three men wore foreign-looking tunics of some sort over dark trousers. None looked like her father. She controlled her urge to run back to the guest house.

The man in front hopped out into thigh-deep water. Emiko could see a large bundle of some kind on his back. She stooped lower, watching, ready to run.

The engine started up again, and the launch slowly backed away from the shore. The man with the bundle began slogging laboriously towards the beach. When he reached the dry sand, he dropped to his knees and looked up the path towards the graveyards. Under his peasant farmer's hat, Emiko caught a partial glimpse of a dark, bearded face she didn't recognize.

The man rose and plodded unsteadily towards the path. It was then that Emiko noticed. He was limping. Her father's slight limp. She ran down the path onto the beach. "Dad! Dad! It's me. Emiko."

Her father held his head as if he might be hallucinating.

"I'm here to take you home." She grasped his hand and held it to her heart. The moonlight reflected in his teary eyes. He touched her shoulder as if to make sure she was real. Finally, he took her in his arms. "I can't believe it. Emiko. I thought I'd never see you again."

"Me either, Dad." She wiped her wet cheeks on her sleeve. "You're wet and cold. Let me help you up the path. We'll talk in the guest house where I'm staying."

"Is Mom waiting there? How did you know to find me here?"

"Oh, Dad! I have to tell you. Mom died. Her heart gave out."

He sank onto the sand. "No, no, no."

Emiko put her arm around him. She pulled off his hat and held his head to her chest, sobbing as much at his grief as at her own. His hair was long and tangled. She'd never seen him with a beard before. In the moonlight, she could see it was newly tinged with gray. She wondered what changes had taken place inside.

Covered with sand, they walked silently up the path past the cemeteries and towards the guest house. She had a lot to tell him but thought it best to save it for later. The only thing her father said on the way back was, "She was so young."

At the corner of a field, there was a rusty oil barrel piled with trash for burning. Emiko stopped. "Dad, do you really need that hat any more?"

He handed it to her, and she tossed it into the barrel.

"And that tunic thing? We could burn that, too. You don't want people to think you're a foreigner sneaking into Japan."

He took off the huge bundle tied on his back and gave Emiko the tunic. It was stiffer than she'd expected. Probably waterproof. But she wanted him to start looking like her father again. She threw it into the barrel. "Also, you smell like fish," she joked. He only said, "Not surprised."

A long bath in the guest house removed the fish smell. He came out with a shaved face but still with hair almost to his chin. In the light of the room, Emiko commented on how darkened his skin had become. That was when his story of the past eight months began.

"When I was helping Beheiren in Tokyo, I met some U.S. military who were buying heroin and other drugs in Japan. I traced their sources and found that a person I used to know was one of the suppliers. I confronted him, gave him a chance to stop the business. The next thing I knew, I was kidnapped by yakuza drug dealers, shipped to northern Thailand, and forced to work as a gardener and cook in a fenced, guarded compound." He sighed. "I escaped once and went to the local authorities. They turned me right back in to the gang."

"Oh, Dad. I don't see how you survived."

"The hard part was being apart from you and Mom. Being held prisoner wasn't new to me. I'd had a taste of that in Soviet Russia." He grinned. "I didn't mind the work itself in Thailand. I'm now a good farmer and a good cook."

Emiko bathed and put on the yukata supplied by the guest house. The memory of Juan saying how beautiful she looked the first time he saw her in hers brought a lump to her throat. When she went back to the room, her father had rolled out two futons and was already asleep on one.

Emiko turned out the light but wasn't ready to sleep. She'd brought writing paper in her backpack and started a letter to Juan in the bright moonlight from the window. *Dear Juan, you won't believe this. I found my ....*

She must have fallen asleep. There was no telling for how long. She was startled awake by her father's voice calling out "Nobuko," her mother's name.

The moonlight streaming through the clouds cast an animated pattern on the wall that wavered above where her father had laid his head.

"Dad!" She crawled over and shook him. "What's wrong? Did you have a dream?"

He sat up. "Did you hear that whistle?"

A chill ran down Emiko's back. Her mother had died holding her father's whistle in her hand.

"You heard it, didn't you, Emiko?"

"No, Dad. It must have been a dream." She wished she were more sure of that. He'd called out her real name—which the acolyte Tōshin in the Nakakuni temple had warned her would call her back if she hadn't been able to completely detach herself from this world yet. "Dad," she said. "Mom's ashes are in the temple back home. We should go back together and bury them. That would bring us some peace."

"Yes," he said. "And I think your mother may already be at peace. In the dream, she was smiling down on the two of us lying side by side."

On the boat back to Kagoshima, Emiko had a chance to share the beauty of the view with her father. On both nights, they stayed up on deck talking until the last light had faded from the sky.

The first thing she needed to tell him about was Juan. "He's … he's an American soldier. I know—the army you were fighting against. I hope—"

"That was ages ago, Emi. Besides, army experience is something we'll have in common." He smiled. "I can tell you love him."

"Dad, we almost ran off to Europe together. I wanted him to desert. I didn't want him to be killed." The thought of that brought a tightness in her chest. "But at the last minute he said he couldn't desert. He's in Vietnam. I'm so worried."

Her father touched her shoulder. "I'm sorry he's in danger, but I'm glad you didn't go off to Europe."

"How much danger do you think he's in, Dad?"

"The odds are he'll make it. That's the best anybody can say." He frowned. "I've learned there's another danger for troops in Vietnam. Drugs." His eyes met Emiko's. "You never saw any signs that he might—?"

"No. Nothing like that."

"Good. Before I was kidnapped, I turned up a lot of information about drug smuggling. I learned even more in Thailand. It makes me want to help fight the drug trade in Japan."

"But when they set you free, didn't you have to promise not to turn them in?"

His eyebrows arched. "Yes. How did you know? So I won't expose that one drug ring that kidnapped me. There are others." He narrowed his eyes. "I found out a lot about yakuza gun smuggling, too."

Emiko realized there were plenty of things she still hadn't told him. She'd save Takashi and Satoru for later.

"One thing I don't understand," her father said. "The Thailand gang said they'd kill me and you, too, if either of us talked to the police. How did they know about you? You still haven't told me how you knew I'd be set free on Yoron."

It was time to tell him about her deal with Genji. She described her second visit to Genji, not her first. "I found your report naming Genji Sato's Trading Company and took it to him."

Her father's mouth dropped. "You blackmailed him?"

"Well, I promised we wouldn't turn him in if he let you go."

Her father stared blankly over the boat rail. She couldn't tell what he was thinking. Was he angry thinking that Genji would go unpunished? Was he angry at her?

He turned to her. "You saved me, Emi? It was you?"

She clutched his arm with a grin. "Of course."

"Weren't you scared?"

"Of course."

On the train all the way from Kagoshima to Tokyo, her father kept periodically chuckling and muttering, "Of course."

Relief throbbed in Emiko's chest as she approached her Narimasu house, not alone this time but with her father by her side—and with his report retrieved from the post office box before Mariko could mail it. No *Rent Overdue* sign was posted on her door. Nothing suggested the police had been there. It was late. They were exhausted. She put two futons side by side on the floor, and they fell asleep immediately.

III

32

Taking a prisoner

I have no great ambition in battle, yet I like to keep my honorable name.

—Zeami Motokiyo, *The Battle at Yashima*

A reporter with tinted glasses passed by the poker game Juan's squad was playing on the hood of a jeep. He stopped beside the ammo case Juan sat on. Juan could see he was Japanese. He stared at Juan's chest. "I am surprised. You are wearing a Japanese omamori talisman. For good luck?"

"It's worked so far."

"I write for the *Nippon Weekly*. Would you let me ask you some questions?"

Juan used this as an excuse to leave a card game he was losing. He led the reporter to a shady spot behind his barracks. The reporter explained, "I'm doing a report on various soldiers in the war. Just a personal profile. Nothing about strategy or specific locations."

That sounded permissible, Juan thought. He said he didn't mind.

"Have you been in Japan?"

"Yes." Juan told him how he'd met Emiko. "She gave me the omamori."

"Has she written to you?"

"Yes." Juan patted his pocket where he kept the one letter he'd received.

"Why were you in Japan?"

Juan gave him a quick version of his hospitalization. The

reporter, Mori, took notes on how he got injured, whether he liked Japan, what he liked about it. "So you're hoping to go back to Japan when you can?"

"Definitely."

"I have some other questions. Last month the order came to begin withdrawing 35,000 U.S. troops from Vietnam. I've talked to many soldiers who say America has given up on winning the war. What do you think?"

"The officers tell us we're turning it over to the Vietnamese."

"Do you think that comes down to the same thing as giving up?"

"The Vietnamese I've fought alongside of are tough, so ... maybe they can handle it."

"You say 'maybe.'"

Juan shrugged. "Probably?"

"On another topic. I've talked to G.I.s who say they'll refuse to obey orders that put them in danger for no reason. Have you heard any talk like this?"

"Some. Not much."

"Have you had similar thoughts yourself?"

Of course, this brought to Juan's mind the attack he'd been wounded in. He didn't volunteer any information about that. He said, "It's hard to know if an order's given for a good reason or not. So it's best just to follow it."

"Next, I want to ask if you've witnessed any drug use among the troops. Narcotics? Amphetamines?"

"Maybe some around the base. Almost never when out on patrol." Lieutenant Joss being an exception, but Juan kept that to himself.

"And have you yourself—"

"No. Never."

Mori turned a page in his notebook. "Finally, I know your platoon has seen action in the western hills since you've been back. I won't name the location, but can you describe what those missions have been like?"

"It's mostly defensive. Search and Clear, they call it. Establishing perimeters to protect villages from the Viet Cong."

Mori tilted his head as if he'd already heard the official reports. "How about your personal experience?"

"We search the area, see nothing, come back to base. Once we took some fire, called in choppers, cleared them out, then came back." When Mori looked up for more, Juan added, "That's about it. Mostly we've been just hanging around the base day after day." He pulled a book from his pocket. "I've been trying to learn Japanese."

Mori slid a camera from his shoulder. "Mind if I take a picture? Let's get the book in it. Now how about one reading your girlfriend's letter?" After snapping these, Mori asked him to get his rifle and pose with it. "If they print my article in Japan, I'll get you a copy."

Juan hoped he hadn't said anything he shouldn't have. "*Arigato*, Mori-san. Guess I'll get back to what we do here as much as anything. Playing poker."

Oct. 29, 1969

Dear Emiko,

I finally got your letter. It took two weeks to get here. It went to the hospital in Oji first.

Your omamori is keeping me safe. They call this the pacification and Vietnamization stage of the war, so that's good.

It's still hot here, but I guess it's getting colder in Tokyo. Keep warm.

Please write again soon and let me know if you have news about your father.

All my love,

Juan

What Juan had told the reporter a couple of weeks ago minimized the troops' demoralized state. Every day in the barracks the talk was about "getting out alive." The fragging of Joss's body was his squad's first slippery step towards anarchy, and this affected the rest of the platoon. In the back of everyone's mind was the order for troop withdrawals. The scuttlebutt was more withdrawals were to come. Poker winnings were bet on which platoon or company might be called home next.

Juan had glossed over the drug use, too. Sergeant Johnson did his best to quell it, but couldn't. The smell of marijuana was everywhere, and the barracks was a trading post of heroin, cocaine, uppers, and downers. The men didn't use them on the rare missions they were sent on. But they made up for it on base. Juan resisted. He saw what they can do to a person. But he lived in fear that he might some day give in.

He lounged in the shadow of the PX studying his Japanese grammar book. When the sun shifted, he moved to the other side. It was hard to concentrate. If Emiko could be with him to help, that would be different. He walked along the fence protecting the base, stopping to pet the guard dogs that were friendly. And he played poker. Day after day.

The monotony weighed so heavily on him that he almost wished to be sent on a mission. He knew some of the other guys felt this way, too, if only a few. When he heard choppers taking off in another part of the base, the excitement there only underscored his boredom.

In his notebook calendar, he marked off another day of service. He'd only been here a month. Five months to go. He lay in his bunk and started another letter to Emiko. Maybe he would try to write something in Japanese using Roman letters. But he'd been up since 0500 and fell asleep long before he finished.

The blare of an alarm woke him up. The whole barracks was in motion, boots scraping on the floor. It was still dark.

"On the double, men! Rescue mission. Full battle gear. Let's go." Sergeant Johnson stood by the door waving the platoon into a helicopter. He was in charge since Lieutenant Joss had never been replaced. Juan folded his letter to Emiko and put it under his pillow.

"Come on, Gomez. Don't want to be late for the party."

Juan had maps, a compass, and infrared goggles. Blake had the radio and GPS. Riley was struggling with the tripod for his M60 machine gun. There was barely time to sit down before the squad's chopper took off.

Juan looked out the open door at the lights of the base. They were following two other choppers off to their right. In minutes, the black jungle canopy below was all they could see. It couldn't be far to the landing spot. The Laos border was less than an hour away by chopper.

Flares shot up from below, and the chopper slowed, circled once, and dropped into a clearing. Johnson jumped out even before it touched ground. The others followed, keeping their heads low. It was a South Vietnamese ARVN squad that had been ambushed by Viet Cong. They had already carried one of their wounded back from the forest and now loaded him on a stretcher into a chopper.

"One more man down up ahead," the Vietnamese lieutenant said. "The fire came from the trees at the foot of that hill."

"Just one?" Johnson queried. "Everybody else accounted for?" He held out his hand. "Gomez, give me the goggles. Fan out, everybody. Keep low. Follow me."

The tall grass made it hard for everybody but Johnson to see where they were going. Before long, he put his hand up. They stopped. "Here he is." Johnson bent and took the man's neck pulse. "Alive. Riley, give Juan the M60. You and Ratcliff carry this man back to the chopper. Gomez, come with me. Let's see who's out there."

A few rounds of an AK-47 rang out. Johnson and Juan dropped to the ground. Juan poured machine gun fire into the general direction of the shots. He waited, listened. With the goggles, Johnson had a better chance to tell how many were out there. Juan waited for him to pop his head up and look. "Sergeant," he whispered. "What do you see? Sergeant?" Johnson groaned. He was hit. "My leg."

Juan crawled over and saw a rip in the thigh area of his field trousers. He pulled gauze from his pack and tied up the large but shallow wound enough to stop the bleeding. He lay still, listened, then took the goggles from Johnson and scanned the forest where the shooting came from. Nothing. "Man down," he called out as loud as he could. "Medic! Bring a stretcher."

Two men came and carried Johnson back. Juan kept scanning through the trees ahead. He was too far away and edged forward. As he neared the forest where the shots had come from, he dropped onto his stomach and kept snaking ahead until he was at the foot of the hill.

A Viet Cong soldier popped up from the underbrush about thirty meters from Juan.

"*Day shoom swong*!" Juan yelled. The soldier dropped his weapon, and Juan stood up. "*Yuh tie len*!" he commanded. The soldier raised his hands.

Juan walked towards him and could see that he was hurt. An AK-47 lay at his feet. Juan tried to remember how to ask how many were with him. He tried something like "*Bao newy*?" and the soldier shook his head. Whatever that meant. Anyway, only one rifle had fired on them. Juan gestured with his own gun for the man to walk in front, hands behind his head. He picked up the man's rifle and managed one more command in G.I. Vietnamese. "*Dee dee*," which was said to mean "Move out."

When they got back to the choppers, the South Vietnamese Lieutenant questioned the prisoner but got nothing from him. He made sure the medics treated his shoulder wound.

When the choppers landed back at the base, a small group of reporters was waiting with cameras. Johnson and the wounded South Vietnamese soldier were carried to the hospital on stretchers. Juan had been keeping watch on the wounded Viet Cong and helped him onto the ground, holding his good arm. Just at that moment, Mori, the Japanese reporter, flashed a picture of Juan leading the prisoner away.

33

Interrupted melody

How now, sinner, why are you so late?

—Anonymous, *The Mirror of Pine Forest*

The first thing Emiko's father noticed when they awoke was the bowl. "Is this ...?"

"No. It's like Mom's, isn't it? Juan gave it to me."

Her father sized up the little house for the first time. "Nice." He smiled. "Cozy. What's that bigger house on the other side of the yard? Is it connected to yours?"

"Let's have some tea, Dad. I still have a lot more to tell you."

She started with Takashi. "I've been working for the man who lives—or used to live—in that house over there. Takashi. I thought he was a Beheiren supporter. My job was translator. It didn't take long to realize he's really an ultranationalist."

"Translator? It's a perfect job for you. But for an ultranationalist?" A furrow formed in his forehead. "I dug up lots of information on those extreme nationalist groups before I was kidnapped. Some of them are smuggling guns into the country. They're dangerous."

"I know." She told how she'd followed Satoru when he picked up guns and delivered them to an office in Waseda. "Satoru was Takashi's naïve delivery boy. It wasn't only guns. Takashi used him to deliver a chemical bomb that ended up killing him. The news reports say it was probably made by amateurs. The police are looking for Takashi."

Her father gave her a hard look. "Emi, I'd feel better if we just moved back to Kitayama."

"I know, Dad. But I can't. The police know I have some connection with Satoru. They questioned me and let me go but told me not to move without letting them know. If I tell them now that I knew about the guns even before the bomb attack and didn't reveal it, they'll want to know why."

"In fact, why didn't you?"

"I was hoping to get Satoru a different job first, get him out of the picture." She dropped her gaze. "Also, at that time, I was in the process of helping Juan to desert. We were going to leave the country soon."

"I see." He frowned. "But after the bombing, you still didn't tell the police? Satoru was dead and Juan was back in Vietnam."

"I was scared. They knew I was working for Takashi and living next door to him and Satoru. I thought if I told them, it would seem like I was in on it." She clung to her father's arm. "Dad, I'm such a screw-up."

He brushed a tear from her cheek. "If you'd been arrested, I'd still be in Thailand. So let's just worry about now. I think you need to go to the police and tell them everything. You say the bomb was set off near the Socialist Party headquarters. From what I found out about one of these groups, that was probably just a test run. They have bigger things planned."

"All right, Dad. I'm ready to take the consequences. But will you come with me?"

As they walked towards the station, Emiko glanced at her father's long hair, which she'd tied in a short pony tail. She liked the look. This was no salaryman. She was proud to walk beside a man who looked like he had other things on his mind besides fitting in. But the light nylon jacket didn't hide the faded, yellowish spots on his shirt and pants.

"Dad, I still have some money from Mom's funeral offerings. If we're going to the Metropolitan Police headquarters,

I could buy you a suit. It might be wiser if—"

"If I didn't look like an escaped worker from a drug camp? You could be right."

They walked to a men's clothing store near the station where the women clerks swarmed around her father to help him. He tried on the cheapest ready-made gray suit, and they gushed, "Ah. Yes. Yes. Oh, my. Yes." Emiko knew it wasn't flattery because she felt the same.

Inspector Fujiwara's assistant in the horn rimmed glasses brought another chair for Emiko's father. Fujiwara began, "We were about to pay you a visit, Miss Ozeki. Your employer is missing. We wonder what you know about that."

"I don't know where he is, but—"

The note taker clicked open her pen.

Emiko poured out almost everything she'd found out about Takashi—the gun shipments from Yokohama, their delivery to the subversive journal office in Waseda, even the radical editorials she'd translated. The only thing she kept to herself was what she knew about Genji's drug business. Her father said nothing at all.

The police had probably drawn their own conclusions about Satoru from the radical magazines in his room and his Tatenokai-like uniform, but she tried to weaken that impression, describing him as a naïve idealist misled by an overbearing employer.

"This is very helpful, Miss Ozeki. I wonder why you didn't tell us when we first brought you in?"

"I was scared you'd think I was an accomplice. I'm not."

Fujiwara thumbed through his notes. "We checked on the American you brought to the Tokyo Beheiren office. He did indeed return to his unit in Vietnam. We checked known associates of radical-right groups. Your name doesn't appear. Can you avow you're not working for any of them?"

"I'm not. The last thing I want is for Japan to revert to colonial imperialism. That's why I support Beheiren." She was about to elaborate, but Fujiwara twisted his jaw, and she thought it best to leave it at that.

Her father spoke up for the first time. "Inspector, some months ago, I did research on yakuza gangs, their smuggling operations, in particular. I never came across the name Nakamura Takashi, but I learned that one gang might be supplying a group that has a plan to attack the Diet when it's in session."

"Why are you reporting this just now?"

"It seemed far-fetched until I heard my daughter say guns were actually being stored in Waseda."

Of course, the real reason was that her father had been held captive in Thailand for the past eight months. Like Emiko, he only mentioned guns, not drugs. He was being faithful to his promise not to inform the police about Genji.

Inspector Fujiwara nodded to his note taker, then turned to Emiko's father. "Please tell me everything you know about this gang of gun smugglers."

Emiko was surprised how closely the information her father had turned up matched what she knew about Takashi. He gave Fujiwara the sources of weapons in America, the names of ships bringing them into Yokohama, and the place where they changed hands.

"And the plans of the groups buying the weapons?"

"The only plot I learned of was the attack on the Diet. It's supposedly planned for some time before the New Year's holiday."

The inspector sat up straight, glancing at his note taker. "Thank you, Mr. Ozeki. And Miss Ozeki. We'll need you to remain in your current residence until further notice so we can contact you."

On the street, Emiko checked her subway map. "My

friend Mariko's apartment is nearby. Would you mind stopping by there with me?" She explained the promise Mariko had made to mail her father's report to the police if she didn't return in three weeks. "I didn't tell her I was going to Yoron. I said I was going home."

"Devious Emiko."

"Well, I didn't want to tell her you were in a drug lord's camp."

"Just kidding. Come on, let's go see your friend."

Mariko squinted under the hall light as she opened the door. Her mouth gaped open. "Emiko. Come in. This must be the handsome man you told me about."

"What? No! I mean, well, yes. My father. That's right." Emiko's face felt like it was on fire. Mariko's turned blood red. "Your father!" she said. "You found him."

Emiko's father bowed.

Mariko pulled her futon aside, tipped the little table onto the tatami, and set out two teacups. Emiko realized she only had two.

"Sorry how cramped it is here. But I have news of my own. I'm engaged. Remember the man I told you about? I'll be moving into his apartment soon with him and his mother. No big wedding. We'll get married at the Tokyo Ward Office. I'll be quitting work at the restaurant. Masa, that's his name, already got me a photo shoot for a clothing ad."

"Congratulations, Mariko. I can see how happy you are."

Mariko grinned. "Our Hi Crass Bar days are far behind, it seems."

Emiko rolled her eyes sideways towards her father. This was another thing she hadn't mentioned to him yet. He raised an eyebrow at her but said nothing.

Before any tea could be poured, Emiko said they had to be leaving. "Oh, and mailing that envelope? I've taken care of it. Got back earlier than I thought. Mariko, congratulations again."

Mariko's life was now settled, determined, set in stone for a predictable future. It was a life that society would approve of—because it was a life like theirs. When Emiko thought of her own future with Juan, that approval was far from certain. The thing was she didn't care.

Even now it was uncertain how she would live. The police had told her and her father to stay where they were. That was fine. She loved being with her father again. The little house was crowded, but they would get by.

Her father could always go back to Kitayama and get his guard job back, she was sure. But he'd been lost so long she didn't want to let go of him. She laughed at herself. She'd brought him to the police station with her and to her friend's house with her. She'd even gone with him to buy clothes. It was as if she was afraid if she looked away, he'd disappear again.

She didn't want to lose Juan, either. She sat at the table and took out some letter paper.

November 7, 1969

Dear Juan,

Thanks for your letter. I'm sorry my first letter was sent to the Oji hospital before getting to you. I waited to get yours before sending this so I could be sure of the address. Just in case, I'm writing "Vietnam" on the envelope of this one.

I miss you so much. You've been gone almost a month. I worry about you being hurt by Lieutenant Joss as much as by the enemy.

You wouldn't believe how much has been going on. Every time I start to write, something seems to come up.

There are lots of things to tell you, but for now I only

want to give you good news. I've found my father. He's here with me now.

Please stay safe. I can't believe we have to wait five more months before we can be together again.

I love you.

Emiko

For days she and her father sat in her little house reading newspapers, listening to the radio, and talking about her mother and Juan. They were settling into a routine, the chance that Inspector Fujiwara would call them back for more questions all but forgotten. Their life became a happy melody played over a persistent undertone of melancholy and longing for two people they missed.

Her father did the cooking. "This is Pad Thai," he said one day. "I know at least ten varieties. I'll let you try them all."

She liked it, but after a while she longed for Japanese food. One day, when he announced, "All right. Pad Thai variation number ten coming up," she had to say, "Um, pork cutlet on rice would be fine. Maybe we could take a break from Thai food. Save number ten for next week?"

While he was cooking, she read Juan's letter once again. It seemed strange that he hadn't answered her second letter yet.

A sound like creaking wood came from Takashi's house.

"What's that?" Her father's frying pan clanked onto the stove burner.

"Somebody in Takashi's house. Should we go look?"

Her father turned off the stove. "I'll go."

Emiko followed him across the yard and through the back door into the hallway. A light was on in Takashi's office.

"Hello," her father called out. "Who's there?" He stepped carefully down the hallway towards the office, Emiko following. The office door was half open. Her father pushed it all the way.

"Takashi!" Emiko cried.

Takashi stood up from the floor beside the desk, a crowbar in his hand. "Get out of my house. Now."

"Put that down," her father commanded. But Takashi raised the iron bar and moved towards him.

Emiko felt something brush by her leg. It was the dog Kuro, growling. He leapt on Takashi, knocked him down. Her father kicked the crowbar away and pinned Takashi to the floor. "I need something to tie his hands," he called to Emiko.

All she could think of was her elastic belt. She pulled it off. Her father tied Takashi's hands behind his back while Emiko called Kuro off.

"We can lock him in Satoru's room," Emiko said. "No windows. The lock is on this side."

Her father nodded. He pulled Takashi to his knees but wouldn't let him stand, forcing him to hobble on his knees into the room. Emiko slammed the door and locked it.

"Go up to the Narimasu police box," her father told her. "I'll stay here and make sure he doesn't get out."

Emiko was out of breath when she got there. An overweight policeman was asleep at his desk. She woke him with a shout. "Attacker in my house. With a crowbar. He's big."

The cop called for help. Another cop, younger and more energetic-looking arrived on a motorbike. Emiko rode behind him up to the house, the other cop following on his own motorbike.

They could hear Takashi kicking on Satoru's door as soon as they went in the office. It took a moment before the cops were convinced Emiko's father wasn't the intruder. "The man in there attacked us with that crowbar," Emiko insisted. "He's wanted by the police. It's Nakamura Takashi. Please call Inspector Fujiwara at the Metropolitan Police. I have his card."

The heavy cop made a radio call, and a police car arrived. Neighbors' lights came on, their dogs barked. Emiko felt faint and sat on the floor leaning against the desk. Her father did the rest of the talking. And there was a lot of talking.

"Help," Takashi yelled. Finally, two cops opened Satoru's door. Takashi was outraged. "They tied me up. This is my house."

The third cop stood by the office door to keep Emiko and her father from leaving. He talked on his squawky radio using some kind of police codes. Twice he said, "Nakamura Takashi" and "Inspector Fujiwara. Metropolitan Police." He asked Emiko the address of the house and repeated that into the radio. He listened, then pointed to Takashi. "Cuff that man and bring him to the station."

He turned to Emiko's father. "We'll also need the two of you to come and give statements."

As Emiko got up, she noticed a tatami section had been partly pried up from the floor. She bent to look, and a cop came over. He pulled the thick tatami piece farther up, shined his flashlight beneath it. "Come look at this." He pulled out a long gun of some sort. "It's a machine gun."

At the station, Emiko and her father were questioned all over again. Finally the chief closed the folder on his desk and made a phone call. "You are to report to Inspector Fujiwara first thing tomorrow."

34

Settling in

Only the happy ones return to contentment.
Those who were sad return to despair.

—Kōbō Abe, *The Woman in the Dunes*

Emiko and her father explained the capture of Takashi once more for the inspector and his note taker.

Fujiwara wanted to know more about her father's military service. He asked for details about how he'd restrained Takashi, and he seemed impressed. After again going over the information about yakuza smuggling her father had given him previously, he said, "I'd like you to tell all this to my contact at the customs office. Would you mind paying him a visit?" He made an appointment on the phone.

Emiko tagged along. The Customs Headquarters was only five stops away plus a short taxi ride. This part of town was new to both of them. Businesses, schools, and industrial buildings lined the sidewalks—no trendy shops or elegant restaurants. A faint smell of the Tokyo port hung in the humid air. Emiko waited in the headquarters lobby while her father went up to the third floor. She was glad he was wearing his new suit.

A low wall by a row of palm-like plants was the only place to sit. The employees, mostly in uniform, rushed back and forth from one office to the next, papers in their hands, without a glance at her. It wasn't long before she got uncomfortable and went outside.

Gray mid-November clouds hung low over the street.

Emiko turned up her collar, crossed a wide street roaring with trucks belching black diesel dust, and walked towards the port. The water was shiny brown and smelled oily, but a group of men and women stood with poles dangling over its edge, confirming Emiko's theory that wherever there is water there will be people fishing in it.

She returned to the customs lobby and paced from one end to the other, reading the names on the doors. *Compliance Director*. *Customs Security*. *Duty Enforcement*. It all seemed a little scary.

"Hey. There you are." Her father's eyes were shining. "Big news. Let's go outside."

In a different direction from where Emiko had walked they found a little park with a pond. It was like a quiet green oasis in the midst of gray industrial clamor. "I got a job," her father announced.

"What? What do you mean?"

"Auxiliary Customs Investigator." He chuckled. "How about that title? The director is the same age as me. He was in Manchuria, too. We talked about those days. He asked how you and I caught Takashi. He'd been looking for him. Without mentioning Genji's operation, I told him what I'd learned about smuggling. So even though my only previous experience was being a guard, he offered me a position."

Emiko was speechless.

"The emphasis is on 'auxiliary.' Just kind of a helper, I guess. But it's a fulltime government job." He laughed. "After a few weeks of paper pushing to confirm it, that is."

"Did you tell him about Thailand?"

"I did. He was particularly interested in that. Said my inside knowledge would help."

"Oh, Dad." She gripped his arm, and he pulled her in for a hug.

As usual these days, the first thing she did when they got

home was to check the mailbox beside her door. A letter was waiting for her. Her heart jumped. But it was her own second letter to Juan, returned for some reason. Something not quite readable was stamped on it about "assignment locations." She slumped to the floor. Was it returned because Juan was missing? Or worse?

Her father looked at the envelope. "Hm. You wrote 'Vietnam' in the address."

"I wanted to make sure they knew where to send it this time."

"Yes, but the mailing code should be enough. The military might not want to reveal the location of the assignment." He put his hand on her shoulder. "That's probably what it is."

Despite her father's encouragement, she went to sleep that night fearing the worst while trying not to let herself think about it.

"A few weeks." That's how long her father had said it would take before he was actually employed. Emiko knew they were living in the house on borrowed time. What if the landlord, whoever he was, showed up and asked for the rent? She'd used most of her savings from her job to go get her father and bring him back. Obviously, her employment with Takashi was over. They were living on the remaining funeral offering money now. She'd never mentioned where the bulk of that came from and didn't want to.

She needed a job herself and wondered if she could really be a translator. She showed her father some reports Takashi had given her.

He looked through them with interest. "Ah, this is one I wrote myself."

"Right. It's one of the few I kept. All the right-wing subversive ones I put back in Takashi's office after the police questioned me."

"And you were supposed to translate these?"

"Yeah, I translated a few for him before. He was going to send them to English-language papers. I don't think he ever did."

"Hm, translations. Why don't you try your hand at writing an original story of your own? You could describe the capture of Takashi and the breakup of the Diet attack plot by the police. You've got first-hand knowledge."

With time on her hands, Emiko decided to give it a try. As soon as she started, she found writing articles in Japanese was easier than translating. You could tell the story in your own words. She showed her first article to her father, and he loved it. "You should see if any newspaper is interested."

She got on the train before she had a chance to change her mind. The *Tokyo Daily* had already taken two of her translations. She'd try there first. Maybe they'd take an original article.

Emiko was definitely getting used to marching into tall glass-walled buildings and getting what she wanted. She checked her reflection in the door, pushed some hair behind her ear, straightened her collar, and took a breath. Inside, there were no pretty young women simpering in childlike voices to welcome her. Just men and women doing their jobs. She went to an information desk.

"I'm Emi— I mean Ushirouchi Nagako. I've brought my latest article in person. I need to discuss it with an editor."

"Who is it who handles your submissions?"

Of course, she had no idea. "I think it's ... no, that's not it. This is embarrassing. I can't—"

"It must be Miss Saeki."

"Yes. That's right."

"Second floor, room 203."

At least fifty dark heads were bent over desktops in room 203. No one looked up when Emiko walked through the open door. A low clicking and the whine of telex machines gave the feeling that the room was in motion. Emiko walked up to the nearest desk, asked for Miss Saeki.

"Saeki-san!" the young man called out. A frumpy woman with crooked teeth and no makeup stood up. She waved Emiko to her desk. A few heads looked up briefly from their desks but immediately dipped back to their work. There was no chair by Miss Saeki's desk. They talked standing up.

"I guess I should tell you Ushirouchi Nagako is just my pen name." Emiko gave her real name and the titles of the Ushirouchi translations the paper had published. "Now I've brought an article I wrote myself."

The editor's eyes seemed to bulge when Emiko mentioned Takashi and the Diet attack plot. She read the first few pages while they stood there. "I see. Yes. Would you like to come with me? I'll introduce you to our personnel manager."

And that was it. Emiko was hired as a *Tokyo Daily* reporter. She would only be paid per article, but she had a job.

Miss Saeki walked her to the door. "Your article mentions gun smuggling. Do you think you could do a detailed report on what you know about that?"

"Definitely."

Emiko's father became a major source for reports Emiko began to submit to the *Tokyo Daily*. She wrote descriptions of radical right-wing groups including the Shield Society admired by Takashi. She gave more detailed information on bribery cases that had already been publicized. As for anything related to Genji's drug smuggling, she kept silent on that. She would not give him and his personal yakuza gang any excuse to come after them.

Finally, Emiko's father's job became official. She walked with him to the station on his way to work on the first day. Together they called the Kitayama factory manager. The manager spoke loud, and Emiko could tell by his voice he was worried her father might be in trouble. When her father said he wouldn't be coming back to the factory, she heard, "As long as you're all right. But come back to see us. Everybody's been concerned about you. We can find you a job here any time you need one."

Emiko asked the manager to put Jun-oba on the phone. "You have to bring that handsome young colleague here to visit," Jun-oba insisted.

"I will. But there's something else. I found my father!"

"Oh, really? That's hard to believe. Well, the house you lived in is rented to another family. I moved all your things to my spare room."

Her father heard that and took the phone. "Jun-oba, it's really me. I'll have a long story to tell when we come back. I don't know when that will be since I'm working in Tokyo now. Thanks for taking care of our things."

Now that her father was working at Customs, Emiko began to do the cooking. She tried to make *sukiyaki* like her mother in a pan on the electric burner on the table. The meat was tough and the vegetables wouldn't absorb the juice.

"Delicious," her father said.

"Just like Mom's?"

"Heh-heh."

Emiko told her father the story of Jun-oba's visit. He laughed, but she could tell it made him think about her mother and their home town. He went to sleep early, as he always did these days now that he had to catch the early train to work.

Emiko sat at the table thinking about her mother. They'd missed holding all seven of her mother's funeral memorials, even the last one. That would have been when her father was on the boat from Bangkok. She didn't see any reason to bring that up.

Now that Emiko and her father both had jobs, they went

together to the electronics district in Akihabara and bought a little black and white television like the one they'd had in Kitayama. With that and the portable radio, along with reading newspapers, their life began to resemble what it had been in Kitayama. Emiko imagined she could hear her mother's voice saying, "Enough talk about the news. Who wants to go look at the cherry blossoms?" She was sure her father heard it, too.

"Dad, there's a park near here," she said one day. "Let's go for a walk and look at the leaves changing color."

He met Emiko's eyes and turned off the TV without comment. They walked in silence along a sunlit path bounded by brilliant red maples and yellow ginkgos. Emiko noticed her father's eyes clouding over and put her arm through his.

Taking occasional walks with her father to admire nature's beauty became a way of honoring her mother. She imagined her mother walking along with them.

"Red sumac leaves," her father said. "Your mother always loved them."

"And she told me not to touch them."

"Those pink cosmos. They were one of your mother's favorites."

"I remember she planted them in front of our house."

"We should plant some in front of the little Narimasu house." Her father's face brightened. "Maybe next spring."

It seemed that the little house was their new home now. They both had jobs they liked. They had settled into a happy routine here. She missed Juan, and they both missed her mother, but she and her father had each other. She planted some tulip bulbs in the yard along the fence. Her father planted beets and endive for his cooking.

The weed-strewn yard had always depressed her. After finishing an article for the *Tokyo Daily* while her father was away at the customs office, she stood in the yard making plans. If she started early next spring, she could fill it with all of her mother's favorite kinds of flowers. She went back inside and began making a sketch for a garden.

A knock at the door startled her.

A man's deep voice called out, "Anybody there?"

Emiko cracked open the door. A short, stocky bald man in a worn, shiny suit stood without bowing. "Are you the maid?"

"Pardon?"

"I rented to a man named Nakamura Takashi. He's been out of touch. So I'm checking at the maid's house." He handed her a dirty business card. "Owada. Real estate agent." He pulled a contract from his coat pocket. "The residence is rented to one person. The owner made it clear that no one else was allowed to live here. If you're not the maid or a family member, you'll have to leave."

Leave? She couldn't do that. She hadn't heard from Juan since his first letter, but she had never given up hope he'd come back. If she moved, how would he find her? She looked Mr. Owada in the eye. "Does the owner know he's been renting to a criminal?"

"What's that you're saying?'

"I'm saying the renter, Nakamura Takashi, is in police custody. It's been in the newspaper."

"Who are you?"

"I worked for him—until I found out he was a terrorist. I used this little house as my office."

"Terrorist! I'll check this out with the police. Meanwhile, you'll have to leave the premises immediately. Gather up any personal belongings before I put a lock on the door."

"May I ask, Mr. Owada, if you might have any difficulty renting a place formerly lived in by a criminal?"

He stared at her without answering. Emiko knew the pay of a rental agent depended on his making sure the owner never lost money.

"Because," she said, "I would like to rent the house myself."

Owada's grimace faded. But his eyes narrowed immediately. "How old are you?"

"Twenty. Legal age to sign a contract. And of course I realize there would be key money involved for your services."

A smile struggled to form on Owada's face. "You realize the contract is for the whole residence, not just the maid's house?"

Emiko's heart jumped. She definitely hadn't realized that. "Of course," she lied.

Owada told her the amount of the rent. She fought to keep a composed face. It was more than she'd imagined. Takashi had told her it was cheap. He must have meant in comparison to places in the center of Tokyo. But she had no choice. She and her father needed to be here when Juan returned.

"You could just give me the key money now," Owada offered. "I'll need to verify that Mr. Nakamura won't be needing the place any longer."

After Owada left, Emiko sat thinking about what she'd done. The key money had taken all of her savings. It was going to be hard for her and her father to afford the rent. Not only that, but the customs headquarters where her father worked and the newspaper office where she took her articles were both on the other side of the city. The reasonable thing would be to look for a place over there.

"Maybe we can afford it," her father said when he came back from work. "We'll borrow money, if we have to. But why here?" Then before she could answer, he tapped his head. "Ah, I see. You're out of touch with Juan. Of course you need to be here when his service is up."

She bit her lip. "Tell me. Do you think he's really coming back?"

"Emi, you just have to presume he will."

"Because, you know, people say soldiers have flings with girls when they're on leave and never intend to come back. I know that's what Jun-oba would say. That's why I told her Juan was just a colleague. I never mentioned he was in the army." She looked down and muttered, "Or that I was in love with him."

Her father's hand on hers encouraged her to go on. "Dad, you were in the army. You knew lots of soldiers. Is it true? Do they pretend to like girls and say they're coming back but never do?"

"Emi, no. It's no different with soldiers than with any men. A few would do this, but most wouldn't. About Juan, you know him as a person. That should give you your answer."

Knowing her father was right, she worked at putting her fears to rest, immersing herself in her writing and listening to her father's stories of customs investigations. She saw it pained him to know things about Genji's drug smuggling operation that he couldn't tell Customs. "Anyway," he sighed, "we're going to shut down the other operations."

One evening in the middle of December when they were eating stir-fried rice and watching TV, a special report interrupted the news. The U.S. president had announced that 50,000 additional troops were being withdrawn from Vietnam.

Emiko grabbed her father's arm. They looked at each other, neither daring to say what they hoped.

35

Flying pillows and boots

Summer grasses—
All that remains
Of soldiers' dreams.
—Bashō Matsuo, *haiku*

Juan hadn't gotten a clear answer from the Viet Cong prisoner he'd brought back. Were more enemy hiding nearby and how many were there? The prisoner had been interrogated, but whatever was learned never filtered down to the patrol level. Instead, a long period of silence followed, as if the whole incident had never taken place.

Juan asked the men in his barracks about this, and the general consensus was to let sleeping dogs lie. "Forget it," Riley told him. "Focus on what's important. It's lunchtime."

The enlisted men's mess hall rang with the clatter of metal dishes and war protest songs. Riley took sirloin steak, potato salad, and beans. Juan couldn't find cod but scooped up some fried ocean perch and crab casserole. It was easy to see how the guys attached permanently to the base gained weight.

They found a table with room to set their trays beside men from a different platoon who kept eating without looking up. They were talking about which dessert was best, cheesecake or banana splits or apple strudel.

A uniformed South Vietnamese sergeant sat down across from Juan. It was Ve, the translator from the Joss incident. Juan nodded. He saw Ve had chosen a spoon to eat the loose American-style rice.

"This table's not for gooks," the private beside Ve slurred with a full mouth.

Ve dropped his spoon and took his tray to an empty table. Riley joined the dessert conversation, advocating tiramisu. Rather than start an argument, Juan got up and went to sit across from Ve. "Sorry about that," he apologized.

"That's all right. I'm used to it." Ve tilted his head. "Aren't you the guy who brought back that VC prisoner?"

"Yeah, did you translate at his interrogation? I've been wondering. It doesn't seem logical that he was the only one out there in the forest."

Ve frowned. "'The interrogation produced nothing conclusive.'"

"He wouldn't talk?"

Ve looked Juan in the eye. "He talked. The captain got the report."

Juan understood Ve hesitated to talk about it. But he couldn't see why the information needed to be kept secret. He persisted. "So was he attached to a larger unit or not?"

Ve swallowed a huge spoonful of rice. "Here's what the prisoner said. There was—still is—a Viet Cong camp near the Laos border, not too far from where he was captured. He was sent out on reconnaissance. One of our South Vietnamese guys surprised him—shot and missed. He shot back and retreated into the forest. Two Americans pursued—you and Sergeant Johnson. One of you fired into the trees, hitting his shoulder."

"The captain knows this? Seems like we would have been sent to wipe out those VC near the border."

"He got the report. That's all I can say." Ve sipped some tea. "The VC are camped there just waiting for the U.S. troops to go home so they can facilitate the North army's march to the south. That's according to the prisoner."

Juan thought this over. It was a détente, as the Vietnamese

called it. Neither the VC commander nor the U.S. captain wanted to engage in a pointless bloody fight. For the first time, Juan had a definite sense that the war was over. And for the first time, like the others, he felt a strong reluctance to be the last person killed.

"The prisoner's shoulder healing OK?" Juan asked.

"Yes. He's on the list for prisoner exchange. I couldn't get any information about Sergeant Johnson."

"His leg was broken. He's enjoying a nice vacation in Yokohama now."

"Lucky guy." Ve eyed Juan over a spoonful of his crème caramel. "That village incident. I want to thank you for not turning that girl's father in when he ... you know, when Lieutenant Joss was going to—"

"It never happened, Ve. Joss was killed by a booby trap."

Ve gave a single nod, more like a bow.

Search and clear missions for Juan's patrol seemed to be paused, at least for now. Maybe they had cleared out the last of the Viet Cong from the vicinity of the "pacified" villages in the western hills. Or maybe they hadn't but the U.S. had abandoned hope of controlling that area. In any case, weeks wore on filled with nothing but sitting around, scrounging for the latest news from the States, playing poker, and shooting the bull.

Juan read in the *Stars and Stripes* that back in the middle of September 35,000 troops had been withdrawn from Vietnam. Word was out that coming up in mid-December even more would be called home. That was only a couple weeks away. Juan's whole unit was squirming like worms in a can. Most of the men thought their unit deserved to be the next withdrawn. Skeptics claimed that "deserving" had nothing to do with it. The troops sent home would simply be those easiest to withdraw.

In the barracks Juan listened as the guys ragged on Williams, who had taken R and R in Japan and met a girl there.

"You really think she's waiting for you, Dummy?"

"I guarantee she's doing the deed with another G.I. right now."

"Yeah, she's probably picked up three or four since you left."

"She reads the casualty reports. She knows the odds. She's not going to waste her time waiting around for you."

"You got one letter. Then nothing. What does that tell you?"

Juan broke in. "Shut up, guys. Williams doesn't need to hear that. You don't know anything about the girl."

"They're all the same," Riley scoffed. Others agreed.

That night on his cot, Juan read once again the one short letter he'd received from Emiko. She'd written it shortly after he left. It said she loved him. But he'd written back, and she never answered.

The next day there was a letter for Juan, but it was from his friend Walter, not Emiko.

November 1969

Juan,

Walter here. Enjoying my mother's cooking and our family conclaves jawboning about old times on Coosaw Island. I guess this letter will get to you eventually no matter where you are through our wonderful APO system. Hope you're doing well.

I keep reading that more troops are going to be withdrawn. I hope that includes you. If you do get sent back to the States, come see me. We'll fix you some shrimp creole that will make you never want to leave.

Your friend,

Walter 803-555-7232

It was a good surprise to hear from Walter. They'd spent some happy times together in Tokyo. Juan would definitely go see him if he ever got the chance.

He checked the postmark. It had only taken Walter's letter ten days to get here from Beaufort, South Carolina. He hadn't heard from Emiko for almost two months. Her one short letter had said she had a lot to tell him. Then nothing. He'd answered that letter right away. What was it she had to tell him? Something was wrong.

Before Juan even reached his barracks, he heard shouts, whoops, banging on the quonset walls. Inside, pillows and boots flew into the air. Blake ran and threw his arms around him.

"What is it? What is it?"

"You haven't heard? We're going home."

Juan tried to share in the wild excitement on the plane flying back to the States. He drank a couple of beers and sang along with the chorus of "Give Peace a Chance." But he couldn't stop wondering why Emiko had only written that one letter. The barracks wisecracks about girls not waiting for GIs to come back kept replaying in his head.

This plane at least had seats. Even windows. He slept off and on until finally the sprawling army base came into view as the plane careened and dove towards the Fayetteville airport. "I'm going to kiss the ground," Riley shouted above a thundering of cheers and stamping feet. "Home at last," Blake cried out. A bus was waiting to take them to Fort Bragg, North Carolina.

Juan was glad to be out of the war, but this felt no more like home to him than any army base. Home to what? More smelly barracks, more mess halls, more sitting around and doing make-work jobs. They were going to have four days leave as soon as they checked into the base. For some, this was enough time to visit their families. For Juan it wasn't. Puerto Rico was too far away. Not to mention Japan.

He sat on his bunk about to read Emiko's short letter one more time when he had an idea. He would visit Walter. There was a telephone right in the barracks. And Walter had given him a number to call.

"Look at you. Sauntering 'cross the yad like you never been hurt."

"Walter! How are you? Looks like you've put on some weight."

"He-he. So I have."

The only direction Walter had given him was "Coosaw Island, South Carolina, right near the Friendship Baptist Church." It was a decrepit but rambling bungalow shaded by trees dripping with Spanish moss. A line of relatives stood on the porch waiting to greet him—white-haired mother and father, gray-haired aunt and uncle, and bare footed nieces and nephews. Every one of them shook his hand.

Before he knew it, Juan was leaning back in a creaky rocking chair, sipping a gin and tonic and laughing with the others at Walter's stories from his four years in Japan. "Tell that one about when you thought that brown seaweed was chocolate," a nephew prompted. They laughed as if they were hearing it for the first time.

Juan had gotten a touch of seasickness on the boat ride from Beaufort, but the gin and the stories had settled his stomach. Here on a little island with a Gullah family he was actually starting to feel at home.

Walter's mother suggested Juan settle down on Coosaw Island when he got out of the service. "Shrimping and crabbing are good business these days. You can make enough to buy yourself a plot of land to build a house on."

"Except the land is getting so dear these days," Walter's father complained, "what with real estate investors luring rich people here from the mainland."

"Um-hum. But we're never selling this place," an aunt chimed in. "Our family's been here since long before there was a United States. Nobody's digging up *our* graveyard to make a golf course."

"You got that right," Walter's father said. "Don't want to call those spirits back from their rest. They worked themselves to death on the plantation. Now let them sleep in peace."

Walter wanted to hear about Juan's recuperation in Japan.

"I met a girl. Emiko. She's all I can think about."

Walter's mother rocked in her chair. "Ooo. Now that's something." Her sister echoed, "Um-hum. Um-hum."

"My service is over in four months," Juan told them. "Then I'm going back. I wish I didn't have to wait so long."

Walter put down his glass. "Maybe you don't. Maybe you could finish your stint in Japan. I have a friend who got reassigned to the Tokyo APO mail center when the Oji hospital closed. He told me they're short on manpower."

"Walter, do you think—"

"I guess it wouldn't hurt to ask. I'll try giving my friend a collect call tonight."

36

House scrubbing and money laundering

It used to be that even people who were guilty of serious crimes escaped this sort of punishment ....

—Murasaki Shikibu, *The Tale of Genji*

Emiko read the newspapers, but they never reported which U.S. troops were being sent home. The one piece of good news was that Takashi had been charged, convicted, and given a ten-year jail term for gun smuggling and conspiracy to lead an attack on the Diet. The news media were calling him the Japanese Guy Fawkes. His followers, mainly gullible students and lost souls like Satoru, received much lighter sentences. She still wished to see Genji's drug ring broken up, but her father was right. If he got him arrested on information he gave the police, Genji had a large syndicate of smugglers spread as far as Thailand who would come after them. They had to let it go.

The rental agent Owada must have seen the TV news about Takashi, too. He knocked on their door with a contract. "Ah, two of you? A family member? Because sub-letting isn't allowed."

Emiko's father had withdrawn some savings that were sitting in the post office bank since before he left Kitayama. That and the last of their funeral offering money paid the rent for a month. They'd be able to pay the following month from her father's salary. That wouldn't leave them a lot to live on. It didn't matter. Emiko needed to stay here until she found out whether Juan still wanted to be with her—and whether he was even still alive.

Her father ran his eyes over the notes and papers Emiko had spread out over their little table, on the floor, on the kitchen counter. "Since we're paying for the whole place, maybe you could use Takashi's office and desk for your writing and translating."

She nodded agreement although actually she didn't like the idea of going into a room by herself to work.

He had another suggestion. "And I could move into one of the upstairs rooms over there. It would give you more space."

"I don't need more space, Dad. We're all right here."

He smiled. "How about we both move over to the big house? We could each have our own room upstairs. There's an office, a big kitchen, a bath. It's a full-sized house."

"All right. If you want. I mean, we'd still eat and watch TV together and talk about the news and everything, right?" She hoped she didn't sound too clingy.

"Of course. Just like back in Kitayama. Except ...."

"Yeah, I know. Listen, Dad. I've been thinking. The New Year's holiday's coming up. Everything will pretty much be closed down for the first two weeks of January. How about we go back home and hold a memorial service for Mom? We could see some of our friends. It's been a long time."

He ran his fingers over the blue and white scarf Emiko had given back to him. "And we could bring back a few more things for our house here."

"Like the kamidana you built?" She'd always teased him about the little shelf they hung on the wall to hold daily offerings to their ancestors. She called it pretending their spirits were still around. His answer was always, "It's just pretending, yes. But it makes me and your mom feel better." Strangely enough, now the idea of hanging it on their wall here in Tokyo made her feel better, too.

Before they moved into Takashi's house, they set about cleaning it thoroughly. They called the toilet man to empty the tank even though he wasn't due to come yet. They wiped down the bath with bleach. They scrubbed the wooden hallway floor. They sanitized the large kitchen and all the utensils left in it. Emiko was trying to wash away all traces—and memory—of her former boss.

She had never realized there was a large tatami room adjoining the kitchen. When they moved in, this is where they put the TV and sat together, talked, and read. It was almost like magazine pictures of a Western-style sitting room, except that they sat on the floor.

They still preferred to eat at the low table in the "sitting room" rather than sit on chairs at the large kitchen table. They listened to the news on TV while they ate. Emiko wasn't interested in the business news. Rice subsidies. Tariffs on grapefruit. Pressure to devalue the yen. Boring.

"Wait," her father said one night. "Listen."

"... investigations into money laundering. Arrested were Sato Genji and another employee of the Gen-Sa Trading Company for sheltering profits from illegal transactions in a German bank."

"Dad! I can't believe it. Genji's arrested?"

"For money laundering. That should bring down his company."

"And we had nothing to do with it."

Emiko sat for a moment, letting the news sink in. Genji was being punished for breaking tax laws, for greed. She remembered him bragging about bypassing import taxes on foreign cars he brought into the country to sell. True enough, he was greedy. But that wasn't his worse offense. His worse offense was telling his yakuza agents to "take care of" her father, not worrying about how they interpreted his order. He didn't do that for money. He did it out of a manic, psychopathic desire for a woman. For her mother.

"Somehow the punishment doesn't fit the real crime," her father mused.

"I know. He did worse things than money laundering." Emiko immediately regretted she'd said "things" in the plural. She didn't want her father to know how much she'd found out about Genji and her mother. And she didn't want him to know what happened between Genji and herself.

"Still," her father said, "the jail time is about the same for drug smuggling."

"And kidnapping?"

Her father closed his eyes. He might have been thinking about his long captivity in Thailand. But maybe also about Genji and his wife. "You're right," he said. "He could get life in prison for kidnapping." He rubbed his temples. "That's not the point, though, is it? All that matters is he's not a danger to us any more. Even when he eventually gets out of jail, his business will be gone. He'll be powerless."

Emiko let out a breath and lay back on the tatami. Now all they had to worry about was Genji's yakuza gang, she thought. But she didn't say anything to disturb the peace of the moment.

In the few days since they'd moved into the big house, they sometimes talked and talked until they both fell asleep on the "living room" floor. Emiko would wake up hours later, nudge her father, and they'd go up to their own rooms.

After the announcement of Genji's arrest, she crawled under her quilt, but had a hard time going back to sleep. Her thoughts jumped from one thing to another without any logical thread—

Genji's yakuza gang—they were still out there even though Genji had been arrested.

Juan—why didn't he write? Was he injured, or missing, or ...?

Her father—she smiled to think of triumphantly returning to Kitayama at New Year's having found him when a lot of people assumed he was one of the "evaporated people" who fled the pressures of society and intentionally got lost.

Thinking of going back to Kitayama for the New Year's holiday, she finally fell asleep. It was just daylight when she awoke to hear Kuro give a short bark, then an excited whimper. There was a man's voice, but she couldn't make out the words. She looked out the window into the yard.

A man in a U.S. army dress uniform stood there, patting Kuro, knocking on the locked door of the "back house." It was Juan.

She grabbed the key and rushed across the yard in her yukata to jump into his arms. She held him tight as if he was an apparition that might fade into the frosty air at any moment. "I can't believe it. Are you really here?"

They pulled close to each other on the tatami floor of the little house. "You're not hurt, are you?"

"No. The war's over for me."

Nothing else was important. There was no more talking. They made love in a dreamlike cloud isolated from the rest of the world.

37

Merry Christmas

... those merchants are bad men. No distinction between right and wrong could be clearer than this.

—Kannami Kiyotsugu, *Jinen the Preacher*

Emiko's father gave a little bow when she led Juan into the big house. Then he held out his hand foreigner-style to shake Juan's. "Very nice to meet you," he said in English. "Ozeki Hiroji."

"Gomez. Juan Gomez. *Hajimemashite.*"

Emiko waited for the two men to exhaust what they knew of each other's language. Her father noted two stripes on Juan's shoulder. "Corporal."

"Yes." Juan turned to Emiko. "I'm a corporal now."

Emiko blushed. She'd never known or even thought to ask what rank he was. "A promotion?" He nodded.

Her father eyed an insignia on Juan's shoulder. "Fourth Division. Lots of fighting."

"Well, yes. *Hai.*"

Her father pointed to two ribbons on Juan's jacket and seemed impressed.

Juan turned to Emiko. "Tell him everybody gets these. They're just for Army Achievement and Good Conduct."

She wasn't about to diminish her father's admiration. "They're for Bravery and Valor," she translated.

It was crazy. Her father was making a connection with a

man in an army that had formerly fought against his. It was a connection that would never have been possible if Juan had deserted and met him as a civilian in Switzerland or somewhere else.

"*Anata wa*?" Juan asked her father. "How about you?"

As Emiko translated her father's unit, rank, decorations, and so forth, her face heated again. She'd never bothered to ask him about any of this. Neither had her mother, as far as she knew.

It was curious that Juan had arrived wearing this fancy uniform. Asking him about it hadn't been her top priority before. She asked now.

"We're supposed to wear civilian clothes when we're not on duty, but I'm going to a job briefing this afternoon. I'm going to be a mailman."

"What?"

"I'm assigned to the Military Post Office in Tokyo for the rest of my service."

Emiko raised an eyebrow. "They gave *you* the job of seeing that letters get through?"

"Emi, I started to write a few times. I was hoping for a second letter from you."

"It got returned."

"I was worried."

"So was I." Emiko noticed her father trying to follow this. It seemed he did. "Anyway," he interrupted in Japanese, "let's help Juan move in. I'll move my things back to the little house, and he can stay in the big house with you."

Juan understood but was confused. "The big house—isn't it Takashi's?"

"It's ours now. We gave the police information to stop Takashi's gun smuggling operation. And his planned attack on the Diet. Takashi's in jail now."

"So you finally went to the police about the guns?"

"My dad and I did." She didn't want to bring up Satoru's death. There were a lot of things she had to tell Juan later on.

Her father obviously understood none of this. "Ask him if he likes Thai food."

Emiko rolled her eyes. "I *know* he likes Japanese food."

Moving her father's few things back to the little house took no time at all. Then Juan and her father walked together to the station for their commute to work. Emiko pranced in to Takashi's office and sat at his desk. Her desk now. Her office. She started working on a news story about political bribes made by yakuza gangs. She'd learned a lot from a couple of the reports Takashi had given her. The *Tokyo Daily* had told her she could come in when she needed to do phone interviews. She was starting to feel like an actual journalist.

Later that afternoon, she cooked curry rice, and when the men got home from their jobs, the three of them ate together in the living room. It was the first time she remembered hearing a conversation about baseball during dinner. She didn't need to translate much. A lot of the baseball words were the same in Japanese and English, and the players' names were the same, just pronounced a little differently. She wondered if her father had missed not having a son.

"Tomorrow's Christmas." Juan said. "I worked just one day, then got a holiday. I surprised my parents with calls from the mail room."

"Christmas. Yes," her father repeated. He had brought a white box tied with red and green ribbon and put it on the kitchen table without comment but with a glimmer in his eye. Emiko was sure it was a Christmas cake, which they traditionally ate on Christmas Eve.

"Delicious," Juan said when they served it. "I've never heard of a Christmas cake. We eat turkey at Christmas."

"Ugh. I'll take cake any day," Emiko scoffed. When the English was simple enough, it seemed her father could follow.

"Me, too," he agreed.

Juan had a lot of questions about her father's job. This was when Emiko needed to translate. She simplified Auxiliary Customs Investigator to "customs guy."

"Speaking of turkeys," her father said, "tell Juan this. Somebody in Canada tried to export a hundred live ones to Yokohama. Here's a bit of advice. One: turkeys need air to survive. Two: they smell really bad when they've been dead for two weeks."

"Don't laugh, Juan. You'll just encourage him."

"Also, if you're producing fake Chanel N° 5 and Johnny Walker Scotch in China, it's best not to get the bottles mixed up."

Her father was having a great time. "A lot of Japanese go out drinking on Christmas Eve," he reminded Emiko. "Ask Juan if it's the same in America."

Juan said no. Christmas Eve was a family time.

"Heh …."

"Besides, Juan and I are too tired to go out tonight."

Her father seemed to take the hint. He looked through the window at the moon and forced a yawn, then got up, shook Juan's hand, and left to sleep in the little house.

Juan pulled open a sliding door. "I didn't know there were two rooms up here. We could sleep in one, and your father could sleep in the other."

"No."

Her definitive reply widened his eyes.

"You see how thin these doors are, Juan?" She drummed her fingers on the sliding cardboard fusuma."

"Hm."

"We need privacy." She slipped her hands beneath the pajamas he'd put on after bathing, stroking his chest. "No new injuries at all? I was so worried you'd be killed by the Viet

Cong. Or by Lieutenant Joss."

"Joss was killed in action. —Hey, what are you doing?"

She dropped her *yukata* sash onto the floor. "Juan, I missed you so much. You don't know—"

He pulled her close. "And I never stopped thinking about you."

They sank to the futon, Emiko's pulse responding to the blue-green intensity of his eyes.

The full moon was high in the sky. They lay exhausted in each other's arms. Emiko was drifting off to sleep when Juan jostled her. "It's past midnight. Emi. Merry Christmas."

"Oh. Merry Christmas." It was something she'd never said before.

Juan dug into his duffle bag. "I brought you a present." It was wrapped in brown paper and tied with string. "I bought it in Saigon before our plane took off for the States."

She unfolded a white silk dress with pale lavender piping, a high neck, and long sleeves. "Juan, it's beautiful."

"It's called an *Ao Dai*. It comes with long trousers."

She stood up, too excited to notice she had nothing on.

Juan's grin spread ear to ear. "I guess you put the trousers on first."

She held his shoulder as she stepped through the billowy white silk, then straightened up, giggling.

"OK, the dress part buttons tight from the neck down to the waist, then just kind of hangs loose. I never knew how they get into them. I could try to help you."

"Ooo, that tickles."

"Hold on. There." He stood back. "Oh, my God. You look beautiful."

"Let me see." She stood before a mirror on the closet door. "Oh, Juan. Thank you."

"Where's your camera?"

"Let me straighten my hair first."

Emiko wore her Vietnamese dress downstairs on Christmas morning. Her father looked up from stirring miso soup. "Oh my, who's this movie star? You look fantastic, Emi."

"It's from Juan."

"I kind of guessed." He bowed to Juan. "Thank you. Thank you. Very nice."

"Take a picture of me and Juan, Dad." Then she had Juan take one of her and her father."

Juan said, "My father wants me to send him a Japanese camera."

"Then let's go to Akihabara," Emiko suggested. "Everybody says they're cheaper there." Besides, she wanted to show off her Vietnamese dress.

The camera Juan picked out was nothing like hers. It was so big you had to hang it around your neck by a strap. Emiko was shocked at how much it cost. Juan didn't care. "My father has never asked me for anything."

"Your mother didn't ask for anything?"

"Actually, she did. A rice cooker."

"That's great, Juan. We can get one in the store across the street, the one with the big picture in the window of Santa Claus cooking rice." Her face flushed with happiness to think that urging Juan to write to his parents might have been the beginning of a reconciliation. She would encourage Juan to continue the effort to make peace with them.

Juan had the rice cooker sent directly to his mother, but he wanted to use the camera himself first. He tried taking pictures of Emiko and her father, but the streets were too crowded. Every time they stopped, people bumped into them. So they took the train two stops to Tokyo station and walked around the Imperial Palace grounds. Before long, the camera was filled with pictures of Emiko posing in front of the palace, many of which unfortunately included complete strangers posing for the same pictures.

At dinner that evening, Emiko said, "Here's what I haven't told you yet, Juan. My dad was kidnapped by a yakuza drug smuggling gang. He was kept a prisoner in Thailand."

"What? You're kidding."

She gave him a short description of how she'd gone to Yoron to get him.

"Unbelievable. Weren't you afraid they'd kill both of you?"

"I was. But I could tell they were afraid, too." She told Juan about the report she'd threatened to send to the police. "I got Dad freed, but both of us had to promise not to turn the drug smugglers in."

"Promise? I don't understand. Your dad's a customs agent. Is he going to let the drug smuggling go on?"

Emiko's father partly understood. "Tell him what Genji said his yakuza will do if we turn them in."

"Genji?" Juan asked. That and *yakuza* were probably the only words he'd understood.

"Genji's arrested, so he's out of the picture." Emiko didn't want to talk about Genji now with her father sitting right there.

"If your dad knows something—"

"Dad knows about a shipment coming in soon. But if he tells Customs, the smugglers will realize the information came from him. They said they'd kill us both."

Disbelief flashed in Juan's aqua eyes. "Emiko, you can't be serious? Oh, my God. This all happened—"

"While you were gone."

Juan jerked his head from side to side as if trying to shake out what he'd heard. "You've been in danger all this time, and I didn't know it?"

"We're safe as long as we don't turn those drug smugglers in. I don't like it, but I can't see any way around it." Emiko spoke to Juan, leaving her father out of the conversation for the present.

Juan put hands to his head, staring at the wall. He closed his eyes for a moment, then looked at Emiko. "Maybe there's a way. What if it was the U.S. Army that arrested the smugglers? Then they could turn them over to the Japanese for prosecution without involving you?"

"Is that possible?"

"The army wants to stop drugs from coming into the country as much as Japan does. They have their own investigators."

Emiko saw what he was getting at. "If it's the Americans who catch them, the yakuza wouldn't suspect Dad and I were behind it."

Juan nodded gravely. "When is the shipment coming in?"

"In three days, my dad says. On a Sunday when the port customs station is closed."

"OK, so if your dad gives me the information, I could get it to the CID, the Criminal Investigation Division, tomorrow. That should give them time to act."

"CID?" her father chimed in. Somehow he knew what the CID was. That alone seemed enough to give him the same idea as Juan's. "Juan could tell the CID about the drugs. Is that what you're saying? Then it's clear to me. If there's anything we can do to get them arrested, we should give it a try."

The plan seemed safe enough. Emiko couldn't believe Juan had been back just one day and had come up with a way out of their dilemma. She wanted to kiss him but held off in front of her father.

Her father drew a sketch of the Red Brick Warehouses and pier. "Here. Behind this building." He tapped his pencil. "This is where the boat will dock. The *Royal Thai*, a small cargo ship."

Her father pointed to his sketch again. "This warehouse

is where they'll probably take the heroin. It'll be in Thai funeral urns, red and gold, packed in plastic bins." He gave the sketch to Juan while Emiko explained it all to him.

38

Car chase

The proud do not endure, like a passing dream on a night in spring; the mighty fall at last, to be no more than dust before the wind.

—The Tale of the Heike

A cold draft rattled the window. Hovering gray clouds looked like they might bring snow. Emiko put on the hooded parka Juan had given her. Sunday morning. Time to go.

Juan had set everything up with the CID investigators. They would be in place near the Red Brick Pier when the *Royal Thai* docked at about noon. At the Narimasu station, Emiko's father called in to his office to say he was doing an investigation. Juan secretly held Emiko's hand on the long ride all the way from Shibuya to Yokohama. None of them said anything.

They walked from the station but didn't cross the bridge to the Red Brick Warehouses. Instead, they found a coffee shop across the way where they could observe the whole pier from the window. Juan again took hold of Emiko's sweaty hand under the table.

A middle-aged waitress in a satin dress came to take their order. She spoke with a Chinese accent. When she left to get their coffee, Emiko teased, "She was looking you over, Dad."

Her father didn't seem to hear. He pointed out a man on the passenger terminal across from the Red Brick Pier. "Strange. He's just sitting there."

"He's looking across at the warehouses," Emiko observed.

"I bet that's a CID guy in disguise," Juan said. "They told me he'd be dressed like a Japanese so he wouldn't be recognized. He'll probably radio the MPs when the ship comes in."

They were stirring cream into their second coffee when the low, muted moan of a ship horn sounded through the window. "There it is," her father whispered.

The man on the pier stood, took an olive green walkie-talkie from his pocket, held it to his ear.

The *Royal Thai* grew larger as it slowed, billowing black smoke, and angled in to the dock. Crew in cone-shaped hats and tunics like what Emiko's father had worn to Yoron jumped out and cleated first the stern, then the bow to the bollards with heavy-looking hemp lines.

"Look! Out in the harbor," Juan said. "Army patrol boats." Emiko counted five gray boats streaming towards the *Royal Thai*. "This is it," her father said.

Emiko pushed back her chair and rushed to the phone by the cashier's counter. She took a note from her pocket and dialed the tip line of the *Asahi* newspaper's Yokohama office. She spoke low. "I'd like to report a raid on a drug cartel by the Americans. It's going on now. Red Brick Pier. U.S. Army boats are coming towards a Thai cargo ship." She hung up.

When Emiko got back to the table, the CID lookout was at the end of the pier signaling to the patrol boats. They slowed and seemed to approach cautiously.

Emiko's father pointed to the Thai ship. "They might be too late. Look."

A gangplank had already been lowered, and a man was wheeling a large cart loaded with plastic bins onto the pier. "I know those bins," Emiko's father said. "They're packed with drugs."

The man leaned forward, hurtling the cart towards a white open-bed truck at the end of the pier.

"I know that guy," Emiko's father said. "He's the middle

man."

Juan rushed to the phone, dropped a handful of coins into the slot, asked for somebody, waited, then finally spoke in an agitated voice. Emiko heard "white truck" and "getting away."

"Come on," he told Emiko and her father. "They want us to follow him." He left money on the table and opened the door. "Taxi!" he yelled, and an orange and white cab squealed to a stop. "Emiko, tell him to follow that white truck up there at the intersection."

As they drove away down Kaigan Street, Emiko looked out the taxi window and saw the U.S. boats had surrounded the *Royal Thai*. Soldiers were rushing on board. Then she noticed a crowd of reporters with cameras already rushing towards the ship along with a crew from a television van.

The taxi beeped and passed one car, but the street was jammed in both directions. They saw the white truck up ahead stopped at an intersection while a steady line of cars, taxis, and small trucks crossed in front of it. Juan squirmed in his seat, looking out the windows on both sides as if for a way to get ahead. That wasn't going to happen. More cars and taxis cut in front of them from side streets until the white truck was even farther ahead.

"He's turning left onto Bangkok Bridge Street," the driver complained. "I can't keep up."

The truck disappeared down the street as they waited for oncoming traffic to come to a stop. "Go down that street anyway," Emiko's father said. "There's not as much traffic. We'll look down every side street." It wasn't long before they saw the truck again. It was stopped at a red light.

The light turned green. The truck turned. And when they finally got to the intersection, it was out of sight. The taxi driver pulled to the curb. "Sorry," he said simply. "Anywhere I can take you now?"

Emiko's father said, "Let's try something else. Driver, do you happen to know where the Gen-Sa warehouse is?"

"There's a warehouse near here. I don't know what it's called." He took them there in only a few turns. The sign in front said Gen-Sa Sōgō Shōsha. Genji's company. Emiko's father wrote down the address. "Drive around to the back, please."

The taxi turned. And there it was. The white truck was parked at a loading ramp. "Stop here," Emiko's father said. "Pull over next to that newsstand." He handed Emiko the address. "Here. Help Juan with the call."

The American office didn't make him wait this time. "Juan Gomez here. Right. The delivery was made to …." He repeated the address Emiko read out to him. "Pardon? That was nobody. Just somebody on the street helping me read the address. I can't wait here, you understand. If there are questions, you can contact me tomorrow at the Military Post Office."

"Now where to?" the cab driver said.

"Yokohama station."

Before they were back on the main street, they heard the low-pitched siren of a U.S. military vehicle moving in the direction of Genji's warehouse.

When they reached Narimasu, Emiko's father stopped to buy beer and dried squid. "Juan likes cod," Emiko suggested.

Juan blushed. "No, that's OK."

"We have to get it, Juan. It's how we met. Remember?"

Her father's eyes opened wide. "Cod, huh? You're serious? All right, I'll get some and cook it for him. And it's almost New Year's. We'll get some *mochi*, too."

With glasses of beer they toasted each other in the sitting room. As Juan and Emiko's father drank, they started spouting whatever words they knew. "*Subarashī*," Juan declared. It wasn't clear what was wonderful, but her father clearly took it to mean the whole day. "Many boats," he added. "Yakuza to the guardhouse."

Emiko felt a little tipsy, too. "Juan, I have a complaint. That man on the pier? 'Dress like a Japanese,' you say they told him? Light gray shirt, dark gray pants, medium gray jacket—that's your idea of how Japanese dress? Come on. He looked more like some kind of twilight ninja."

"OK, maybe that was overdone. But I have a complaint, too. The Yokohama coffee shop? What's the deal with the Santa Claus vases that had flowers growing out of their heads? There was one on every table. You can't do that to Santa Claus."

"Santa Claus," Emiko's father repeated, miming flowers blooming out of his own head. "Ha-ha-ha."

"Well, I thought they were cute—*Kawaī*," she added for her father's benefit.

He smiled and shook his head.

"And the car chase?" Juan shook with silent laughter. "You have to admit our taxi driver was no Steve McQueen."

"Taxi driver—no Steve McQueen!" her father echoed. "Ha-ha."

Juan was on a roll. "Well, I guess there isn't a need for one in a country where even the criminals stop for red lights."

This one her father didn't understand, but he burst into a guffaw when Emiko translated.

Soon everybody was hungry. Emiko and Juan cooked the cod fritters while her father went into the yard to dig a little pit and build a fire for later.

"How do you like the bacalaitos, Dad?"

"Very good."

She knew he was lying. "I love them, too. Maybe we should have them two or three times a week. You know, instead of Thai food? What do you think?"

"I will seriously consider it." He gave the diplomatic Japanese reply that often meant *Hell no*.

After dinner, they took the hardened rice cakes out to roast over the fire with tongs. "We eat *mochi* on New Year's," Emiko explained. "After it softens over the fire, I like to put sugar and soy sauce on it." She fixed one for Juan on a plate. "How does it taste?"

"Like sugar and soy sauce."

"Smarty." She gave him a light punch on the shoulder.

"Well," her father said, "work tomorrow. I'm going to get some sleep."

Emiko and Juan sat alone on plastic milk crates, warmed by the fire. Juan said, "Your dad seemed a little sad when he went in to bed."

"The New Year's holiday. It's the most important time of the year for us. We go home to our families, eat lots of special food, talk."

"Sounds good."

"Except this year my mother won't be there."

He put his arm around her. "I'm sorry, Emi. When are you going back?"

"In two days. We'll probably stay there a week. I wish you could come with us. But I know you just started your job."

"I can come. I know it doesn't make sense to take a week off as soon as I started. But it's the army. Things don't have to make sense. Besides, I cut my leave short to come back here as soon as I could. So actually I started early."

"You mean you'll come? This is going to be wonderful."

The night air was cold, and they moved their seats closer to the fire. Juan said, "I haven't told you about my job yet. It's stupid-easy. Sorting mail, making some pouch deliveries. I have a housing allowance. I'm going to use it to pay the rent here."

She put her arm through his. "But do you really like doing a 'stupid' job?"

"Here's the thing. It's not all military. When my service is over in April, I'll be able to stay on as a civilian. I'll even be paid more. And veterans benefits will pay for my last two years of college."

"College? Where?" She was starting to panic.

"My supervisor says there's a program at Sophia University in Tokyo that's taught in English. Asian Studies. I could look into that."

Emiko resumed breathing. "That sounds perfect. And if you have to go full time, I can help. I have a job now, too, writing reports for the *Tokyo Daily*." She twisted her jaw. "Too bad I had to forgo today's drug-bust story and let the *Asahi Shimbun* cover it. I could have—"

"Don't even think of getting your name connected to that arrest, Emi. There are plenty of other articles you can write."

"I know. They've already given me a new assignment. I'm getting paid per article now, but I'm hoping they'll put me on a regular salary soon." She was getting excited. "Then when you finish, maybe I can go to college, too."

"Emi, you can go first if you want. Keep writing articles just every now and then until you graduate. I'll pay your tuition." He cleared his throat. "I mean, how much does it cost?"

She chuckled. "A lot. But I'm sure I could get a scholarship to pay part of it. I was pretty good in school."

They were planning their future. She couldn't believe it. "Either way," she said, "let's agree we'll take care of each other." She held out a curled little finger, and he hooked his into hers.

Emiko held tight to him, her eyes closed, her heart beating fast.

"So, Emi, we can be together as long as we want."

"Forever. That's how long I want to be with you."

"Do you think your dad likes me?"

"You're kidding. He loves you."

"So here's what I'm thinking. Maybe we could get married."

"Oh, Juan. That's what I'm thinking, too. That's what I've been thinking ever since we met."

The embers glowed in Juan's widened eyes. "So, how do we work this?"

"You ready to do it? We could go to the Tokyo Ward Office like my friend Mariko plans to do. Just sign some papers, and that's it."

"Hm."

"What's wrong?"

"Is that how your mother and father got married?"

"It was the Kitayama Ward Office. But yeah. They had a marriage ceremony after that."

"Ah. Not just the paperwork?"

"No. They had a Shinto ceremony."

"So there was something holding them together besides a piece of paper?"

"Well, no, actually. Religious ceremonies aren't recognized. It's the piece of paper that's binding. Tell me what you're getting at, Juan."

"Before coming back to Japan, I visited my friend Walter on Coosaw Island. His family has lived there for three hundred years. They believe the spirits of all their ancestors still live in the graveyard and are protecting them. It keeps Walter and his family going. They feel like they're all connected. Crazy, maybe. But it's something like the kami in your shrines, isn't it?"

Emiko nodded.

"I want our spirits to be connected."

"In a shrine, you mean?" Emiko felt tears clouding her eyes. "Sure. We can get married in a shrine if you want to."

"I do."

She climbed into his lap, hugging his head to her breast.

"Then I do, too."

As they walked back to the big house, Emiko couldn't resist commenting, "I have to warn you, though. The priests wear hilarious hats."

"Oh?"

"You'll be expected to keep a straight face."

"Oh, God. I wish you hadn't said that."

39

Old friends and relations

The train came out of the long tunnel into the snow country. The earth lay white under the night sky.

—Kawabata Yasunari, *Snow Country*

Problems arise when everybody in a country takes a vacation at the same time. During the New Year's holiday, it was absurd to expect to get a seat on a train. What made things worse for Emiko, her father, and Juan was that this was ski season, when tourists flocked to Kitayama. That and the fact that Emiko was determined to take the local train.

The aisle was stuffed with bodies, backpacks, furoshiki bundles, and skis. Emiko couldn't stand upright. She was pushed over in front of a seated woman, forced to hold onto the rail behind her chair to keep from falling into her lap. When the train started, the mass of humanity lurched backwards, but nobody fell. There was nowhere to fall. They simply became momentarily more compressed.

"Emiko," Juan whispered. "Six different people are touching my body right now."

"At least you don't have a backpack jammed into your ribs."

"Actually, I do."

When the train stopped at Nakakuni, Emiko struggled to straighten up, take Juan's hand, and force their way off. Her father slipped out just before about twenty more passengers squeezed inside.

"I still don't understand why you wanted to stop here." Her father straightened his jacket, which had twisted around so the zipper was on the side.

"We'll continue on the next train. Like I said, I really want to put some flowers on the grave of somebody I knew in Tokyo."

Juan asked, "Want me to go with you, Emi?"

"That's all right. How about you and Dad get dinner in a restaurant and I'll meet you here on the platform in an hour?"

Emiko bought a thin metal vase and a few chrysanthemums at the stand beside the station and made her way up the path to the temple. She didn't remember seeing a cemetery when she'd been here before, but there must be one.

There it was, behind the weathered temple wall. There must have been a hundred flat stones lined close together, some with little stone figures of the Jizo Buddhist deity clothed in caps or bibs. She looked for the newest stones, not knowing if Satoru's parents had put him to rest here, but it was likely.

And there it was, a sleek new stone with his name carved on it. She squatted to dust it with her handkerchief and put the vase of flowers in front. Then she needed to use the handkerchief to dab her eyes. "Satoru," she whispered. "You never meant anybody harm. I should have made you quit that job. I hope you reach the enlightenment you were seeking."

She rose and turned. Back against the temple wall Tōshin stood watching her. She walked towards him. He bowed, said nothing.

"Do you remember me, Tōshin? I know Satoru was a friend of yours."

"Sachiko. Yes. Satoru wrote saying he had a good friend in Tokyo. But he said her name was Emiko." He ran his hand over his shaved head.

It came back to her. She'd given Tōshin a fake name, she didn't even remember why. "Emiko's my real name. I hope you've said some prayers for him."

"Yes." Tōshin's eyes seemed focused on something far off in the cool twilight.

"Well, good-bye."

He turned to her. "Did you find your father? I prayed for you, too."

"Oh. Yes, I found him. Thank you." She started to reach for his hand, but it didn't seem right. Instead, she bowed and walked slowly back to the station.

Juan and her father weren't back from the restaurant yet. The bench was empty. She sat and dug through her backpack to pull out the fortune paper she'd got on her first visit to the temple. *Uncertain luck*. The failure to make a prediction annoyed her less now. The words seemed to mean "Don't count on luck. You're on your own."

A few passengers trickled onto the platform, but the late train was obviously not going to be as crowded as the earlier one. Before she saw them, she heard Juan and her father engaged in one of their elemental two-language conversations. They sounded like they'd had a few beers.

"We brought you this." Juan gave her a boxed dinner.

"And ...." her father pulled a can of beer partly from his jacket with a questioning look.

"Yes. Thanks, Dad. I'll drink that right now."

Whether it was hearing that Satoru had called her a good friend, or the beer, Emiko's spirits lifted. She felt ready to make her happy, triumphant return to Kitayama.

As the train moved farther north, the air blowing in at each stop grew colder and colder. Emiko tightened her parka and looked through the window at a clear blue-black sky filled with stars. When the train entered the tunnel, she felt a chill, remembering the trapped sensation she'd had in Kitayama before she left—the mind-numbing work in the factory, the pressure to fit her life into a ready-made pattern. And now she was coming back. But it was different now. She'd been on her own and had muddled into a life that suited her. Jun-oba and the rest of the town would have to accept her as she was. She was returning with a father who was more a close friend than a traditional authority figure, and a husband-to-be who was unlike anyone they'd ever known.

When the train came out of the tunnel, Juan gawked at the snow glistening in the moonlight. "It's beautiful. Look at those mountains. Emiko, take a picture."

She burst out laughing.

"Ah. I guess the view isn't as new for you guys as it is for me."

"No. But I'll take a picture for you."

At Kitayama, tourists hauling skis on their shoulders clattered out of the train. The snow had been shoveled from the station walkway, but the line of bicycles stood covered in white. Under a light, Emiko noticed a purple fender beneath partly melted snow. "My bike! I want to take it back with us when we leave. I can ride it up the road to the Narimasu station, bring groceries back in its basket."

She walked away without it, and Juan seemed confused. "You just going to leave it there? Nobody will take it?"

Emiko didn't understand. "Why would they take it?"

Juan rubbed his head. "They wouldn't, I guess. In some countries they would."

A young woman leaving the station stopped short. "Emiko?"

"Naomi! Hello. It's been since last New Year's." Of all the high school friends Emiko had lost touch with, Naomi was the one she missed the most.

"I only get home on holidays. The university keeps me busy." Naomi bowed to Emiko's father.

"We're living in Tokyo now." Emiko introduced Juan.

"My fiancé."

"Waaa. So glad to meet you."

Juan made use of his trusty "*Hajimemashite*" introductory greeting. And Emiko felt a little thrill to see her friend's mouth pop open and no words come out.

"We're getting married on Sunday at the Shinto shrine. We'll have a little reception afterwards at the Mountain Hotel. Ten o'clock. Please come. Tell any of our friends you happen to meet."

"Heh .... Congratulations. I'll be there for sure."

They shared a taxi as far as the guest house where Emiko's father had reserved rooms. Naomi went on to her parents' house.

The Happy Times guest house was bulging with skiers clomping down the hallway in their boots.

"Let's go skiing tomorrow." Emiko tugged at Juan's sleeve.

"Um, we don't do a lot of skiing in Puerto Rico."

"You're saying you can't? Oh, this changes things. I'm calling the wedding off."

"Heh-heh." Somehow Juan wasn't bubbling with excitement like she was. Neither was her father.

"What's wrong, Juan?" She asked her father, too.

Juan apologized. "I was wishing my parents could come to the wedding."

Emiko tilted her head "I've been thinking about that. Here's an idea. How about we go to Puerto Rico for a honeymoon as soon as we can save up enough?"

Juan's eyes brightened. "Really? I've saved most of my pay ever since I've been living on the army. We could go next month."

She held out her little finger to hook his. "It's a deal."

Her father seemed to get the main idea. "Puerto Rico? Honeymoon? Wonderful."

"I can guess why you're a little gloomy, Dad. New Year's

without Mom. I'm trying not to think about it."

"Tomorrow morning we'll take her urn from the temple and bury it in her family crypt."

Jun-oba and two of Emiko's mother's best friends from the factory accompanied them to the cemetery. Her father lifted the heavy stone over the crypt where urns holding the ashes of her mother's parents were kept. His hands trembled as he placed the urn beside theirs.

"Nobuko was a wonderful person," one of the women said.

Goose bumps raised on Emiko's arms as her mother's name was said. Only her Buddhist spirit name was to be used until she had passed completely into the other world. Otherwise, her spirit would be called back. Genji had made this mistake once. So had her father.

But no ghost was aroused. Emiko knelt staring into the crypt, her father's hand on one shoulder and Juan's on the other. A deafening silence rang in her ears. Her mother was at peace in the other world.

As they left the cemetery, Emiko's father pulled her aside and took something from his pocket. "I found this whistle when I packed up the things Jun-oba was storing for us. I want you to keep it—a reminder that you can call on me any time you need me."

Emiko clutched it in her hand, turning away to hide her tears.

When they got back to the guest house, Emiko's father said, "It's the last working day of the month. The Ward Office is closed on New Year's Eve and will be closed for at least a week. If you guys want to get officially married ...."

The office was walking distance. They stepped into a dim room with a wooden floor. Behind a counter, a gray head was leaning against a stack of files. The clerk was asleep.

He sat upright when Emiko's father coughed. "Welcome. I was just …."

Emiko said she was here to register her marriage to Juan.

The little man stood up, only rising above the counter from his chest up. "Congratulations. What a wonderful occasion."

Emiko got out her health card. Juan followed her lead and took out his passport and military ID. The clerk asked the name on the Family Registry. "Ozeki, let me see." He pulled out an oak filing cabinet drawer, sifted through folders, and took one out. "Here we are." He opened the Ozeki Family Registry on the counter.

The clerk ran his finger down the notations. "Oh, dear. I see Mrs. Ozeki has recently passed away. My condolences."

His finger continued along the record. "Ozeki Emiko, born 1949 to Ozeki Hiroji and Ozeki Nobuko. This must be you. Correct, young lady?" His finger found the place to list the marriage to Juan. He had Juan write out his information on a piece of paper and copied it into the registry himself, as if neat handwriting was the main requirement of his job, which Emiko believed it was.

When the clerk folded up the registry, he said, "Just a minute, please." He took a sheet of paper and in impressive calligraphy wrote, "Juan and Emiko Gomez. Married December 30, 1969" and handed it to Emiko. "A present from me," he said. "Please keep it forever."

More people were on the street when they left the office, lots of them shopping for food and treats for the New Year's holiday. Two friends from Emiko's high school days saw them and stopped. They were guys she'd helped with their English lessons.

"Emiko! It's been so long."

"Sorry to hear about your mom."

"You're back for New Year's?"

"Yes," she said, "and to get married." She held up the paper the clerk had given her. "This is Juan, my husband."

"Waaa. Congratulations."

They wanted to take Juan to a coffee shop—to practice their English on him, Emiko was sure. Juan accepted the invitation and left with them. "See you back at the guest house in a while."

As Emiko walked along with her father, she thought about the carefully kept details of the family registry. Looking at the entries had reminded her of something she'd been refusing to think about for a long time. When they got back to the guest house, she thought now she might dare to bring it up.

"Dad," she began, "the registry clearly states that you and Mom are my parents, right?"

"That's what it's for, to keep family records. I was sure you knew that."

"I do. Dad, this is embarrassing. Can I tell you something? All right, somebody—I won't say who—told me Genji Sato is my biological father."

"Jun-oba."

Emiko's face warmed. "Of course, it doesn't matter. You're my dad. But once the idea that somebody else might be my biological—"

"He's not." He closed his eyes as if recalling something painful. "When I came home from the war, your mom told me she'd slept with Genji—after she was sure I was never coming back. When you were born about forty weeks after I got back, I heard rumors, mainly spread by Jun-oba, that the baby might be his. I wouldn't have cared. I would have loved you all the same."

She threw her arms around him. "Dad, I never should have mentioned it."

"But you're not Genji's child. You're mine." He said this with an air of absolute confidence. "Let me tell you. Genji's father heard the rumors and sent Genji away to Tokyo. He wanted to know the truth, too. I went to talk to him. He showed me his wife's Mother and Child Health Handbook that she got from the hospital when Genji was born."

"The one that lists blood types?"

"Right. Your mother's is type O. Yours is A. That means your father has to have type A or AB. Genji's blood type is O. He's not your father." He added, "Mine is A. I am your father."

"Did you tell people?"

"Jun-oba was the only person who seemed to care. I told her." He laughed. "The blood-type talk went over her head. She thought I was making stuff up. She probably still does."

Emiko knew she did.

"Everybody else seemed to forget about it. As you grew up, people were always commenting on how alike you and I are."

40

The bell and the ring

> *...he heard a sound that only a magnificent old bell could produce, a sound that seemed to roar forth with all the latent power of a distant world.*
>
> —Yasunari Kawabata, *Beauty and Sadness*

The next day was New Year's Eve. Juan was surprised to hear there were no fireworks, heavy drinking, or wild parties. "So people just go to a shrine, say some prayers, ring the bell? That's it?"

Emiko couldn't remember her family ever going to a shrine on New Year's Eve, but she wondered if her father might want to go tonight.

He did. She offered to go with him, and Juan wanted to come, too.

The night was cold and the moon was hidden behind heavy clouds. It would snow before the morning. The shrine was off the main street and up on a little hill. They had to be careful not to slip on the icy stone steps. Emiko's father thought there would be few people there on a night like this, and he was right. They were alone.

They passed under the red torii gate. The water for cleansing their hands was frozen, so Emiko's father lit a stick of incense and waved the smoke over the three of them. They bowed in front of the entrance to the inner haiden hall. Her father must be asking the spirits to look after Emiko's mother. He pulled the thick rope and the long bronze bell echoed out with a low, booming reverberation that startled Emiko.

Wishing for her father to find his way onward without her mother and for Juan never to stop loving her, she pulled the rope with both hands, and it resounded into the night.

"Let us always be together," Juan whispered, giving the rope a resolute pull.

The next morning they went to Jun-oba's house for the New Year's feast. Her table was spread with countless little dishes of food she and her friends had spent days preparing. Emiko was sad to be celebrating without her mother, but it was exciting to be spending her first New Year's Day with Juan. She had no idea what the English word was for lots of the food and tried saying things like "something from fish" and "some kind of root." But sometimes Juan wasn't willing to eat it until she looked it up in the dictionary. Even when she did, Juan wasn't always familiar with the English word. He ate a lot of fish and rice and drank a lot of beer.

Naomi came to Jun-oba's door with some other friends of Emiko's to wish them a happy New Year. The young men who had taken Juan to a coffee shop tried out their English on him.

"You are congratulate the New Year."

"Please to come my house drink the saké." This was Naomi's brother. Naomi nodded enthusiastically, as if she might have put him up to the invitation.

Emiko hated to leave her father with Jun-oba, but she jumped at the chance to show off Juan to her friends. They stopped by four different houses by the end of the day. Emiko invited them all to the reception after her wedding on Sunday.

Wedding day. Juan sat in a corner of their room reciting over and over the Japanese vow he would have to read at their wedding. Emiko had transcribed it in Roman letters for him. She said it meant something like "We, Juan and Emiko, make our vows together on this great day to become husband and wife with the blessing of the kami ...."

"Which kami?" Juan wanted to know.

"Um, there's no special one at the Kitayama shrine. So all of them, I guess."

Juan seemed pleased. "All of them. Good."

Naomi came to help Emiko put on her rented *shiromuku* trailing white kimono, white makeup, and white *wataboshi* hood. Juan and Emiko's father wore formal rented tuxedos. Naomi rode in the taxi with them to the temple. Emiko wanted her to be designated the matchmaker, but her father said they'd better give the honor to Jun-oba.

The priest in a flowing white robe and towering, thin black hat was followed to the altar by two *miko* shrine maidens in white *kosode* upper robes over loose red *hakama* trousers. Emiko stood beside Juan, who held his blue-green eyes wide open as if not wanting to miss any of this.

Holding a flat wooden stick in front of him, the priest recited a purification for the couple, then read out a ritual prayer announcing to the kami that they were married from this day on and asking for blessings and protection for them. Emiko knew Juan would have appreciated this. She'd explain it to him afterwards.

Next, one of the shrine maidens brought a tray to Juan with three red wooden saké bowls on it. She poured some into the smallest bowl and offered it to him.

"Drink it in three sips, I think," Emiko whispered. She'd seen parts of the ceremony on television and in movies.

As soon as Juan drained the first bowl in three sips, the shrine maiden filled the second-largest one. Emiko knew Juan didn't like saké. But he seemed to welcome this as a way to take the edge off his nervousness. Emiko could see what was coming next: the biggest bowl. Juan closed his eyes and downed it in three sips. His eyes reddened, and Emiko had to bite her tongue to stifle a laugh.

But the kami must have taken offense at her irreverence because the shrine maiden now came toward her with three bowls. She'd never drunk more than a tiny cup of saké in her life. She hated the taste. Juan knew it. His face flushed, he eyed her with a mischievous half-smile, all his nervousness obviously gone now.

Three sips. She did it. She could feel the heat rising from her throat. The shrine maiden poured a bigger bowl. Emiko took two small sips, paused, then finished it off. Her face was burning, and now it was time for the biggest bowl. She'd never even drunk this much tea in three sips. She closed her eyes, sipped, swallowed, took a breath.

"You don't really have to finish it," Jun-oba whispered. "Just pretend." Emiko had never been so appreciative of the old woman's advice.

Juan, on the other hand, hadn't pretended. He was warmed up and ready to read out the marriage vow. He stumbled over some words, and it didn't sound like he had any idea what he was saying, but the saké clearly kept him from caring.

After the ceremony, Emiko's father gave the priest a gift. Or maybe it was money. All Emiko could think of was getting out of her heavy kimono and hood and wiping the thick makeup off her face. They taxied to the guest house, where she washed and dropped face down on the futon in her underwear.

"You all right, Emi? Your cheeks are red."

The room was spinning. "I think I'm going to—" She ran to the toilet.

"Hm. I didn't expect this reaction to our marriage," Juan laughed in the hallway, waiting for her.

When she came out, she felt much better. "I must be just love-sick." She put her arms around his neck. "I'm sure that's it."

Juan wanted to know, "My vow—did I read it OK?"

"It was perfect, Juan. Nobody could have read it better."

Emiko changed to her Vietnamese dress for the reception. It was snowing when the taxi pulled up to the Mountain Hotel, where the reception guests were gathering. As soon as the cab door opened, Naomi ran towards them from the hotel without a coat, followed by another former classmate, Haruko. They were holding copies of a magazine. Emiko held her dress up off the snow and went to greet them, but they headed straight for Juan. "It's you," Naomi practically squealed in English as if she'd spotted a rock star.

"Sign, please." Haruko held out a copy of a magazine and a pen.

Before Emiko knew what was going on, a stream of her friends from high school ran towards the cab. Michiko also had a copy of the magazine and a pen. So did Fumiko and Akiko and Reiko and Chieko and Kiyoko.

Protesting he couldn't be who they thought he was, Juan signed Haruko's magazine. The others stood in line.

"Emiko, your husband is famous."

"So are you. Why didn't you tell us?"

"You married a hero."

Emiko's father spoke out, "It's snowing, ladies. Let's go into the lobby."

Naomi showed Emiko her copy of the *Nippon Weekly*, a popular magazine featuring articles on politicians, actors, and people recently in the news. "See? Three pictures of Juan. You haven't read what it says about him and you?"

Emiko never read the *Nippon Weekly*. She needed to ask Juan what this was about, but he was surrounded in the lobby by her former classmates, now including some of the men who'd seen the article.

Mr. Kobayashi came to the doorway of the reception room. He was Emiko's father's friend from the factory and had agreed to host the gathering. "Ladies, gentlemen," he called out. "Please come in and take a seat."

Still in the dark about what the magazine article buzz was about, Emiko sat beside Juan at the head table with her father next to her and Jun-oba in the matchmaker's position next to Juan. The way Jun-oba was talking suggested she'd convinced herself she really was the matchmaker.

Even the reception was going to be too formal and conventional for Emiko's tastes. Mr. Kobayashi stood to welcome the guests and introduce the newlyweds. He knew Emiko quite well since he'd been a frequent guest at her parents' house. He described her as "a star high school student and conscientious worker at the factory who has now become a journalist for the *Tokyo Daily* newspaper."

Of Juan, Mr. Kobayashi knew next to nothing—just the few details Emiko's father had given him, which mostly amounted to "He's a nice guy." But he had the *Nippon Weekly* in his hand. He read out the title of the article. "American soldier in love with Japanese girl hopes to return to Japan."

Emiko shook her head at Juan, mouthing "What?"

Juan shrugged. He whispered, "Some reporter interviewed me. Tell you about it later."

"I know a lot of you have seen these pictures," Kobayashi said. "Here—he's studying Japanese. And here—he's reading a letter from Emiko-san."

Emiko felt a lump in her throat. If she turned to look at Juan, she knew it would be hard to hold back tears.

"... and there's more." Kobayashi held up the picture of Juan escorting the Viet Cong prisoner by the arm. "He is pictured here capturing an enemy soldier."

Jun-oba snapped open her purse, took something out, and passed it to Juan—the photo of him posing with her after the tea ceremony. "Sign, please," she said.

Emiko's high school English teacher stood next, calling

Emiko "an exceptional student." She pronounced the word in a way that made it somewhat ambiguous. There were a few titters. Then she looked around the room and drew laughter by adding, "And I happen to know she helped a lot of you get through my class."

The factory manager spoke next. "For two years, Emiko did excellent work on the assembly line without complaining," he began. "Although the management might have had a complaint or two about her ignoring some company rules." Again laughter. Emiko had the urge to stand up and ask him what those widgets were that she'd been assembling. But she let it go.

There was cake, as seen in Western films, and she and Juan cut it together, as seen in Western films. There was also a champagne toast, as seen in Western films. Emiko chuckled to see that Juan hated the taste as much as she did. In fact, nobody took more than a tiny sip before planting the glass on the table for the rest of the meal, which was Japanese, and which they clearly did like.

Being in the public eye all day long had been exhausting for Emiko. She was relieved to get into the taxi and head back to the guest house. Minutes after it drove away from the hotel, she heard light snoring beside her. Juan was asleep. She looked on the other side. So was her father.

"Here we are," the driver called out. And Emiko realized she'd fallen asleep, too.

After long soaks in the bath, she and Juan lay together on the thick futon. "We're married now. Can you believe it, Juan?" She rested her head on his shoulder. "The reception was kind of stiff and boring, didn't you think? What are they like in Puerto Rico?"

"There's a whole lot of music and dancing."

"That sounds like fun. I can't wait to go there and meet your parents. Maybe we can have another reception there."

"Let's plan on it."

"And what did you think of the wedding ceremony?"

"Even though I didn't understand a thing?" He grinned. "Seriously, I still found it moving. I feel like our lives are joined now. And our spirits will always live together."

Emiko held him closer.

"But one thing," he said, "was missing from the ceremony." He stretched a bare arm out from under the quilt and retrieved something from his wallet. He took her hand and slipped a gold ring on her finger.

Epilogue

Soon after returning to Tokyo, Emiko and Juan flew to Puerto Rico for their honeymoon. Juan's parents both told Emiko she was like the daughter they'd always hoped for, and the marriage seemed to bring Juan and his parents closer together.

In early February, when they returned to Japan, Emiko was hired as a full-time reporter for the *Tokyo Daily*. Her friend Mariko and her husband became regular visitors.

In late February, Emiko's father received a commendation from the Customs Headquarters for his help in exposing multiple smuggling schemes, none of them related to Genji's operation. His job kept him too busy to take part in protest movements any longer, but some of his goals had been achieved. Throughout 1970, the U.S. continued to withdraw troops from Vietnam, and in February Henry Kissinger began secret peace negotiations in Paris.

In March, Genji was convicted and sentenced to seven years in prison. His trading company was forced into bankruptcy. After some discreet inquiries, Emiko learned that Genji's wife had managed to keep part of the company money and was living in a sanitarium in Dusseldorf, Germany.

In April, Juan received an honorable discharge from the army and continued to work at the Army Mail Center as a civilian.

On September 30, 1970, Emiko gave birth to a beautiful baby boy. They named him Ken. They invited Juan's mother to come and visit. She stayed with them for a month and was a big help with the baby.

After the fall semester began, Emiko's friend Naomi began to visit her, sometimes staying over instead of returning to her university dormitory. She frequently offered her services as a baby sitter. Emiko planned to apply to the same university as Naomi in a year or so.

In October, while Emiko was caring for the baby and temporarily working from home, Juan began taking courses at Sophia University in Asian Studies and the Japanese language.

In early November, Emiko read that Takashi was denied a sentence reduction. None of his plots had succeeded. The Japan-U.S. Security Treaty, which he had opposed, was left to stand and remains in effect to date, as Emiko and her father had hoped.

On November 25, 1970, while watching TV, Emiko was shocked to hear that Mishima Yukio, the well-known writer and political radical admired by Takashi, committed ritual suicide after failing to convince the country's Self-Defense Force soldiers to stage a rebellion, overthrow the government, and re-establish the Imperial regime. Emiko liked Mishima's novels and plays but had always recognized a sado-masochistic undertone in some. It was sad to remember how Takashi had brainwashed Satoru into thinking of this man as a hero.

Towards the end of 1970, Jun-oba sent Emiko a letter announcing she had completed her tea ceremony apprenticeship and was now a certified Tea Master.

Emiko, Juan, and her father took the fifteen-month-old Ken to Kitayama for the 1972 New Year's holiday.

Then, in the spring of 1972, another of Emiko's father's causes was successful. Okinawa was finally returned to Japan. It was about this time that Emiko noticed her father began talking about a woman he met at the Customs Headquarters.

Despite the Paris Peace Talks, the war in Vietnam dragged on. It wasn't until January 27, 1973, that the Paris Peace Accords were signed, bringing American troops' participation in the war to an end.

By this time, little Ken was over three years old and speaking both Japanese and English.

List of epigraph translators

Chap. 1. Murasaki Shikibu, *Genji Monogatari* (*The Tale of Genji*). Trans. Edward G. Seidensticker.

Chap. 2. Kanze Kojiro Nobumitsu, *Dōjōji* (Noh play). Based on Donald Keene translation.

Chap. 3. Osaragi Jirō, *Kikyō* (*Homecoming*). Trans. Brewster Horwitz.

Chap. 4. Masaoka Shiki, *haiku*. Trans. Harold G. Henderson.

Chap. 5. Kōbō Abe, *Suna no Onna* (*The Woman in the Dunes*). Trans. E. Dale Saunders.

Chap. 6. Ōe Kenzaburo, *Man'en Gannen no Futtoboru* (*The Silent Cry*). Trans. John Bester.

Chap. 7. Dazai Osamu, *Ningen Shikaku* (*No Longer Human*). Trans. Donald Keene.

Chap. 8. Sōseki Natsume, *Botchan*. Trans. Umeji Sasaki.

Chap. 9. Tanizaki Junichiro, *Tade Kū Mushi* (*Some Prefer Nettles*). Trans. Edward G. Seidensticker.

Chap. 10. Zeami Motokiyo, *Atsumori* (Noh play). Trans. Arthur Waley.

Chap. 11. Kawabata Yasunari, *Senbazuru* (*Thousand Cranes*). Trans. Edward G. Seidensticker.

Chap. 12. Sōseki Natsume, *Kokoro*. Trans. Edwin McClellan.

Chap. 13. Ki no Tsurayuki, *Kokinshū* No. 471. Trans. Helen Craig McCullough.

Chap. 14. Ono no Komachi, *Kokinshū* No. 636 Trans. Helen Craig McCullough.

Chap. 15. Sei Shōnagon, *Makura no Sōshi* (*The Pillow Book*). Trans. Ivan Morris.

Chap. 16. Kawabata Yasunari, *Yukiguni* (*Snow Country*). Trans. Edward G. Seidensticker.

Chap. 17. Anonymous, *Heike Monogatari* (*The Tale of the Heike*). Trans. Helen Craig McCullough.

Chap. 18. Jōsō, *haiku*. Trans. Harold G. Henderson, adapted.

Chap. 19. Kakinomoto Hitomaro, *Man'yōshū*. Trans. Hideo Levy.

Chap. 20. Bashō Matsuo, *haiku* from *Oku no Hosomichi* (*The Narrow Road to the Deep North*). Trans. Nobuyuki Yuasa.

Chap. 21. Mishima Yukio, *Yūkoku* (*Patriotism*). Trans. Geoffrey W. Sargent.

Chap. 22. Mishima Yukio, *Gogo no Eikō* (*The Sailor Who Fell from Grace with the Sea*). Trans. John Nathan.

Chap. 23. Ihara Saikaku, "Gengobei, the Mountain of Love," *Kōshoku Gonin Onna* (*Five Women Who Loved Love*). Trans. William Theodore de Bary.

Chap. 24. Ōgai Mori, *Gan* (*The Wild Goose*). Trans. Burton Watson.

Chap. 25. Ihara Saikaku, "What the Seasons Brought," *Kōshoku Gonin Onna* (*Five Women Who Loved Love*). Trans. William Theodore de Bary.

Chap. 26. Bashō Matsuo, *haiku*. Trans. the author.

Chap. 27. Mishima Yukio, *Kinkakuji* (*The Temple of the Golden Pavilion*). Trans. Ivan Morris.

Chap. 28. Ihara Saikaku, "The Barrellmaker Brimful of Love," *Kōshoku Gonin Onna* (*Five Women Who Loved Love*). Trans. William Theodore de Bary.

Chap. 29. Anonymous, "The Death of Kiyomori," *Heike Monogatari* (*The Tale of the Heike*). Trans. Helen Craig McCullough.

Chap. 30. Murasaki Shikibu, *Genji Monogatari* (*The Tale of Genji*). Trans. Edward G. Seidensticker.

Chap. 31. Ono no Komachi, *Kokinshū* No. 552. Trans. Helen Craig McCullough.

Chap. 32. Zeami Motokiyo, *Yashima* (*The Battle at Yashima*). (Noh play). Trans. Makoto Ueda.

Chap. 33. Anonymous, *Matsuyama Kagami* (*The Mirror of Pine Forest*). (Noh play). Trans. Makoto Ueda.

Chap. 34. Kōbō Abe, *Suna no Onna* (*The Woman in the Dunes*). Trans. E. Dale Saunders.

Chap. 35. Bashō Matsuo, *haiku*. Trans. the author.

Chap. 36. Murasaki Shikibu, *Genji Monogatari* (*The Tale of Genji*). Trans. Edward G. Seidensticker.

Chap. 37. Kannami Kiyotsugu, *Jinen Koji* (*Jinen the Preacher*). (Noh play). Trans. Makoto Ueda.

Chap. 38. Anonymous. *Heike Monogatari* (*The Tale of the Heike*). Trans. Helen Craig McCullough.

Chap. 39. Kawabata Yasunari, *Yukiguni* (*Snow Country*). Trans. Edward G. Seidensticker.

Chap. 40. Yasunari Kawabata, *Utsukushisa To Kanashimi To* (*Beauty and Sadness*). Trans. Howard S. Hibbett.

Japanese words used in the novel

The first appearance of these words in the novel is italicized, and an explanation is given or implied at that time. This list may serve as an additional reference.

Anata wa? – How about you?

Arigato gozaimasu/gozaimashita. – Thank you very much.

Atsukamashī. – Impudent, shameless, brazen.

bacalaitos – (Spanish) codfish fritters.

Beheiren - the Citizen's League for Peace in Vietnam.

chakin – white linen cloth for wiping the edge of a tea bowl.

Chikushō. – an expression indicating disgust.

daikon – a long, white radish.

Dō desu ka? How's this?

donburi – a simple rice bowl with fish, meat, or vegetables on top.

edamame – steamed green soybeans.

ema – a votive tablet offered at a Shinto shrine.

enka – an old style of singing.

furoshiki – a large wrapping cloth for carrying anything.

fusuma – a sliding door made of cardboard on a wood frame.

genkan – a small street-level area to leave shoes before stepping up into the main area of a house.

geta – wooden clogs which keep the feet elevated above the ground.

Gomen kudasai. – Excuse me.

Hai. – Yes.

haiden – the main worship hall of a Shinto shrine.

Hajimemashite. – Pleased to meet you.

hakama – loose trousers worn below an upper robe.

hamegu – (English: ham and eggs).

Higan – spring and autumn equinox holiday.

higanbana – spider lilies.

hinoki – a fragrant kind of cedar often used to make bath tubs.

Ichi ban ii no. – Number one best.

Ikura desu ka? – How much is it?

Irasshayimase. – Welcome.

Itekimasu. – I'll be back.

Jama shitakunai. – I wouldn't want to inconvenience you.

Jizo - a Buddhist deity.
kami – spirit.
kamidana – a shelf or altar for offerings to the spirits of dead ancestors.
Kampai. – Cheers.
kanji – Chinese character(s).
karatsu - an ancient style of glazed pottery, mostly in earth colors.
kawaī – cute.
kendo - a Japanese martial art using bamboo swords.
kōban – police box or booth.
komorebi – the speckled effect of sunlight filtering through trees.
Korareta. We were inconvenienced by someone's coming to see us.
kosode – the white upper robe of a Shinto shrine maiden.
manga – comic books, graphic novels.
matcha – powdered green tea.
miko – a Shinto shrine maiden.
miso – fermented soybean paste with flavorings.
mizuwari – whiskey and water.
mochi – hardened rice cakes.
mompei – baggy patterned cotton working pants.
mono no awaré – sadness from knowing beauty or pleasure cannot last.
noren – a slit curtain hung across an entrance, often of a shop.
nori – a kind of seaweed processed into flat dried sheets.
obi – a broad sash used to tie a kimono.
ocha – green tea.
Oishii. – Delicious.
Okaeri. – Welcome home.
okazu – general term for any side dish to go with rice.
okoden – a funeral offering of money.
omamori – talisman to keep one safe, bought at a shrine or temple.
omikuji – a fortune prediction obtained from a temple or shrine.
omiyage – a gift brought back on returning from a trip.
onigiri – rice formed into wedges or balls covered with nori, filled with pickled plums or other ingredients.
otsumami – any side dish, usually to go with an alcoholic drink.
reba - (English: liver).
reikin – key money: an upfront gift of money to a landlord.
rōmon – roofed gateway to a Buddhist temple.

sabi – stark beauty.

sabisu (English: service, i.e. free).

sadō – tea ceremony.

seiza – way of kneeling with feet folded beneath the haunches.

seppuku – ritual suicide by disembowelment.

shino – an ancient style of glazed pottery, mostly white.

shiro – small intestines of a chicken.

shiromuku – a trailing white kimono worn at a wedding.

shōchū – a clear alcoholic drink distilled from rice, barley, or sweet potatoes.

shoji –sliding door with semi-opaque paper panels.

soba – buckwheat noodles.

Subarashī. – Wonderful.

sukiyaki – thin slices of meat simmered with vegetables in a pan.

Tadaima. – I'm back.

takoyaki – octopus fritters.

tara – cod.

tatami - thick mats on the floor covered with woven rush.

Tatenokai – Shield Society, Mishima's private defense force.

tebasaki – chicken wing tips.

tempura – batter-fried fish or vegetables.

tonkatsu – breaded pork cutlet.

torii – the tall gateway at the entrance to the grounds of a Shinto shrine.

uyoku dantai – ultranationalist far-right groups.

wabi – rustic simplicity.

wabi-sabi – appreciation of transience and imperfection.

wataboshi – a kind of white hood worn by a bride.

yaki udon – stir-fried noodles with meat and sauce.

yakitori – grilled chicken.

yakuza – Japanese criminal gang or member.

yukata – a loose cotton kimono worn in the summer.

yūrei - a ghost who comes back because of an attachment to life that cannot be dismissed.

Zengakuren - a league of various groups of communist and anarchist students.

Japanese words which are commonly used in English, for example, saké, futon, ramen, hibachi, pagoda, and kimono, are not identified by italics in the novel.

CPSIA information can be obtained
at www.ICGtesting.com
Printed in the USA
LVHW041824231120
672479LV00017B/696/J

9 781733 052498